DEVIL'S LAKE

Aaron Paul Lazar

Devil's Lake

First Edition, July, 2014
Cover art by Kellie Dennis

Published in the United States of America.

Cover Art by Kellie Dennis at Book Cover by Design

www.bookcoverbydesign.co.uk

Dedication

To the women kidnapped and held hostage for ten years by
that monster in Cleveland, Ohio. No names will be used to
protect their privacy, but you know who you are. I pray you are
able to heal and enjoy life again. The decent people of this
world are so very sorry that this fiend took you, exerted control
over you, and stole so many years from you. God bless you all.

PART I
Home

Chapter 1

Portia hauled on the wheel and dragged the old truck around a sharp corner, wincing when the engine popped and belched black smoke. The beat-up Chevy had been running rough since she left the highway an hour ago.

Come on, keep going. Just a few more miles.

Dust clouds marked her progress along the dirt road. She glanced in the rear view mirror for the millionth time, expecting to see the police chasing her.

Or *him*.

Tears streaked her cheeks, and she hiccupped a few sobs. She'd been weeping all the way from Wisconsin and felt dry, as if she had no more tears to shed. Of course, that was insane. She'd probably cry all day, every day for the rest of her life.

Around yet another corner, and Cupcake slid toward her, scrabbling toenails on the vinyl seat. She steadied the little mutt, who snuggled close to her, blinking round black eyes.

"Sorry, baby." Her voice cracked, roughened from all the crying.

Cupcake leaned into Portia, nuzzling under her arm.

She stroked the dog's soft white ears. "Good girl. You're my good little dog."

She'd stolen the mongrel and the truck when she escaped—was it really only two days ago? Hurriedly thrusting her little friend into the front seat, she'd roared away from the cabin.

When she'd emerged from the woods in the old Chevy, bleary-eyed and shaken, completely disoriented, she'd followed the dusty road toward a village, where a row of eclectic stores lined both sides of a narrow street. In search of directions, she stumbled into the first gas station she could find.

There she was. Hungry. Weary. Traumatized. Skinny as a twelve-year-old boy. And the store clerk hadn't even given her a second glance. He'd pointed down the road in the direction of the highway, and had gone right back to texting without meeting her eyes.

Glancing into the rear view mirror, filled with irrational fear, again she half-expected to see him chasing her.

She forced herself to relax.

Just calm the hell down.

Sighing, she patted Cupcake with her free hand. "We just need to get home. That's all."

Home.

Internally, the need to scream clawed at her. Somehow, she stifled it and told herself she'd be there soon.

As if welcoming her, the Green Mountains surged into the clouds in the background, guarding the rolling hills of the valley where her family's farm nestled in the hollow.

Oh, how she'd dreamed of this day.

Two long years. Two years of wishing. Of wanting. Of daring to hope.

She hiccupped another sob.

Bittersweet Hollow. She'd desperately yearned for it, picturing her mother's kind face, the smell of her bread baking in the oven. She'd imagined her father quietly helping to deliver a new foal and the scent of fresh pine shavings on his wool shirt. She remembered leaning into his broad chest, feeling so safe. So protected.

Every night, she repeated the farm name as a mantra before sleep, after the man tied her to the bedposts. The memories of her parents had comforted her then, and the thought of coming home filled her with a twisty sense of near-maniacal joy.

Her heart slammed against her ribs, quickening with every milestone she recognized.

Almost there.

Portia peered through the dusty windshield, savoring the view of the mountains that rose from the undulating wheat fields and indigo blue foothills in the distance. The scent of fresh-mown alfalfa entered the cab, prompting sweet memories of her childhood. The road dipped into the valley—affectionately called The Hollow by locals—into the protected basin cradled by hills on one side and mountains on the other.

Cupcake raised her head, sniffing the air.

"We're almost home, baby."

The dog licked Portia's outstretched hand.

"When we get there, you can run free."

Her voice shook, and she realized her words came fast—too fast, really. She'd been holding herself together like a cracked vase hastily glued to hide the broken shards and missing pieces. She knew she'd break apart soon, but if she could just make it a few more miles...

The scruffy dog sat up on her haunches, balancing like a circus dog, sticking her nose out the partially opened window.

They rolled around the last bend. There it was!

A surge of shuddering joy passed through Portia. They drove under an archway made from twining grapevines that reached out to twist together from both sides of the road. Beneath the natural arch, a rustic sign hung, swaying in the faint breeze, proclaiming a welcome to *Bittersweet Hollow, a Morgan Horse Farm.* Beneath the name in dark blue script: *Dirk and Daisy Lamont, Proprietors.* Orange berries adorned the edges of the sign, celebrating the farm's namesake, the beautiful but dangerous berries that filled the woods and burst into vibrant color in the fall.

In the distance, several barns emerged, flanked by emerald pastures encircled with expansive rectangles of white

7

post and board fences. Dozens of horses populated the acreage, with coats ranging from blazing red chestnut to bright bay to dark seal brown. In his own separate paddock, her family's black stallion, Mirage, raised his head and trotted to the fence near the driveway. He stood proud and strong, his long curly mane rippling in the breeze.

In spite of the lingering pall of darkness, Portia's heart swelled with uncontrolled exhilaration. After all this time of wanting, wishing, and yearning for The Hollow.

Finally, she was home.

꺵ᴏᴈ

Boone Hawke watched the old Chevy truck rumbling toward him along the driveway, spewing a trail of smoke. He straightened, wiped his brow with a blue bandana, and stepped closer to the open hayloft door. Another customer, horse hunting? He couldn't assume they had no money because they drove an old wreck. It wasn't unusual for good old Vermont stock to keep their vehicles until they rattled to the junkyard and died. In spite of their frugal ways, they still valued horses and would spend good money on a well-bred mount. He figured if he could sell one of the young mares today, he'd put cash in Dirk and Daisy Lamont's bank account for when they came home.

If they came home.

It hadn't been easy taking care of his neighbors' horses while they were gone, especially in the winter. One month turned to two. Two months became four. Now it had been six months since they left.

The checks they sent to keep the farm running had been just about enough for expenses, but he'd had to pitch in from his own farm's funds on occasion when the Lamonts' tractor broke, or when the barn roof needed patching. He didn't want to add to their troubles, so he kept a ledger of his expenses and figured he'd pay himself back the next time a horse sold. The poor people had already been through enough, what with losing their eldest daughter to God-knows-what and now with Daisy's illness.

With a grunt, he lifted and tossed the last hay bale onto a pile that almost reached the roof peak. He straightened, dusted off his hands, and started down the wooden ladder. Swiping at his unruly blond hair, he summoned a smile and ambled out into the sunlight.

Chapter 2

Portia parked in back of the barn to hide the truck. Her heart pounded, and sweat popped on her brow.

Cupcake danced in the seat, her eyes sparkling with excitement. She put her front paws on the door and barked, a surprisingly low-pitched sound for such a small dog.

With a shuddering sigh, Portia thrust open her door. "Okay, baby. We're getting out."

For one frozen moment, she watched the little dog scamper to the grass beneath a large oak. And then, released from bondage, Portia burst from the truck as if being chased by the Devil himself, heading for the kitchen door.

"Mom? Dad!" She pounded up the steps, sobbing again, tripping over her own feet. "I'm home," she screamed.

"Mom!" Yanking open the screen door, she crashed into the kitchen. "Dad?"

Tears streaked her cheeks, and she darted into the living room, searching for her parents. "Mom, where are you?"

Like a tornado on a rampage, she raced from room to room, finding no one. Up the stairs, two at a time. At the top, she had to stop to catch her breath.

"Mom? Are you up here?"

Dashing from along the hall, she ran again, sobbing harder. "Where are you guys?"

As she left her parents' bedroom, someone grabbed her from behind. She screamed when he pinned her elbows to her side.

"God damn it, let me go," she wailed, trying to jab the man who held her tight in his locked arms.

"Stop struggling," a rough voice commanded. "And tell me what you're doing here."

10

She collapsed to the floor, pulling away from him until she backed up to the wall. "Get away from me," she cried. "What are you doing in my parents' house?"

The man jumped back. He leaned against the doorjamb, arms crossed, peering at her from under a shaggy mass of wheat-colored hair. "What? Your parents?"

She looked up at him, wiping her cheeks. "I live here, you moron."

Light dawned in his dark gray eyes. "Wait one damned minute." He moved closer, bending down. "Portia?" His face drained of color. "Oh, God. Is it really you?"

She pulled aside a curtain of dark copper hair. "Yes. It's me. Question is," she said, with as much defiance as she could muster in her tear-drenched voice. "Question is, who the hell are you? And where are my folks?"

"Hold on now. Let me explain." He crouched closer to her. "Don't you recognize me?"

Portia stared at the hulking man. He vaguely resembled the boy from the neighboring dairy farm.

They'd ridden the hills together ages ago, when he was just eighteen and she was fifteen. *Ten years.* He must be twenty-eight now. No wonder she hadn't recognized his face. She hadn't seen him much after he went off to agricultural college, and by the time he came home again to run his family's dairy farm, she'd left for college. "Boone?"

"It's me." He offered her a hand, but she pulled hers away.

Slowly, she stood, putting a hand to her brow. "Now, tell me. Where the hell are my folks?"

☙❧

Boone stared at the woman who hunkered before him like a ghost from the past, her hair glistening in the light shining through the bedroom window. She looked thin, and very pale, unlike the robust teenager he'd known years ago.

11

And very unlike the photo in all the posters he'd helped her parents plaster across the county.

She must've lost forty pounds.

"I can't believe it," he whispered. "It's really you."

She nodded, but didn't smile. "It's me." Her voice quavered as if she'd break down any minute.

"Geez, what *happened* to you?" He stepped toward her and almost took her arm, but she jerked away from him.

"Please. Don't touch me."

A sense of dread filled him. Heat rose to his cheeks. "I..." He hesitated. "I didn't mean anything by it. It's just...we've been searching for you, for so damned long."

A flash of anger filled her eyes, and she stood up. "Right. And you never found me." She crossed her arms. "One more time. Where are my folks?" She choked out the words and lost her balance. Stumbling toward the wall, she leaned on it to steady herself.

"Whoa, hold on now. Won't you let me help you?" he asked, eyeing her with concern.

Her face hardened. "No! I need my parents."

He answered slowly. "I know. But like I said, they're not here."

She shot him a teary glance. "Then where are they?"

He slid his hand into his jeans pocket and rocked on his heels, not sure how to tell her. He had so many questions. So much to tell her. Where had she been for the past two years? Was she kidnapped like they originally thought? Or did she run away, like the cops began to think, when the investigators had seemed to give up hope.

He watched her face turn a chalkier shade of gray, then realized he hadn't answered her. "Um. I'm sorry. They're in New York City."

She seemed disappointed, but the panic left her ravaged face. "Oh. A vacation? They used to love going to shows in the city."

He stalled, scuffing the carpet with one well-worn boot. "Not exactly."

Distrust filled her eyes. "What, then?"

"Um. Your mom isn't well. They went to a clinic. It's a special place where they're doing experimental studies. You know, a research hospital. It's called Sloan-Kettering."

Her eyes searched his, already flooding with tears as if she knew the answer. "Research for *what*?"

He hesitated, then blurted it out. "Cancer. I'm sorry, Portia. But they're hoping the new meds will—"

Her eyes rolled. She crumpled to the ground before he could catch her.

෩෧

Portia woke in her own bed, in the lacy pink bedroom of her dreams.

She opened one eye, taking in the filmy curtains blowing softly in the window, the white bureau with blue, red, and yellow horse show ribbons fluttering on the mirror. Cupcake slept on the bed next to a big chocolate Labrador retriever.

"Boomer?" she croaked. The dog lifted his head, flapped his tail on the bedspread, and squirmed closer to lick her hand enthusiastically.

A voice came from the doorway. "He's been staying at my house. Would have been too lonely all by himself, y' know?"

In a flash, it all came back to her.

She was home. Home in her own soft bed, in her safe, pink bedroom. Home, at her family's Vermont horse farm, with the beautiful Green Mountains all around. It wasn't a dream this time. It was real.

In the next second, the awful truth stabbed her and she bolted upright. "My mother. I have to see her. How can I..."

Boone sailed across the room in three long strides. "Whoa, there. Doc's coming out first. We've got to make sure you're okay before you go gallivanting off to New York."

"I'm fine," she lied. She felt horrible. Weak and wobbly, she could barely sit up. "I think I just need food."

His face darkened. "When's the last time you ate?"

She frowned, as if trying to remember. "Um. I think yesterday."

"Crap. I'll be right back." Turning, he disappeared into the hall.

She heard noises in the kitchen below. While she lay under the comforter trying to collect her thoughts, the phone rang.

Boone's deep voice reverberated from the first floor, but she couldn't make out every word. He hung up quickly, and within minutes, appeared in the doorway with a tray of steaming soup and crackers.

"There isn't much in the cupboards," he said apologetically. "Just some Campbell's soup and a box of Saltines. Hope you like chicken 'n stars."

"I have so many questions," she said. "My mother. This place. The horses. What's happened in the last two years? And what about my sister? Is she still in school? Is she okay? She was such a mess back then."

He raised an eyebrow. "Whoa. Hold on, let me set this tray down first." He laid the tray on the night table. "Can I help you sit up?"

She froze inside, suddenly reminded of *him* and his ministrations after he'd hurt her. "No. I've got it." With a huge effort, she scooted up on the pillows.

"Blow on it, it's hot," he said. He stepped back and grimaced. "God, you'd think I could come up with something

14

more original than that." He sank into the chair in the corner. "Sorry. I want to answer all your questions, in order, but I have so many of my own, they're jamming up my brain, y' know?"

She nodded and bit into a cracker.

He leaned back and looked toward the ceiling. "You already know about your mother. She's getting the best care in the country, and there's hope for her yet."

Portia felt her knotted stomach relax, just a little.

Boone continued. "Grace is okay." He frowned when he mentioned her little sister's name.

Portia figured it was because Grace had given her family such trouble.

Drugs. Court. Rehab. More drugs. More rehab.

Life had been tough with Grace.

But Boone had been there for her family when her sister had fallen apart, when she'd even dragged criminals into their lives. Portia had been away in college when they dealt with the worst of it, but her mother told her Boone helped her father take Grace up to the rehab clinic—three times. They'd finally gotten the rebellious girl to a point where she agreed to stay clean and study art, her favorite subject, at the University of Vermont. Portia wondered if she'd kept with it.

"Is she still in college?"

"No. When you disappeared, she went nuts."

Portia almost stopped breathing. "I thought she hated me."

"Don't think so. She helped us put posters all over town. Made phone calls. Went on the radio to appeal to whoever took you. The whole enchilada."

Portia suddenly remembered the newspaper clippings he had put up on his corkboard, showing the whole family and each of their appeals to the kidnapper. He'd collected them from all over, relishing the news coverage.

15

"Did she go back to drugs?"

"No. Your mother finally convinced her to return to school, even though it didn't last." Boone shifted on his chair. "It might be hard for you to imagine, but she's married now. She met a professor who wanted to take care of her. Older guy. At first your folks were against him, but he sort of won them over. Happened really fast, too."

"She's married?" A sense of loss filled her. There had been a wedding while she was gone. White dress. Flowers. Family and friends. And she'd missed it all.

Anger built again in her gut. He'd taken that away from her. He'd taken it all away from her.

"Yep, she's a married lady now. Still struggling, goes to therapy twice a week, and occasionally she disappears for a few days, but she comes home again. Poor old Anderson has a hell of a time keeping her in line. But she's better than when you knew her."

He stood and looked out the window. "Aside from dealing with your disappearance, everything's been sort of okay. The horses are fine. But I think Mirage missed you." He took a deep breath, and then turned to her, his clear gray eyes searching hers. "Now it's your turn. What the hell happened to you, Portia?"

Inside, she felt her throat freeze, her heart drummed against her chest. The words would barely come. "I can't...I can't talk about it. Not yet. I'm sorry."

He dropped back into the chair, stretching out his long legs and clasping his fingers over his stomach. A long, soft sigh escaped his lips. "It's okay. You take your time."

She tore her eyes away from his and leaned over to take a sip of soup, swallowing several mouthfuls greedily now that it was cooler, then ate four more crackers and drained the water glass.

"Is it okay? You want more?"

16

She looked at him with weary eyes. "No. I'm good, thanks." She pushed the tray back. "Who just called?"

He gave her a crooked smile. "My brother. Dad's prize cow just had her baby. Looks like it's gonna be a nice one."

She relaxed. Not the police. Not *him*. "Did you tell your brother about me?"

"Not yet. I thought you might need a bit of time before the whole village descends on you. Figured I ought to get your permission first."

Grateful, she smiled, for the first time. "Thank you."

As if called to duty, he suddenly stood. "I need to tell your father. What do you want me to tell him?"

"I'll call him," she said, pushing back the dishes. But as much as she tried to sit up straighter and before she could ask for her father's hotel number, against her best efforts to keep her eyes open, she felt herself being drawn into sleep. Within five minutes, she'd succumbed.

Chapter 3

Boone watched her sleep for half an hour. She seemed exhausted, completely wrung out. And she'd been hungry. Starving, really.

Why?

Where had she been? And where'd she get that old wreck of a truck with Wisconsin plates that she parked behind the barn? If she escaped from a kidnapper, wouldn't she have gone to the cops?

If not, why not?

If she did, they should've arranged transport home. Right? Or at least to a hospital? Why hadn't they fed her?

And where the hell did she come across that little scruffy dog?

Maybe he was all wet. Maybe Portia had just left home for some unfathomable reason. Maybe she'd been living on the road, hand-to-mouth, never enough to eat.

He'd have to ask her again about the details, when she seemed calmer, when that scared, panicked look faded from her eyes. And maybe she'd tell it all to her folks. Why had he expected her to open up to him, anyway?

Meanwhile, he needed to call the Lamonts. He leaned over to pet Boomer and Cupcake, checking to see that they still had water in the big stainless steel bowl he'd set in the corner. Earlier, Cupcake had drunk her fill, then settled on the bed beside Portia, as if she knew she were home.

He slipped out the door, pulling it closed. Downstairs, he dialed Dirk's number.

The phone rang once and Dirk's no-nonsense voice answered. "Lamont here."

"Dirk? It's Boone."

"Boone." He hesitated. "I'm...I'm sorry I didn't call last week. It's been crazy here."

"No problem. Listen," Boone said. "I have something important to tell you. Are you sitting down?"

He could almost feel Dirk stiffen. "What is it? Are the horses okay?"

"It's Portia, Dirk." He shifted the cell to his other ear and looked up the stairs, as if she might wake up. "She's home."

Dirk's phone must have clattered to the floor. Boone heard him cry out, then the sound of him scrambling to get it back to his ear.

"Boone? Oh my God. Is she okay?"

Boone tried to sound calm. "She's alive. But she's skin and bones and totally exhausted. She hasn't told me much yet." He glanced up the stairs again. "She wants to see you both. And I had to tell her why you were gone. I'm sorry."

Dirk expelled a long breath, and he choked out the words. "I can't believe it. She's really home? Did she tell you what happened?"

"No. She hasn't said much about it, like I said. Seems pretty messed up to me. You know, like whatever happened to her was bad, really bad." He paused, waiting for Dirk, but the man didn't say anything for a few beats. "You want me to get her on a plane down there when she's fit to travel?"

Dirk finally answered. "No. I'm bringing Daisy home tomorrow. She's on this new medicine, and so far, she's holding her own."

"Whoa. Excellent news," Boone said. "Glad to hear it. And you three need to be together."

"Can I speak with her?"

"She just fell asleep. Want me to wake her?"

"No, let her rest. I'm going back up to the room to tell Daisy. She's gonna go ballistic. It'll be all I can do to keep her in bed 'til tomorrow."

They hung up and Boone headed for the door. There were chores to be done. His father and brother could manage the dairy farm while he helped out at Bittersweet Hollow, and the Lamont horses needed their stalls cleaned. Straightening his shoulders, he headed outside.

֍֎֍

Dirk flew up the hospital stairs two at a time, his heart hammering beneath his ribs. He burst into his wife's hospital room, bending over to catch his breath. "Daisy, I..."

Daisy sat on the edge of the bed, disconnected for the first time in months from multiple IV lines. Tomorrow's hospital release looked like it might actually happen.

Her eyes danced with worry. "Dirk?" She stiffened, turning toward him. "Honey? What is it?"

Dirk caught his breath and went to her side, taking her hands in his. "Baby, listen. It's gonna be a shock."

She huffed. "Don't torture me. Just spit it out."

"Sorry." He straightened and locked eyes with her. "It's Portia. She's home."

There wasn't much color in her cheeks to start with, but now she drained to pale gray. "*What?* Portia?"

"She's alive, honey. And she's home. Boone just called."

Tears sprang to her eyes, flooding her cheeks. "Oh my God. My baby. She's alive?" She jumped up, wobbly and weak, flinging herself onto him. "I knew she would come home!"

"I know," he said, distantly aware that his own cheeks were soaked and his shoulders shook as they held each other.

After a few minutes, they pulled themselves together, and the questions tumbled one after the other. Dirk tried to answer her rapid-fire inquiries, but realized he knew very little. "She didn't tell Boone much. Guess she was exhausted, fell asleep right away. But we'll call her later, okay?"

"Call her?" Daisy snorted. "Sure we will. But we're going home. Now."

Pride welled within him. He knew she'd react this way. Hell, he'd felt the same, wanted to rent a car and drive right up there, cancel all previous arrangements. But he tried to stay calm. "You know our flight's arranged for morning, right? And the hospital plans to discharge you at ten o'clock?"

"We're leaving, I don't care who we have to kiss to get out of here today. Change the flight. I don't care what it costs. I want to see her. Tonight."

Dirk straightened, knowing it would be tough to get Daisy released from the hospital, collect all the experimental meds, and arrange flights within the next few hours. But he would do it, for Portia. She needed them. And they needed her. His mind raced with thoughts of seeing his daughter again. *Alive.*

Alive!

He hadn't realized how deep the fear had penetrated, how low his hopes had fallen. He kept thinking that she would certainly have contacted them if she were alive. Wouldn't she? The idea had taken hold too deeply, entrenched in his subconscious. He realized with a start he'd almost lost all hope before this call. Almost.

"I'll do my best," he said, grinning and kissing her wet cheeks. "You call Grace while I work on it, okay?"

The sisters had fought like she-cats growing up, but when Portia disappeared, Grace went through hell. He thought that her sister's reappearance and her mother's sudden improvement with the new experimental meds just might be enough to bring her out of her depression.

With resolve, he collared Daisy's oncologist, Dr. Kareem, in the hallway, and began to beg. Come hell or high water, he would bring Daisy home as soon as humanly possible.

Chapter 4

Portia woke on her side with Boomer pressed behind her legs and Cupcake snuggled in her arms. She made a purring sound, yawned, and stretched.

Nobody stood over the bed, leering at her. Her legs were free from bonds.

She rubbed her tender ankles absentmindedly, although the sores had started to heal two days ago, when she'd broken free, when she'd left him, unmoving on the cabin porch.

The sun had just dropped behind the Green Mountains, and she wondered what time it was. Her stomach rolled with hunger.

A distant whinny thrilled her, filling her with an urgent desire to race out to the barn, throw her arms around Mirage's neck, and head to the hills for a ride. But the weakness running through her arms and legs was palpable; she felt shaky, exhausted. She realized it was a miracle she'd even made it home in one piece.

She needed to forget. Really forget. But it was hard to push him away, the memories bubbled beneath the surface of her consciousness, always nudging, always threatening to burst free and paralyze her.

She shook her head.

Don't think about him.

The kitchen door downstairs opened and closed. Water ran in the sink and she heard the clinking of a teakettle being filled and set on the stove.

Portia sat up in bed, her head swimming.

How had she even made it here? Sheer willpower? Probably the two cups of coffee and burger she'd had before she headed for the road.

She felt debilitated, damaged. Needy.

I want my parents.

My parents.

My mom.

My mother has cancer.

A wave of fear and worry burbled into her throat, and a raw sob escaped her just as Boone stuck his head in the doorway.

She tried to bite back the cry, but it didn't work, spewing forth in a harsh wave.

Boone hurried to her side, but he didn't speak. Instead, he sat on the chair he pulled up to the bed, one hand on the bedspread beside her—near—but not touching her hand.

"I'm...I'm sorry," she said, wailing. "It just hit me. My mom...has cancer?" Guilt slid through her. She should have escaped sooner. She should have—

"Portia, listen. She's coming home tonight. They're on a plane. Your dad called an hour ago. They're coming home."

He reached out to pat her hand, but she shrank back from him.

He tried again, his voice even gentler now. "Your folks are coming home, Peaches. Home. And your mom's doing better. The new meds are helping."

Peaches? Why is this stranger using my childhood nickname?

She sat and rocked, heart pounding, trying to figure it out.

Stop it!

It's just Boone, all grown up. No need to be scared.

But she couldn't push the raw fear from her chest, or open her arms for the hug she needed so desperately. She shifted back against the pillows and tried to force a smile, stuttering her words. "She's...she's coming home?"

"They're on their way now." With a sigh of relief, the big man hoisted himself to his feet and grinned, standing over her. "Well, then. Things are looking up, right?"

Inside, she trembled. His shadow fell over her, and this presence, this monstrous big form near her made her want to scream.

She could scream now.

Yes.

Her mouth was free.

She let it out.

∽∘∾

Boone watched the girl shy away from him, like a skittish filly, unused to human hands stroking her fur. Her eyes had grown wide, as if he'd pointed his rifle at her and threatened to shoot. But he'd just delivered good news. Great news. Daisy's getting better, and—

When she opened her mouth and let out the scream, his jaw dropped.

"Portia. It's okay. It's just me, Boone."

The sound pierced his soul, sounding almost feral, like a coyote in pain. But this poor young woman who lay before him was quite human.

She pulled back again and buried her head under the covers, sobbing uncontrollably.

"Listen, Peaches." He stepped back. "I'm not going to hurt you. Please. Don't be afraid. It's just me. Your riding buddy. Remember?"

The weeping slowed a bit.

"Remember when we used to ride up to the gully? When Monty threw you and I had to bind your ankle with my shirt? Remember that?"

She slowed. Sniffled. And peeked out of the covers. "Boone?" The name came out in a child's voice. Uncertain. Shy. Soft.

"Yes, hon. It's me. Now don't you worry. We're gonna take good care of you. Doc's on the way. He just had to close his clinic and finish up. Should be here soon to take a look at you. That okay with you?"

Fear stamped her face, but she seemed to pull together and gave a quick nod, answering in a small voice. "I guess so."

Chapter 5

Doc Hardy looked into the trembling girl's eyes with his penlight. He'd approached her very carefully. She'd been crying, and according to Boone, she'd let out a huge scream when he stood over her bed. Portia was in advanced trauma, nearing psychosis, if his analysis was correct. She needed serious help, and he prayed for wisdom while pulling up a chair beside her.

"Honey, do you remember when I used to be your doc? When you were little?"

She nodded, still not speaking.

"Well, good. We had some pretty exciting times, especially with all your broken bones. You were a real daredevil, I must say." He chuckled, trying to get a response.

There it was. A tiny flickering at the edges of her mouth. An almost-smile.

"I remember," she said in a hoarse whisper.

"You're thin, dear. You haven't had enough to eat. You'll need lots of tender, loving care."

She stared at him with big, frightened eyes, but she let him check her reflexes, gently tapping her knees and ankles. Boone said she hadn't allowed him to touch her, but he figured his white hair and familiar old face might have relaxed her a bit.

He took out his scope and leaned forward. "May I listen?"

"Okay," she whispered.

He warmed the metal first, gently laying it against the girl's chest, sliding it inside her buttoned blouse. "Sounds good and strong."

Doc watched Boone hovering in the background. The poor guy seemed overwhelmed. He meant well, had a great big heart, and was a hard working farmer, but somehow Doc didn't think he'd ever had to deal with a woman in trauma before.

"You wanna talk about where you've been, honey?" Doc asked. "We sure were worried about you. The whole county's been searching for you, you know."

She closed her eyes and shuddered. "No. I can't. Not yet."

With a reassuring pat on her shoulder, he sat back. "No problem, you just take your time. If you want, I can arrange someone for you to talk to. There's a gal who..."

"No! No thank you." She turned away, her mouth tight.

"Okay, hon. Well, listen. I need to get home to my mutts. I've got seven now, all rescues. And they like their dinner on time." He stood and zipped his bag shut. "You call me if you need me, okay?"

∽◦∾

Portia watched the doctor put his stethoscope back into his old-fashioned leather bag. He'd always reminded her of Abe Lincoln: tall, lanky, bearded, with kind eyes and wise words. But now his hair and beard were white.

When had *that* happened? She hadn't really needed to see him in the past decade, because she'd been pretty lucky with her health.

He smiled and nodded to her. "I'll be back tomorrow after I close up shop. That okay with you?"

She wanted to say, "Yes. Please come back," but no words flowed from her lips. She raised one hand and slowly wiggled two fingers. He lifted his hand in a half-salute and disappeared into the hallway.

Boone stood looking out the window, his face drawn. A sense of guilt flooded her, surging through her heart, arms, and legs.

"I'm sorry," she croaked. "I've brought you a lot of trouble."

"No worries," he said, his voice deep and gentle. "I'm just glad you're home."

"You've been taking care of our horses?" she asked, surprising herself with the attempt at conversation.

"Uh huh. And the hayfields, riding the fences, handling the brood mares who come to mate with Mirage. The usual." He moved toward the chair the doctor had vacated. "Okay if I sit with you for a bit?"

She stiffened, then forced herself to relax. *For crying out loud, Portia, it's just Boone.* "Okay."

He settled beside her, his eyes on his hands. After a few seconds, he lifted his gaze to her. "You gonna be okay, Peaches?"

She almost winced at the near-intimate contact of his gaze, so personal, so warm, so...connected. She'd been connected to only one person for two, torturous years, and her instinct was to block him out, to pull back, to force herself into the cardboard cutout who felt nothing, responded to nothing, needed nothing.

But she sat up a little and forced herself to answer. "Honestly, I don't know."

Boone nodded, as if that were the answer he expected. "Understandable."

The fact that he didn't pressure her to spill the truth relaxed her. "What time are my folks coming?"

Boone twisted his wrist. "If the flight's on time, they should be getting here around eight. About an hour from now."

"Okay." Time had ceased to mean much to her. She'd even been deprived of that. No clock. No television. Nothing but walls and ugly old furniture and locked doors. She'd learned to guess when dawn was approaching, when dusk would fall, but that had been about it.

"You wanna eat something? My mother brought over a chicken pot pie. It's in the oven."

Her stomach lurched. She'd grown accustomed to hunger. Long periods of nothing. Then gorging on the fast food he'd bring her. "Okay. Maybe just a little bit. Did you tell her about me?"

He shuffled his feet, looking embarrassed. "Sorry. I kinda did."

"That's okay. I always loved your mother." She tried to continue with the civil conversation, forcing the words from her mouth. "Thank her for me?"

"Sure. I told her not to say a word, though the secretary at the doc's office knows now, and you know how Penny talks." He made a face. "It might not be long before everyone knows you're back." He straightened, stretching his arms toward the ceiling and covering a yawn. "Sorry. Been up since four."

She nodded, her eyes still on him.

"When you're up to it, there will be lots of folks who want to welcome you home."

She winced, and he noticed. He held his hand up as if to calm her. "Not now. Not ever, if you don't want it. You call the shots."

Gratefully, she nodded toward him with a faint smile. "Thank you."

Chapter 6

After eating a good portion of Mrs. Hawke's chicken pot pie, Portia dragged herself to the bathroom and gratefully accepted Boone's suggestion that she soak in a hot bath. He'd run the water for her, steaming and sudsy, and left a few towels on the chair by the tub before disappearing back out to the barn to see to the horses.

The flight from New York was delayed by half an hour, so she still had time to clean up a little and try to regain some semblance of control. Some semblance of normalcy.

Normal? *What is normal now?*

Normal had become the bizarre and horrific life she'd led for the past two years. Normal was being petrified all day long. Normal was being restrained, often tied to the bed. Normal was giving in to a monster, to stay alive.

Stop it.

She found a pink disposable razor in the cupboard below the sink, placed it on the side of the tub, then lowered herself into the hot water and luxuriated in the feeling of smooth porcelain and suds. Sweet-smelling soap bubbles tickled her nose. She sighed, dunked under the water.

Warmth encircled her arms, legs, torso, and head. It felt so good. She popped out of the water again and stretched, reaching for the shampoo.

She'd missed amenities like this. Shampoo and conditioner. Oil of Olay bath wash. Soft fluffy towels.

The showers he'd forced her under had been swift and cold; the soap harsh. One big yellow bar for hair and body. Her hair hadn't felt right the whole time she'd been with him.

Now she lathered and re-lathered, scrubbing fingertips against scalp as if she could rub away the memories of him. She turned on the water again. Using a cup from the side of the tub, she rinsed her hair clean for the first time in years, and then carefully shaved two years of fuzz from her legs and underarms. It took a long time, and she had to get up soaking wet and find another razor to finish the job properly, but it felt so good to feel smoothness beneath her fingertips.

Feeling better, she eased out of the tub, trying not to look down at her skeletal body. She wrapped her hair in a towel and dried off quickly, avoiding the mirrors. Feeling strangely privileged, she slipped into the pajamas Boone had found in her old dresser.

Mom kept all my stuff. She knew I'd come home some day.

She almost sobbed at the thought, but reminded herself one more time. *I am home. Home.*

After finding her old toothbrush in the cabinet, she squeezed out a dollop of Colgate and furiously cleaned her teeth until her gums hurt. She'd have to get to the dentist soon, because there were a few spots she feared had started to turn into cavities. He hadn't exactly provided her with the world's healthiest diet.

A commotion downstairs made her turn toward the window.

Below stood her Dad's Dodge Ram truck, headlights still shining onto the porch. Portia watched him help her mom out of the cab, and in seconds, tears scalded her cheeks.

She wobbled out of the bathroom, reached the head of the stairs, but stopped when Boone appeared, holding up a warning hand from the first floor.

"Whoa. Hold on. I'll bring them up to you." He bounded up the stairs, guided her back to bed, and hurried downstairs to greet Dirk and Daisy.

☜☞

Daisy felt her strength build as the anticipation of seeing her daughter grew like a tsunami inside her. She let Dirk help

31

her out of the truck, pushing ahead toward the warm kitchen light spilling onto the porch.

Boone ushered them inside, looking both flustered and relieved. The poor boy certainly hadn't signed up for this.

"Come on. She's upstairs," he said breathlessly.

She and Dirk exchanged an excited glance, then hurried into the kitchen, through the living room, and up the stairs. She barely noticed how winded the climb made her.

Boone pointed to the bedroom. "She's kind of weak. I put her back in bed."

"Portia?" Daisy's voice sounded hysterical, even to herself. She tried to calm it down. "Honey? It's Mom and Dad."

They heard her before they saw her.

"Mom? Dad?" If Daisy's voice sounded frantic, Portia's heart-wrenching cries were worse.

Daisy raced ahead, in spite of the weakness simmering in her body. Dirk followed close at her side.

She stopped short in the doorway, barely recognizing the girl under the pink comforter. "Oh my God. Portia. You're really home."

Portia threw back the covers, lunging toward them. In a tumble of hugs, tears, and kisses, Daisy, Dirk and Portia fell into each other's arms, sobbing and chattering. Daisy embraced her daughter, feeling the bony body beneath. Dirk put his arms around both of them. Boone stood to the side, smiling, wiping a few stray tears from his own eyes.

"Oh, honey." Daisy's heart beat fast beneath her ribs. She couldn't stop patting her daughter's hair, cheeks, and arms. "Oh, baby. You're home. You're so skinny! What happened to you?"

Portia finally spoke through choking tears. "I'll be okay. But you're thin, too, Mom."

Dirk corralled them both with his strong arms. "Your mom's gonna be just fine, honey. Looks like we've gotta put some meat back on both your bones, huh?"

Daisy stepped back for the first time. "We are quite a pair, aren't we?" She laughed, crying again, then climbed into bed and pulled her daughter in beside her, unable to let go of her hand.

Portia put her head on her mother's shoulder, still sobbing. "Mom."

Daisy held her tight, stroking her hair. "Our girl's home, Dirk." She smiled through tears at her husband, the amazing big lug who'd always been so strong for her, but who'd really surprised her with his strength and dedication since Portia went missing, and even more so when she fell ill with cancer.

Dirk had always been a man of simple tastes and interests, none of that fancy kiwi or sprouts for him. A meat and potatoes man. Family. Farm. Horses. That was all he talked about in the old days. And she'd been okay with that. More than okay with it. The guy had a heart of gold. When someone was hurting, he showed up at their place and helped out. If a farm was about to go under, he'd donate equipment or labor to help them get out of the hole. He didn't often go to church, but Dirk had a strong faith and was the most genuine Christian Daisy had ever met.

He never faltered, this bear of a man, and she thanked God every day for his solid presence and corny sense of humor.

Dirk sat on the edge of the bed, holding his daughter's hand. "Welcome home, both of you."

Daisy pulled him over to kiss his lips. "Thank you, honey."

Boone shifted in the background, "Guess I'll be heading back to my place, then."

Dirk rose to shake his hand, but impulsively pulled Boone into a bear hug. "Come back in the morning, son. We can catch up on the farm stuff, okay?"

"Sure thing." Boone smiled, nodded to Portia and Daisy, and stepped out of the room. "See you all tomorrow."

Chapter 7

When Boone emerged into the starlit yard, he stopped for a moment to lean against his truck, glancing up at Portia's bedroom window, which spilled warm yellow light for the first time in years.

A broad array of emotions flooded his heart.

Joy. Relief. Apprehension.

What had happened to the girl?

It must have been awful. Something dreadful. So bad the fear still raged within her and broke through with certain triggers. Like when he'd stood over her bed, too close to her. Or when he tried to touch her. Of course, his approach had been completely innocent, just him wanting to help. But the act of him looming over her, reaching for her, had caused her to lose it.

When she'd screamed, it had been so primal, so full of horror, dread, and panic, he'd felt the hairs on the back of his neck stand straight up, like a dog's hackles.

What the hell had that brute done to her? Or had there been more than one?

Anger coursed through him. It would be a lot simpler if he had a name or a face. A face he could smash with his fists.

Hitting that bastard would feel so good right about now.

He was convinced she'd been kidnapped, definitely abused.

But by whom? How had he grabbed her? And why?

He knew there were sickos out there. Guys who were pure evil, somehow seriously damaged. Or people with no conscience.

What did they call them? Sociopaths? Something like that. Like they were born deficient, without any sense of right or wrong. Without any concern for others.

He shook his head and glanced over to the paddock, catching Mirage staring at him.

The horse snorted, shook his head, and turned in a tight circle.

He seemed to know something was up.

Boone wandered in his direction. Immediately, the black stallion approached him. Boone fished a few chunks of carrot from his jacket pocket and offered them, palm up. "She's home again, buddy. Your girl. You remember her, don't you?"

Mirage pushed his soft muzzle into Boone's hand and delicately plucked the first piece from his palm, chewing it with a rhythmic crunching sound that Boone found comforting.

He reached up to stroke the horse's thick forelock. "That's a good boy."

Mirage thrust his head against Boone's chest.

"Okay, okay. Here's the last piece."

He patted the horse's sleek neck and muscled shoulder, listening to the sounds of the night. Crickets chirped in the fields. Tree frogs chorused their nightly songs. An owl screeched from the deep woods.

He straightened and took Mirage's halter in both hands, looking at him straight on. "We'll both help her get well, won't we, big guy?"

Whistling a tune, Boone ambled back to his truck, turned the key in the ignition, and headed down the bumpy dirt road toward home.

෪෪

Portia snuggled and wept against her mother, lying beside her in her childhood bed with both dogs pressed against her. They didn't speak for an hour. She felt her mother's soft fingertips stroking her hair, just like when she was a little girl. Inside, deep caverns shifted and yawned, threatening to let the terror escape. But somehow, safe in her mother's arms like a little child, all that emerged were wracking sobs.

She cried until she was wrung dry. She cried for the missed years. She cried for the pain she'd endured, the humiliations she'd suffered, the fear she'd held in, the disabling horror that had been her life for the last two years.

Throughout, her mother murmured soft nothings, little cooing sounds she'd used when Portia had fallen off her bike or took a tumble off her first pony. She patted her arms, her back, rubbing her hands in circles.

Sometime during the night, her father came into the room. He wrapped himself up in a comforter and slept in the chair by the window, softly snoring.

At midnight, with both parents close by, she finally drifted off to sleep.

Chapter 8

Portia woke with a start. Her mother and father had left the bedroom, but she heard their voices downstairs. She smelled the comforting aroma of coffee and listened to the sound of clinking dishes in the kitchen.

Sun streamed in the windows and both dogs pressed against her, Boomer behind her knees and Cupcake on the pillow by her head. She reached up to stroke Cupcake's soft curly fur, thinking randomly she should get her groomed.

What a strange, yet decidedly normal thought to have.

An everyday, regular-person thought.

No worries of survival, escape. No thoughts of murder or revenge.

Murder.

She shuddered, trying to push the horrible memories away…far away. It didn't work. Unbidden images of him lying on the cabin porch flashed across her mind's eye.

Had she done it? Did she actually kill him? Or was he only knocked unconscious long enough for her to grab the keys, get the dog, and steal his lousy truck?

Would he come after her?

He knows where I live.

She started shaking, but Boomer woke, stepped over her, and began to lap her hands and cheeks industriously, as if the sweet ministrations of his soft tongue could make her whole again.

Maybe it could.

She buried her face in his furry neck, quietly sobbing. "Thanks, Boomer."

As if to help with the nurturing, Cupcake started to nuzzle Portia's hands, pushing her cold, wet nose into them. She snuggled closer, her body nestled into the curve under the girl's arm.

With dogs like this, she thought, maybe there is hope.

Maybe I can survive. Recover. Heal.

Maybe.

The scent of bacon sizzled up the stairway.

Her stomach wrenched in hunger.

Bacon. *Real bacon.*

She sat up tentatively, waiting for a wave of dizziness to pass. Slowly, she slid her feet into the slippers her father had lined up next to her bed last night.

One, two, three. *Up.*

She steadied herself on the headboard, feeling stronger than the day before. Both dogs jumped off the bed and shook themselves, trotting around her in excited circles.

"You guys want to go out, huh?"

She leaned down to pat them both again, and their tails wagged in unison.

Still feeling relatively steady, she reached for the robe she'd torn off during the night when she got too hot under the covers. She'd flung it to the floor, but someone—probably her mother—had folded it over the edge of the chair. She slid into it and tied the terry cloth sash into a snug bow.

Somehow, this innocent, everyday action felt supremely good.

To have a bathrobe to wrap up in....

To be able to choose her own clothing, rather than be forced into wearing something bizarre that *he* made her wear.

She might just stay in pajamas for the rest of her natural life.

She let out a half-smile, and headed for the hallway.

∼∘∾

Boone finished tossing hay to the mares in the east pasture, then dragged the hose out to the big water tub extending through the fence for both the stallion and the mares. He watched the water fill, letting it overflow for a few minutes so all the dust and dirt and stray pieces of hay were flushed out of the container.

Leaning back against the fence, he surveyed the property, loving the feel of the early morning sun on his face. Dozens of horses grazed in the distance and several lowered their heads to the flakes of hay he'd strewn on the ground near the barn. A bay filly, almost a year old, approached the water tank, ears perked straight up. After drinking her fill of cool water, she ambled closer to Boone, nudging him with her wet muzzle.

"You want a treat, Laurel?"

She pushed him again, this time gently nipping at his jeans.

"Okay, okay. I'll get you a piece." He fished out a few chunks of carrots and let her take them from his palm. "There you go."

Patting her neck, he admired her conformation. Broad chest, strong neck, flat topline. A perfect Morgan, maybe even top show quality. She arched her pretty neck, tossing her head and flipping her wavy black mane.

"What? You want more?"

Laurel nickered softly this time.

"I take that as a yes." Boone dug out one more piece and offered it to the filly. "Here you go, sweetie. But I've gotta save some for the others, you know."

Mirage trotted to the water tub and sloshed his big head back and forth in the water, spraying some over the fence onto Boone's chest.

"See?" He pointed to Mirage. "He wants his treats, too."

As if to prove the point, Mirage moved closer to the fence and stomped a hoof three times.

"Okay, okay." Boone ducked through the fence and gave Mirage his carrots.

Just as he finished checking all the gates and making certain the place was secure, Dirk waved to him from the porch. "Morning, Boone."

Boone waved back. "Morning, Dirk."

"Come in for breakfast."

Boone's stomach growled and he smiled. "On my way."

Chapter 9

Daisy heard the footsteps first. She bounded up from her chair and met Portia at the bottom of the stairs. "Baby! You're up."

Portia leaned into her mother's hug. "Is Dad cooking bacon?"

Daisy nodded. "He is. Scrambled eggs. Blueberry pancakes. The works. He just can't stop cooking, he's so glad to be back home." She kissed her daughter's cheeks and forehead with loud "mwah!" sounds, over and over again, letting go only when she heard Portia's stomach growl.

"Morning, princess." Dirk turned from the stove where he flipped pancakes with a large spatula. "Hungry?"

Daisy glanced at her husband and smiled. She loved the way he acted as if this were any old morning. As if they'd done this every day of their lives. As if Portia hadn't just come home from God knew what horrors.

If anyone could bring their daughter back to health, it was Dirk, with his quiet, unassuming ways.

Portia settled in a seat next to Daisy, and looked up as Boone entered from the back door.

"Morning, all." Boone eased into the room and went to the cupboard to take down a few cups. "Anyone else want coffee?"

Portia nodded with a weak, "Please."

As if he lived there—and Daisy realized he probably felt as if he did after the last six months—he poured a cup for Portia and himself, then glanced at Portia again. "You still like cream and sugar?"

The frail girl nodded again. "Uh huh."

Daisy watched Boone go about the task of pouring the coffee and milk, adding and stirring sugar. The boy who'd grown up next door had matured into a rugged, good-looking man. With a heaving heart, she realized how very much they owed this good neighbor. She and Dirk would never be able to pay him back. But she also knew he'd never expect or want to be compensated. He'd just taken over the farm because that's what good neighbors do. She sighed, smiling so wide at her daughter she felt her face would break.

She's home.

My baby's really home.

Her heart fluttered a little, and she realized she hadn't felt such joy since long before Portia disappeared. Oh, there was a tingle of happiness when she saw Grace finally married to Anderson. But even that was so tainted by Portia's absence, it had been bittersweet.

Dirk uncovered the hot eggs and slid huge portions onto four plates, laid bacon beside each with tongs, and tossed two pancakes next to the eggs, dealing them out like cards. Next, he walked around the table like an experienced waiter, deftly filling their orange juice glasses.

"Hope you're all hungry. There's more where this came from."

Daisy looked at her husband in awe. It suddenly struck her. When had he become so self-sufficient and helpful in the kitchen?

Thinking back, she realized it was when Portia disappeared. She'd gone berserk for a while, not eating, acting crazy with grief and panic. And Dirk had stepped up and done it all. Horses. The haying. Meals. Laundry. The bills.

He'd taken such good care of her.

But who'd taken care of him?

She felt a stab of guilt.

No one.

Yet, he'd continued with his solid, comforting presence. He'd been there at her side, tending to her needs. He'd been her rock.

She watched her daughter bend over her plate and inhale the food. Another stab of worry hit her.

Hadn't she eaten at all? She was skin and bones, and it was obvious she'd been deprived of food. Would she get sick eating so much with a shrunken stomach?

She started to say something about it, but before she could, Portia stopped, looked at her father, and teared up.

"What's wrong, honey? Don't you like it?" Dirk said.

A small sob escaped the girl, but she stifled it. "No, it's just..."

Daisy's heart constricted, and she put an arm around her shoulder. "Oh, honey. We know. It's so good to have you home again."

Portia straightened, wiping her eyes. "I'm sorry."

Dirk made a motion with his hand as if shooing away a fly. "No worries any more, darling. You're home. You're safe."

A car door opened and closed out in the yard.

Portia froze and looked nervously toward the window. "I hope so."

"You're with family now, honey," Dirk continued. "And if you have reason to think there's danger, you let us know." He smiled at her, though his eyes darted to the window and back. "When you're ready."

Daisy repeated his words, running her hands over her daughter's arm. "When you're ready. Like Dad said."

Portia nodded, but didn't say anything. She took another sip of coffee and began to eat again.

When the food was gone and the conversation waned, Dirk stood to clear the table.

Boone rose quickly. "No, sir. You relax. I'm on dish duty this morning. Spend time with Portia. Maybe she'll be strong enough to take a tour around the barn. She hasn't met—"

Before he could finish, the kitchen door flew open.

Grace stood wide-eyed and expectant in the morning light, her gaze fastened on her sister.

Chapter 10

Portia blinked, staring at her sister.

Grace stood frozen in the doorway. She had grown from a gawky teenager into a curvaceous young woman, reminiscent of a Renoir beauty, with creamy skin and big eyes, long flowing honey-colored hair, with a trim waist and full hips.

"Portia!" The girl broke the trance and stumbled toward her sister.

Portia pushed back from the table and stood, meeting her weeping sister with surprise. The last time she'd seen her, Grace had said she hated her, and that she hoped Portia would just "disappear from the face of the earth."

Well, she got her wish.

As if reading her mind, the young girl sobbed words full of remorse. "I didn't mean it. I didn't want you to go away."

Portia couldn't answer. Hot tears spilled from her eyes.

Her little sister spoke so fast, the words tumbled over one another. "You're skin and bones! What happened to you? Where were you? We searched and searched..."

Again, the words froze on Portia's lips, but she clung to her sister and listened while the girl wept and babbled on about all they'd been through, how they'd tried so hard to find her.

Finally, with a deep gulping breath, Grace stopped and released her tight grip on Portia, turning slightly toward the sound of the kitchen door swinging open.

A tall man in his early forties ducked inside, rolling two suitcases behind him. Brushing aside his sandy hair turning silver at the temples, he searched the room until his gaze fell on the two sisters, still holding tight to each other.

"Anderson," Dirk said. "Come on inside. I'd like you to meet my daughter, Portia."

The man her father called Anderson left the bags at the door and ambled forward, a quiet humility accompanying him. When he reached the girls, Grace slipped an arm around his waist and drew him close. "Honey, this is my sister, Portia. Portia, this is my husband, Anderson Rockwell."

When Anderson gently clasped her hand, Portia felt her initial panic dissipate. This was a gentle man, whose eyes spoke of past sorrows. She liked him immediately.

"Anderson," she said. "Nice to meet you."

She noticed her mother's relieved smile out of the corner of her eye.

Relieved that she hadn't screamed at the big man's approach? Relieved she'd acted civil?

Another layer of fear was shed, and she felt herself relax even more. "I'm so sorry I missed your wedding." Turning to her sister, she touched her face. "You must've been a beautiful bride."

And then it hit her again. The great losses. The missed wedding. The wedding she was sure *she'd* never have, because she'd probably never get over this whole rotten mess.

Boone nodded to Anderson and Grace from the sink, where he'd just started washing dishes. "Nice to see you two again."

To Portia's surprise, Grace turned quickly toward Boone. "Oh! I didn't know you were here! What a nice surprise." She left her sister's side and hurried to the sink. "How are things on your family's farm? Are you managing to keep it all together?"

The words were innocent, but the fluttering of her sister's lashes and the way she canted her hips made Portia wonder about her intentions.

Am I imagining it?

47

Anderson didn't acknowledge the overt flirtation. "We're very glad to see you home again. Your sister's been sick with worry. Never, ever gave up. She was just on the news last week, for the second anniversary of your disappearance, appealing for help. She made it her job, you know. To find you."

"Really?" Portia raised one eyebrow. "She used to hate me."

Anderson chuckled. "She's grown up a bit since you left."

Really?

Portia watched Grace giggle and walk her fingers up Boone's arm. He shifted sideways, looking uncomfortable.

Was she really acting like this in front of her husband? In front of the whole family?

With a huge effort, Portia spoke, clearer and louder this time. "I want to see my horses."

❧

Boone turned away from Grace, sliding the last of the dishes into the dishwasher. "I'll do it," he offered, glancing at Portia.

Cripes, what the hell is Grace doing?

He pulled away again. She'd have to get the point pretty soon.

Sure, Grace had developed into a beautiful girl, gorgeous, even. But she was married. And the nice guy who'd rescued her from her past life with drugs stood not ten feet away.

What is she thinking?

She'd made passes at him before, when he and Dirk had driven her up to the rehab clinic. She'd sat on his lap in the truck and slung her arms around his neck when her father disappeared into the gas station to get coffee.

On other occasions, she'd plastered herself against him at every chance when she needed money for drugs, had even stalked him at his own farm once, waiting for him to come in from the fields. He'd never given her a penny, and she'd always stormed off, furious at him.

He tried to forget that time when he'd almost succumbed to her ripe lips pushing eagerly into his. She'd ambushed him, reaching down and stroking him that one summer night, and he'd had to forcibly remove her hand from him, but not before his body had reacted to the sudden touch.

He hadn't been about to take advantage of a kid whose next fix depended on her seducing a dumb farmer.

Since the wedding, she'd calmed down, according to Dirk's reports. But he really hadn't seen much of the little vixen since then. And now, here she was, reverting to her childish behavior in front of her husband and the Lamonts.

Hell.

He shook off Grace's hand, which had somehow grabbed his again, and approached Portia.

"May I?" he said, offering her his arm and gesturing toward the barn. "There are several horses who are very eager to see you again."

Portia paled when he approached, so he slowed and backed up a step. "You still want to go?"

She forced a weak smile. "Uh huh. Long as no one cares that I'm in my pajamas."

Boone snorted a laugh. "I don't think the horses will care." He turned toward Dirk. "Maybe your dad would like to come with us?"

Dirk jumped up, kissed the top of Daisy's head, and smiled widely. "I've missed those critters way too much. Come on. Let's go get reacquainted."

Chapter 11

Boone wasn't surprised when Portia had shrunk from him, and frankly had been almost relieved she didn't scream in panic.

When she faltered on the porch steps, her father grabbed her arm, and kept his hold on her until they reached the barn.

Boone followed at a safe distance. Good thing she trusts somebody, he thought.

Dirk Lamont was pretty good at hiding his feelings, but today glints of joy flashed from his eyes. The man couldn't stop staring at his daughter's face, and he touched her hand, shoulder, and back frequently, as if to assure himself she was actually there.

After two tortured years, Boone didn't blame him, not one bit.

Impressed with the way the family held back asking the obvious questions, he found it hard not to burst out with "Where were you?" and "Who took you?" But he'd seen the panic in her eyes when Grace asked, and he'd pushed his own questions down, much as they begged to be blurted out.

He watched father and daughter walking—no, it was more like shuffling—toward the barn. Portia looked so small and frail.

She'd always been an open and honest girl. He'd admired that. But now she was changed, severely damaged.

What *in hell* had happened to her?

As they approached the barn, he came up beside them and noticed her eyes brighten, her step quicken. She stood a bit taller beside her father.

"Where's Mirage?" she asked, searching the paddock by the driveway.

"He was outside a little while ago, but I saw him head for the barn, so I expect he's eating breakfast in his stall," Boone said. "I told him you were coming and he's kind of excited to see you again."

Dirk flashed him a grateful smile, and opened the sliding barn door with a well-practiced shove. "Here we go. Let's go say hello."

Dirk had been gone to that cancer center for so long, it must've killed him being away from his beloved farm and horses. Living in the city he hated, waiting for the woman he loved to respond to some new fangled treatment. *Waiting for her to die?*

Thank God one of the meds had finally worked.

Boone couldn't believe they were actually home. He'd often pictured the worst. The phone call from the city, saying it was over. The funeral. The sadness that would permeate the farm forever.

But it hadn't gone down that way, and he thanked God as they walked across the rough floorboards toward the stalls.

Portia's heart swelled when Mirage's big head turned toward her. He nickered softly, and swiveled away from his hayrack, ears pricked in her direction.

"Hey, big fella." She lifted a hand to stroke his forelock.

The gentle stallion nosed her, pushing his soft muzzle against her neck.

She reached up to hug him, and he stood still, letting her cry against his black coat. Running her fingers through his thick wavy mane, she inhaled the pungent but wonderful scent of horse, feeling his whiskers tickle her neck.

Dirk and Boone spoke in low whispers about the farm, the mares, the fences. She knew they were being polite, turning away from her as she had her private moments with Mirage. For that, she was grateful.

On the other hand, it was humiliating. Being such a wuss. Being so scared and crying all the time. She wanted badly to move past this new fragile creature she'd become.

Problem was, she wasn't sure where to begin.

She felt no control over her own body anymore. It was as if the mechanism that used to make it walk and smile and talk had completely corroded. And the old "I won't cry in front of people" filter had frayed and blown away in the wind.

She was a mess.

And it was all *his* fault.

Her darkening mood was broken when the kitchen door opened and both dogs bounded outside, raced to the barn, and leapt on her, madly licking her hands. The expressions of joy on their faces made her smile, and she dried her tears with the back of her hand, trying to stay standing under their assault.

"Oh, you sweet pups. Look at you. Cupcake, this is Mirage."

The big horse lowered his head, snorted, and tossed his mane, as if to show his superiority.

Boone leaned down to pat Cupcake. "You're right, this little scruffy critter hasn't met him yet." He loosed a wide smile. "She isn't your usual farm dog, Portia. More of a lap dog, I think."

Portia felt a smile tug at her lips. "I know. I always loved the big dogs, like Boomer, here." She knelt down to give both dogs hugs. "But she is the best pal a girl could ever wish for."

As if to milk the situation, Cupcake stood on her hind legs and turned in a circle, both paws in begging position.

Portia felt something tickling her throat, and with surprise, realized it was the beginning of a laugh. "I think she was a circus dog in her past life."

She jumped when Boone bellowed and slapped his thigh. "She's a corker, that one."

She tensed, then stopped the stupid emotions and forced a smile. "You think so?"

He nodded. "Absolutely. I was just picturing her in a little pink tutu, jumping through hoops."

Portia felt another layer of darkness crack and peel away, and for a moment she actually felt...what was it? Happy? Pleased?

It was a foreign sensation, but she relished it.

Her father crouched down beside her and patted Cupcake, who nuzzled his hand. "Yep. She may not look it, but I think she'll be a fine farm dog. She's got spirit, that's for sure."

Cupcake barked, then noticed the orange cat jumping down from the loft. With legs flying, she tackled the startled feline and began to sniff her from head to tail.

"Riley might not take to that dog-slobbering," Boone chuckled.

The cat swiped at Cupcake, causing her to yelp and back away.

"She'll learn," Dirk said, leaning down to scoop the cat into his arms. "Riley won't take much guff from anyone."

Portia raised a hand to stroke the cat. "I don't know this one, Dad."

"He's one of Buttermilk's kittens. Remember her?"

She smiled. "Of course."

"She's around here somewhere," Boone said. "She's still the boss."

Portia glanced down the aisle. "Can I see the rest of my horses now?"

Boone stepped aside and swept an arm before him. "Thought you'd never ask. Let's go hunt up some of your old favorites."

Chapter 12

After spending an hour meeting and greeting her old friends and learning the names of some of the new foals, Portia left the men to talk farm business on the porch. Exhausted, she shuffled back inside where she found Grace and her mother cuddled together on the couch.

The aroma of baking cornbread filled the air, and in that one swift moment of recognition, she knew she was really truly home.

Cornbread. Warm, buttery, crumbling in her fingers. She almost melted with the idea of it.

Leaning against the kitchen doorway, she watched Grace laughingly play with her mother's hair. A stab of jealousy pricked her. There was a new closeness between her mom and sister, one that hadn't been there before.

When had *that* happened? Since the wedding?

Portia had always been the "good" girl, and even had suspected she was her mother's favorite. But now she felt so removed from everything, so distant. Sure, she got some welcoming hugs when she came home, but it felt like everyone was tiptoeing around her because of what happened.

Of course they were. She still hadn't told them. She'd have to face it before long.

Dread grew in her stomach.

To talk about it...oh, God. Even to *think* about it, made her nauseated.

Grace trilled a laugh. "I like it. It grew in real nice, Mom. I think you have a little more curl than you used to."

Daisy reached up to pat her short gray hair. "I'm so glad to be done with that danged chemo."

Portia glanced up at the ceiling, wondering at the footsteps overhead. In a flash she realized it must be Anderson walking around upstairs in the guest bedroom, opening and closing drawers and closet doors.

He's too good to Grace, bringing in the suitcases, putting away their clothes. An uncharitable thought hit her. *She doesn't deserve such a nice guy.*

Immediately, guilt struck her.

Just because I suffered doesn't mean my sister shouldn't be happy.

She shifted against the cool paint of the doorframe. *What's wrong with me? Why am I so mean now?*

She sighed, realizing she had a lot of family history to overcome. All the pain Grace had put her family through with the drugs and court and rehab...it was still there. She hadn't seen her sister recover, or even apologize. She hadn't had two years to forgive and forget. It all felt so fresh. But it wasn't fresh. She had simply stagnated, pulled out of life by the bastard who took her. Put on a shelf to dance to his needs, while the rest of life went on and on without her.

And then of course, there was that weird display earlier, where Grace flirted with Boone right in front of everyone.

How do I feel about that?

She let her mind free up a bit, but one wandering thought wouldn't go away.

I'm jealous.

Jealous? Why?

You ninny, you were jealous of Grace and Boone.

After all, Boone was *her* friend, *her* riding pal, *her* childhood crush.

Sure, she shrank from him in the beginning. He was just so *big* now, so different. But inside, he was the same old Boone. Gentle. Caring. Funny.

Wasn't he?

She faced the thought full on. She *had* been jealous of Grace flirting with Boone. She felt possessive of him, although she wasn't ready to have him touch her or get too close. She didn't know if she'd ever let any man come within a foot of her now, except her father and Doc—and maybe Anderson. There was something about Anderson that put her at ease. Maybe it was the kindness filling his eyes, the gentle smile on his lips? Either way, she liked him already.

But Boone was all male, so big and muscled and...such a cowboy.

Her mother turned, suddenly noticing her in the doorway.

"Honey, come inside." She patted the seat next to her. "Sit with us."

Portia walked over and sat on the other side of her mother, leaning into her embrace. "Hi, again, Mom."

"Hi, sweetie."

Grace smiled at her from the other side, and when her eyes shifted to a quizzical glance, Portia was afraid she was going to ask her again about what happened.

She braced herself.

Before her sister could ask the dreaded question, the sound of tires on crunching gravel filled the air.

Portia stiffened. "Oh my God."

Daisy frowned. "Honey? What's wrong?"

Portia scrambled to her feet, her heart hammering hard beneath her ribs. She broke into a cold sweat and ran to the window, but couldn't see the car. "It's *him*. Oh, God. He's here." She hurried toward the cellar stairs. "No, no, no!"

Jerking open the old wooden door, she flipped on the switch and stumbled down the rickety stairs, fell at the bottom, then got up and raced for the small room at the end of the dirt floor cellar. The cold storage room stood waiting, its flaked blue-painted door ajar.

Quickly, she eased herself through the crack and pulled on the overhead light.

The smell of rotting turnips hit her full force. With a shock, she realized the storage room had been deserted last year, and the few remaining vegetables had been left to wither and rot.

Uncaring, she pushed the door shut behind her and shoved a large garbage can full of sand behind it, using every ounce of her waning strength. Trembling all over, she headed for the far corner and sank against the rough stone wall, ignoring the nasty cut on her knee that seeped blood through her pajama pants.

Sobs escaped her, slow at first, then they built to a wailing crescendo. Shoulders shaking, heart pounding, she cried so hard she was sure *he'd* hear her. Trying to muffle the sound, she pressed her mouth into her sleeve, pushing so hard she bruised the inside of her lip against her teeth.

NO. NO. NO. NO. NO!

Help me, dear God. Please help me.

Footsteps descended the stairway and she panicked once again.

Someone's coming.

Oh, no. Please. No.

"Portia?"

The voice outside sounded vaguely familiar, but she couldn't relax. Not yet. He could be tricking her, like he used to.

Someone pushed open the door a crack, shoving the sand bucket a few inches toward her.

Realizing with a start that her mouth was free, that no tape held her sounds captive, she screamed, long and loud. The shuddering sounds echoed through the damp stone room.

Chapter 13

"It's just me, sweetheart. It's Dad."

With a shaky sigh of relief, Portia opened her eyes. "Daddy?"

Her father pushed the door open, knocking the sand over. He rolled the bucket aside and eased into the room, crouching beside her. "It's okay. Nobody's going to hurt you. I promise."

A new torrent of sobs flowed from her. She clung to her father, rocking back and forth.

He stroked her hair, and held her tight. "You just breathe, now, princess. Just breathe."

She caught a glimpse of Boone in the doorway, worry written on his handsome features.

His deep voice rumbled in the cold stone room. "Is she okay?"

Dirk nodded over Portia's shoulder. "She will be. We just need a little time."

"Okay, then. I'll be upstairs if you need me."

Portia hiccupped and coughed, then tried to regain control. She looked up suddenly. "Wait. Who drove into the yard?"

Her father didn't answer straight away.

"Dad? Who was it?"

"I sent them away, but they'll be back tomorrow. It's Sheriff Dunne and Deputy Mills."

Shrinking away from him, she shook her head. "I can't talk to them."

"I know. That's why I asked them to come back."

"What did they want?"

"Just to know what happened, sweetie. They've been following your case since the day you disappeared. They have reports to file, a case to close."

"What did they say? Did they tell you anything new?"

"Like what?" he said, frowning.

She kept the words from coming out, but her brain poured through all the questions.

Did you know he was dead, ma'am?

Did you kill him, ma'am?

Did you steal his money and truck, ma'am?

What did he do to you, ma'am?

She shuddered again. "Nothing."

"Honey?" He tilted her chin up so she was forced to meet his eyes. "Do you want to see a doctor?"

"I've seen Doc," she said.

"No, I mean a psychiatrist. Someone you can talk to. They might prescribe something to—"

"No drugs!" she yelled, instantly embarrassed at the volume of her voice. "I'm sorry, Dad. I don't want to be drugged up. I just want to be home. With you, and Mom. And my animals."

He stood, helping her straighten up beside him. "Okay, sweetie. If that's what you want, that's what you'll get."

With a final hug, she leaned against him, her words muffled in his shirt. "Thank you."

"We'll worry about the Sheriff tomorrow, okay? Right now, let's get you upstairs and comfortable. I don't think I can take the smell of those old turnips one more minute." He leaned over and kissed her forehead. "Okay?"

She sighed, long and low. "Okay."

Together they made their way toward the stairs and back up to the living room, where everyone busied themselves with something, generous in their intent not to embarrass her.

Her mother flipped through a magazine, pointing out fashions to Grace, who tried to seem interested, but kept shooting furtive glances at her older sister. Anderson sat quietly beside them on the couch, reading Bury the Hatchet in Dead Mule Swamp, by Joan H. Young.

Boone ran a dishcloth over a glass carafe, then set it carefully into the coffee maker. "Anyone want another cup?" he asked.

Dirk helped Portia to the stairs. "I'll have another when I come down, Boone. Thanks." He turned to his wife. "You want to go upstairs with her, honey? I think she could use some Mom-time."

Portia shot him a grateful smile, grateful that her father was so in tune with her needs.

Grace jumped up as if to join them, but to Portia's relief, her father waved the girl away. "Just one at a time right now, sweetie. I think that'll be best." He gave the girl a conciliatory glance. "You two sisters can chat together later. Maybe we'll play some Scrabble or something, huh?"

Grace stared after them, her expression pouty. "Okay. I guess." She plopped back onto the couch next to Anderson. "I only came all the way from Albany to see her."

Daisy chided her, climbing the stairs behind Portia and Dirk. "Now, honey. Give her time. You'll be here for the whole weekend, right?"

To Portia, her sister's response sounded like she had when she was a little girl.

"Yes, Mom. I know you're right."

Arm-in-arm, Portia and her mother ascended the stairs.

Chapter 14

Daisy watched Portia flop onto the bed and roll sideways into a ball. She slid onto the mattress behind her shaken daughter, wrapping her own weakened arms around her. "Oh, my sweet girl."

She nodded thanks to her husband, who had been standing by the bed as if he didn't know what else to do to help.

"Go ahead back down, Dirk. I've got this," Daisy said.

"Okay." He leaned down to kiss both of them, then backed out the door, closing it softly behind him.

Laying her head against the girl's back, she began to sing. "Hush little baby, don't you cry..."

For the next ten minutes, she sang the song, over and over again, not sure of the lyrics, but carrying the tune with her warbling voice until the room was full of a mother's love and her daughter finally stilled, breathing quietly.

"You awake, honey?" Daisy asked in a whisper.

Portia's head nodded once. "Uh huh."

"Please talk to me. Talk to your momma. Can you do that for me?"

Slowly, Portia turned on the bed to face her mother. With eyes reddened from crying, her tortured expression pulled at Daisy's heart.

"My God," she said, gently pushing back a stray lock of hair over her daughter's brow. "What did they do to you?"

Portia's eyes welled with tears again, but she didn't lose control. "It wasn't 'they' Mom. It was one guy. One horrid man."

"Oh, my poor baby." She hugged and stroked her daughter's back, murmuring comforting words.

Daisy held back, much as she wanted to pepper the girl with questions, get answers, find out who did this and bring the wrath of God raining down on his head. As enfeebled as the cancer had made her, she felt strength rising up within her, and it was laced with a lust for vengeance.

Surprised at herself, she almost recoiled at the intensity of her emotions. She wanted to kill this man, whoever he was. Whoever had taken and hurt her girl.

"Honey?"

Portia raised her eyes to meet her mother's inquiry.

"It's time. We need to know what we're facing, here." She took both of Portia's slender hands in hers, squeezing them gently. "Are we in danger, baby?"

Portia collapsed against her mother's chest, her words muffled. "I don't know, Mom. I just don't know."

Daisy pulled back a little, infusing a bit of stern mom-talk in her voice. "Okay. I'm going to ask your father to brew up a pot of tea. Then we're going downstairs to see if my cornbread is ready, and you're going to do your best to fill us in." She tilted her daughter's chin up and looked into her haunted eyes. "Okay?"

Portia nodded, misery written all over her face. "Okay."

~∘~

Boone sat at the kitchen table with Dirk, going over the farm records. The air filled with the scent of cornbread, and as if they both had the same thought, Dirk looked up suddenly toward the oven.

"Oh, drat. I'd better check that. Daisy will kill me if it burns. It's our first cornbread in over a year."

He hopped up and opened the oven door, releasing even more of the heady aroma into the room. Grabbing a butter knife from the drawer, he inserted it into the middle of the bread. "That's how Daisy does it," he said. "If it comes out clean, it's done."

Boone watched expectantly. "It'll go good with my mom's pea soup. She's bringing it over in a bit."

"Yep. It's done." With red oven mitts, Dirk slid the hot bread out of the oven and set it on a rack on the stovetop. "That's real nice of your mother, Boone."

Boone smiled. "She doesn't know how else to help. So she cooks. And cooks. And cooks."

Dirk laughed. "It's in our genes, I think. Good food, good neighbors. It all goes together."

The men glanced up when Daisy and Portia came down the stairs. Boone noticed the girl had dressed in jeans and a sweater, had washed her face, and her hair hung neatly in a ponytail down her back. She offered him a weak smile, then sat at the kitchen table and took a deep breath.

His heart broke for her. Every little action seemed to take so much out of her. Just getting dressed, taking a short walk. She seemed to get winded real easy, as if she had some kind of breathing problem going on.

Maybe she did?

No. Doc has listened to her chest. That couldn't be it. And she never had asthma, as far as he knew. Could it be she was just so out of condition that she had to build up her strength again? Hadn't she been able to walk, or move around wherever the hell it was she'd been kept?

When Daisy started toward the teakettle, he jumped up to help. "Let me do that. Why don't you sit with Portia?"

She tossed him a grateful smile. "Thanks."

He noticed Daisy's warm glance at Dirk when she saw the cornbread—unburned—on the stove. "Oh, it's done!" She turned to Boone. "Make a lot of hot water for us. We're going to need plenty of tea."

He wondered why, but filled the kettle to the brim and set it on a burner on high.

"Lipton okay?" he asked, rummaging in the cabinet to the left of the stove. "I don't see much else here."

63

Daisy smiled. "Check that Teavana canister in the back. I think we have some Mohito Blackberry in there."

"Got it." Boone took it down and popped open the lid. "Wow. Still smells good."

Daisy took Portia's hand, as if she were trying to give her strength. "It'll be okay, honey. Let's get everyone settled with their tea and cornbread, and then we can start."

Boone watched Portia's eyes dance from him to the living room and back. She looked scared, and again, he wondered what was going on.

"Portia?" he asked. "Can I get you a nice big chunk of cornbread? Your father bought some supplies early this morning for his breakfast feast, and I know I saw butter in there."

Her eyes met his, held his gaze, and for a split second, he sensed a tremor of appreciation in them. "Yes, please."

Glad to have something to do while the kettle boiled, he grabbed a narrow spatula from the drawer and carved out a big square. He popped it on a plate, added a pat of butter, and slid it onto the table in front of her. "Want a napkin?" he asked.

She nodded. "Thanks."

The tension in the room grew when Daisy called Grace and Anderson to the table.

"Honey," she said, leaning in to Portia. "I know it's gonna be hard talking in front of all of us, but we all need to know what happened so we can help you to the best of our ability." She looked around the table at the circle of concerned faces. "And if we've gotta worry about someone coming here who may threaten you, or any of us, we need to know the scoop."

Boone took down the large tea infuser and with a few hints from Dirk on how to work it, he got it set up. He took six clean mugs out of the dishwasher and set them on the table, where eager family hands quickly distributed them. It felt good to be helping, instead of sitting on his hands. These guys had been through hell and back, and he'd missed them all. Well, except maybe Grace.

He glanced at her and was relieved to see she sat close to Anderson, one arm linked through his and her head resting on his shoulder.

Good. Maybe she's come to her senses.

Dirk passed dessert plates around, set the butter on the table, and put the cornbread dish and spatula on a hotplate in the center.

Boone liked the fact that they were modern men, unafraid to jump in and help.

In his parents' house, his mother had done all the serving her entire life, and when he'd gone to college he realized how unfair it all was. He'd shocked his mother when he came back to run the farm and started helping her in the kitchen, insisting she sit while he passed around the food. He'd even started doing dishes.

It just felt right.

The old ways were fine, if all parties agreed. But his mother was getting older, and he felt like helping. So, he did.

Dirk had jumped into that role, too. With Daisy so upset about the loss of Portia, then with her cancer coming on so fast, Dirk had needed to become the caretaker. And it made Boone proud to watch this rugged farmer cut the cornbread and pass out napkins.

Maybe that was the test of a real man. He could do kitchen work and still maintain his manly ways.

The family talked quietly, but the air remained taut with expectation.

Boone handed the infuser to Daisy, who filled everyone's cups. Then he set it up for another brew.

"Okay," Daisy said. "Boone, take your seat. You're family."

Boone pulled up between Dirk and Anderson. Portia's parents flanked her on either side.

Silence fell, and all eyes were on Portia, who sat like a stone statue, straight and unmoving. With a deep heaving sigh, she began to speak.

Chapter 15

"It happened at work," Portia said. "I was just closing up the greenhouse for the night."

Portia's thoughts went back to the day he'd taken her, and as she replayed the scene in her mind, she spoke the words aloud with eyes closed. She tried to separate her inner self from the voice that spoke, and not react to the gasps and comments of surprise that occasionally erupted from the ring of people around the table.

After she'd earned her undergrad degree in biology, she decided to take a year off before applying to grad schools. To make some money and start paying off her exorbitant school loans, she'd taken a nice no-brainer job at the local garden store.

To her surprise, she'd fallen in love with the job, and had secretly realized if she made enough to live on, she could happily work among the plants for the rest of her life. She'd checked out a few grad schools, but only half-heartedly. There was something so calming and satisfying about working with plants, her hands in the soft soil, the fresh green sprouts that popped up from the dirt, the aroma of flowers that filled the greenhouses...It had become her oasis, and she'd begun to wonder if she really wanted to go forward with her childhood dream of becoming a horse veterinarian.

The Green Mountain Nursery was open from nine-to-nine in the summer. Over time, Portia had moved into a trusted position, quickly becoming indispensable to owner Marty McGorkin, a seventy-something woman who still spoke with a Scottish accent and who was stronger and more energetic than most twenty-year-olds Portia knew.

That night, she'd been left to tend the register and close up. Marty had left at five, to get ready for her usual bridge date with her gal pals. Since it was mid-June, most of the vegetable gardeners had already bought and planted their tomatoes, peppers, and other hothouse vegetables, so the crazy planting season had begun to wane.

A few couples wandered among the herb plants, rubbing leaves and sniffing their fingers to decide which scents they preferred. One elderly gentleman examined the berry bushes just outside the main building, and a family with three kids pushed a green cart through the annuals, choosing a bright assortment of potted zinnias, African daisies, and petunias.

She'd noticed the man puttering around the leftover geraniums an hour earlier. The big push had been in May, for Mother's Day, but they still had a good assortment of reds, pinks, and whites, and they were on sale now, which probably attracted the man to the display.

He wasn't a local customer, at least not one of her regulars. He'd put three plants in his cart, taken them out again, and chosen two more twenty minutes later. As the rest of the customers checked out and drove off, she checked her watch. Almost closing time.

She wondered if he needed help, but he hadn't raised his eyes from the plants for the past half hour, so she'd held back. Some folks just needed time to choose the perfect plants for their yard or porch.

He was a tall man, probably six foot two or three. Broad shoulders, ruddy complexion, pitted cheeks where he'd obviously suffered from a bad case of acne in his youth. A baseball cap mashed down the straight gray hair that reached to his collar, and he wore the regulation jeans and tee shirt that most folks did when they visited her store.

At five 'til nine, she headed over to him. "Sir?"

He looked up, and with a start, she reeled back from the intense expression in his black eyes.

Why had it seemed so odd? The focused, stabbing look he gave her didn't match the image she had of a doddering, indecisive shopper.

68

"Sir, I'm sorry, but we're closing in five minutes. Can I help you decide?"

With a sigh, he put all the plants back except one bright red geranium. "No. I think I'll just get this one."

His voice was deep, gravelly sounding. Almost as if he had something wrong with his throat, like surgery or something on his vocal chords that made it sound a little bit mechanical or robotic.

She'd smiled automatically and led the way back to the counter. "Of course. Come on over and I'll ring you up."

He'd paid with cash, his cap pulled low over his eyes again.

Those eyes.

They'd almost burned her when they lit on her face earlier.

He pocketed his change and picked up the plant, heading toward his car in the back of the lot. "See you around."

Although she felt unsettled, she went through her usual nighttime routine. Count the money. Put it in the safe. Shut off all the lights except the few they left on for security reasons. Lock the greenhouse doors. Lock all doors in the main building. Grab her purse and sweater.

She backed out of the main door, checking it to be sure it was locked up tight. Feeling hungry, she began to plan a run to the local Chinese restaurant for a container of wonton soup. She loved the crunchy noodles they served with it, and always felt good about all the fresh broccoli and pea pods they mixed in with the savory stuffed wontons.

Her old, beat-up Camry sat alone by the back of the greenhouse. With keys in hand, she hurried toward it, feeling a slight chill in the night air. Behind the building, the outline of an unfamiliar vehicle took shape.

Someone's truck?

Why had they parked it there, and left it? Was it one of the delivery guys? But why wouldn't they have told her they'd left it out back?

When she bent down to unlock her car door, a dark form loomed out of the shadows and a strong arm reached around her body, pinning her to him.

No! With quick instincts, she jabbed backwards with an elbow, like her self-defense teacher had taught her in college.

The big man uttered a low "oof" but didn't release her.

"Shhh," he said, and in that moment, she recognized the mechanical sound of his voice. "It's okay. You're with me now, sugar."

Struggling harder, she twisted and turned but couldn't evade his strong grip. A sharp odor filled the air, and within seconds, he'd clamped a rag over her nose.

She slumped against him and everything went black.

Portia roused herself from the memory. "That's it. That's how he did it."

Chapter 16

Daisy folded Portia in her arms when she finished. "Oh, baby."

Portia let her mother embrace her, but this time the tears didn't come. Leaning against Daisy, she listened to the snippets of conversation around the table.

Grace: "I knew it! I knew she wouldn't leave on her own. Stupid cops and all that crap they started about her running away..."

Dirk blurted, "Where did he keep you? Was it near here?"

Boone said, "How'd you get that truck? And what part of Wisconsin did it come from?"

Anderson shouted, "What was his name? We ought to report it to the police, right now."

Portia stiffened, feeling bombarded by all the questions. "I don't know his real name. He made me call him Murphy. I don't know if it was his first or last name."

Her father leaned toward her. "Okay. Murphy. Over six feet, longish gray hair, well-muscled, funny sounding voice. Is that right?"

Portia nodded. "And pockmarked skin."

He started to jot down the particulars. "Where did he take you, honey? Was it all the way up in Wisconsin, like Boone said?"

She sat up straighter. "Yes. I don't know the town name, but maybe we could find it from the registration papers in the truck? When I left the cabin, I just drove like a maniac to the interstate, and didn't look back."

"A cabin?" Grace said, with wide eyes. "In the woods?"

"Yes." Portia looked down at her hands, finding it harder to go on. "It was surrounded by woods, with just dirt tracks going in and out of the place. But I never saw the outside. Until the day I escaped."

Boone leaned forward, his face a study in horror. "He kept you inside for two years?"

Portia's hand flew to her face, which temporarily crumpled. "Yes." She reached for strength, found it in her father's hand that squeezed hers, and took a deep breath. "Except when he tied me to the porch on that last day."

Boone stood up and started pacing. "We've gotta tell the cops who this guy is, the sick f—" He stopped, realized there were ladies present, and turned to Dirk and Anderson. "Or we could go out there, find the bastard, and beat him to death."

Anderson held up a hand. "Not that the idea doesn't have merit," he said quietly. "But he may be armed."

Boone's face turned dull red. "I've got a rifle and I know how to use it. I'm not afraid of that bastard."

Daisy's face went gray. "What if he has another girl in there? Maybe someone else's daughter."

Portia stiffened and squirmed in her seat. She needed to tell them. "Um."

Her father picked up on her distress. "What is it, sweetheart?"

"You can't tell the police where he is."

Boone almost shouted his answer, seeming angrier by the moment. "Why the hell not?"

She put both hands over her face and mumbled her words. "Because," she said. "Because I think I may have killed him."

She felt her father stiffen beside her. *"What?"*

Now the tears came, freely again. They traced her cheeks and made her voice hitch. "I think I may have... I may have killed him. It was the only way I could get away."

Grace jumped up and ran to her sister, pulling her into a hug. "It's okay. We'll take care of you. And I don't blame you one bit. That prick should've been strung up to die from the worst kind of torture. If you killed him," she wailed, suddenly in tears herself, "then good for you."

Anderson added his counsel again, the voice of reason in a sea of chaos. "But Portia's right. The innocent don't always get the benefit of the law. If she did kill him, they might charge her. But if they don't know who she is..."

Boone stopped pacing and looked toward the barn. "We've gotta dump that truck. And its plates. It needs to disappear, forever."

Her mother's face had turned paler than before. "I don't know about this. We're talking about conspiring to break the law."

Portia sat still, crying silently, but the tears still wet her cheeks. "Mom? Do you want me to go to jail?"

Daisy turned to her, resolve stamped on her face. "Goodness, no, baby. I'm sorry." She stood, placing her hands on Portia's shoulders. "I'm with you all. Let's do what we have to do to protect our girl."

Dirk stood, looking out the window. "We've got to go out there, find out if he's dead or alive."

Anderson nodded solemnly. "It has to be done quietly. There needs to be a good excuse for us to be there. Something completely innocent and believable."

Grace swung toward Anderson. "Us?"

His face hardened. "Of course, us. I'm not going to let your father and Boone face this monster alone."

Grace slumped back in her chair. "Right."

"No!" Portia bolted from her seat, ran to her father, and started pulling on his arm. "You can't go out there. If I didn't kill him, if I just knocked him out...he'll kill you. He's ruthless. He's strong. He's smart." She sobbed the last words. "He's a monster."

Boone stepped toward her. "How would he know us, Peaches?"

"He had no television. But you guys were all over the newspapers. He bought several papers each week, clipped the articles. He knows you all by name." She turned to Anderson. "Except you. I don't think he knew you guys were married."

Grace looked scared. "Oh my God."

Dirk turned from the window. "We can't assume he isn't capable of retribution." He thought for a moment. "We've gotta find out what happened to him. Carefully. Without alarming anyone."

Grace said, "What about the papers? We can do a search on the town. Look at the obits online. That kind of thing."

"That'll work if his body was found," Boone said. "But if he lived like a hermit, which I'm assuming is why Portia was never found, he could still be lying there." Boone pulled out a chair again and sat down, running his hands through his shaggy blond hair. "I've got some ideas. Let me think on it. Meanwhile, Peaches, can you tell us more about the place? What did you see the first day you arrived?"

Chapter 17

The ride to the cabin had been long and filled with blackness and distortion. He had settled Portia on the seat beside him, and when she began to wake up, he'd clamped the horrible cloth over her face again, pushing her back to the darkness.

"I remember a few things on the way up there, but mostly I was drugged. Chloroform, I think. He poured it out of a bottle and put it on a cloth over my nose."

They listened closely while she mentally returned to the trip that had begun her two years in hell.

"He threw my purse out the window at one point. I remember feeling a sense of terrible loss. Everything was in there. My license. My cell phone. Everything."

Boone spoke up. "No one ever reported finding it."

"It was very rural. I'd just woken up because cold air came in the window, and when he leaned over to toss it out, I saw it go sailing past me in what felt like slow motion. I was so dizzy. But I seem to remember going over a bridge. Maybe a river."

"That would explain it," Boone said.

Dirk continued to take notes. "Bridge. River. Okay. What else?"

"There was a town called Middleton. I remember signs for hotels lit up. It was night."

Anderson looked up. "I know where that is. I did an undergrad semester at the university in Madison, Wisconsin. It's just next door."

Grace and Daisy watched and listened with intent expressions on their faces, as if they were trying to absorb as much as possible and somehow, through the powers of their minds, find answers.

Portia turned to Boone. "In the truck behind the barn, there are papers in the glove box. Probably his registration and insurance. Can you get them?"

He was out the door in a flash, and back in a few minutes with the folder in hand. "Here you go."

"Give it to Dad, please." She motioned to her father. "Check out the address."

Dirk rummaged through the papers and peered at them closely. "Daisy? Have you got your glasses on? What's that say?" He handed the paper to his wife.

"Looks like his name is Budley McVail. And it's a place called Baraboo, Wisconsin. What a funny name. For both of them."

"I don't think that's his real name," Portia said, sounding defeated. "He might have stolen the truck."

Portia's father jumped up and grabbed a US Atlas from the desk in the living room, flipping through the pages until he found Wisconsin. "Let see. Here's Madison." He moved his finger up the map. "And here's Middleton."

Boone and Anderson got up and watched over his shoulder. Dirk's finger moved on the map. "There it is. Baraboo. Looks like it's about thirty or forty miles north of Middleton."

Portia sat quietly while they talked about the landscape, and possible approaches. She waited until their comments had slowed, and said. "There's more. We were right next to a lake."

"Hmm. There's a lake just south of the town called Devil's Lake. Could be a possibility. Lots of woods and state land there, too."

"That's it!" Portia said with a shiver. "Devil's Lake."

Her father looked up with an encouraging smile. "Please, go on."

"The road to the cabin woke me up. It was so bumpy, like it wasn't even meant for cars, you know? I remember hearing the axle hit roots or rocks, and occasionally he'd have to back up and go around another way."

She paused, closing her eyes to remember. "There was a pole at one intersection with deer antlers nailed to it. Like some sort of trophies. I remember the truck headlights lighting them up. Disgusting." She shook her head and grimaced. "Of course, when I drove out of there I was in such a panic I don't remember a thing about it. It was a miracle I found my way out."

Daisy leaned over and touched her hand. "Could you see the cabin? What did it look like?"

Portia sighed with trembling breath. Exhaustion started to creep over her and she didn't know how much more she could share before she'd need a break.

Her mother picked up on it. "That is, honey, if you're up to it? Do you want to stop for a bit?"

"No. A few more minutes will be okay." Portia steeled herself. "It was a hunting cabin, I think. Heated by wood. It had a tin roof, and I only know that because I'd hear the rain on it, beating away..." She focused inwardly. "There was a front porch. All the windows were boarded up. It had a generator which ran the lights and well pump."

Boone said, "That might make it easier to trace. He'd have to feed it with gas all the time. He'd have to go out for that on a regular basis."

Anderson agreed. "Good point."

Portia let out a tired sigh and leaned back against the chair. "He did. He often went out for gas for the generator."

Grace said, "What was it like inside?"

Her sister's face fell. "It was my prison for two years. I could draw you a picture of every square inch of the inside." The emotion that hit her came swiftly, surprising her with its sudden intensity. She collapsed onto her arms on the table, weeping softly.

Daisy stood suddenly. "That's enough for now. I'm taking her upstairs."

Portia raised a tear-stained face to her mother. "No. I don't want to be cooped up anymore. I want to be outside."

Daisy's eyes widened. "Well, okay, honey. Wanna sit on the porch?"

Portia shook her head. "No. I don't want anyone to see me."

Boone stood and held out a hand with a tentative smile. "How about that old glider behind the barn? We can set you up so you can see all the horses, the hills. Want to try that?"

She nodded, tears still trickling down her cheeks. "Thank you. That would be perfect." To her own surprise, she took his hand and let him walk her toward the door. Before they went out, she turned to the group with a hitch in her throat. "Thanks for listening."

The returned murmurs of affection gave her a renewed sense of strength, and surprising herself even further, she let Boone lead her around the barn.

Chapter 18

Boone settled Portia on the glider, then ran back into the house to bring out a quilt, pillow, bottle of water, and a few magazines Daisy pushed on him.

"Here you go," he said, slightly breathless from running. "You can even use the little bathroom in the groom's apartment. Remember? It's right through this door, here."

She snorted. "Of course I remember. I'm not totally brain dead." She tucked her legs under her, covering her lap with the quilt.

Boone grinned. "Okay, Peaches. Settle down there, girl."

"I'm not a horse!" The corners of her mouth twitched. "Except I think I'd rather be one, at this point in my life."

"Don't blame you. It would be one nice life. Especially if you lived on this farm." Boone pointed to the far end of the glider. "May I?"

"I guess." She nodded, sliding closer to the other end, away from him.

He sat down and began to move the seat back and forth in a comforting, rhythmic motion. "Remember when we were kids? We'd come out here after we had a long ride, have your mom's lemonade... Those summer days were some of my best memories ever."

Portia began to relax. The sun-dappled patterns from the lilac hedges growing near the barn warmed her face and fluttered on her eyelashes, soothing her. "Me, too."

"Remember the time we went up to Deacon's Point? And we got—"

"—caught in that thunderstorm?" she said.

"Yeah. That was so cool."

She actually chuckled, welcoming the sound. "We got drenched!"

"And ran for that cave, where you heard the mysterious growling sound."

"I wonder what lived in there. Was it a big cat? Or a bear?"

"I didn't hear it. I still think you imagined it," he said, tilting a smile toward her so she'd know he was just kidding.

"I didn't imagine it!" She unfolded her legs and put them on the ground, pushing back and forth in the same rhythm as Boone. The simple feeling of gliding gave her comfort, and for the first time since she returned home, she felt safe.

But Portia jumped when her father came around the corner with Anderson, who wielded a long screwdriver. With a nod, they headed for the beat up blue truck and knelt at both ends, removing the license plates. She watched her father tuck the plates into the incinerator by the back shed. Would they burn? Or would he dispose of them later?

They opened the driver's side door and using the blade from a box cutter, scraped off all the stickers from the window.

Boone watched them work. "I think they're trying to get the VIN number off now. There's probably a metal plate on the dash... Yup. They've got it. And now the one on the engine block. Okay, good. All traceability is gone."

Anderson and her dad conferred for a minute, and then disappeared. Her father got in the truck and started it up, heading down the dirt track that wound toward the woods. He leaned out the window with a small wave. "Back in a few hours."

Anderson's Jeep appeared around the corner, following the truck. She watched until they vanished into the deep woods at the base of the mountains. "Where do you think they'll hide it?" she whispered.

Boone squinted in the sunlight. "I'm guessing No Bottom Pond. They could drive it right up the ledge and push it over.

80

They've never been able to measure the depth of that hole. It's at least a mile down, some say. You'd never see it again."

She nodded. "That's probably where they're headed." She frowned suddenly. "But what if someone sees them?"

He twisted his wrist and checked the time. "Not too likely. No hunting this time of year. It's all your dad's private property. Unless there's a random hiker up there..."

"Yeah. I guess you're right. And they'll be careful."

"There's no one on earth more careful than your father," he said. "And he really loves you, Portia."

She smiled and started the glider going again. "I know. He's the best."

Boone's face changed, and she wondered what had upset him. "What?" she asked.

"I just wanted to say I'm really sorry about what happened to you. It's so damned unfair."

She didn't say a word, just pushed the glider back and forth, but his words comforted her.

"And I hope, I pray... that someday you will realize not all men are like that Murphy creep. He's the exception, not the rule." He reached over to touch her hand, but hesitated mid-air.

"I'll get there," she said with a sad smile. "Just give me time."

Boone pulled his hand back, laying it palm-down on his thigh. "Deal."

∾

They glided for another hour. Boone made small talk about the horses and the farm, filling her in on who'd had what foals and which pastures they were settled in. He talked about the roof leaking, the big tractor getting stuck in the mud last spring, and how the local farrier had thrown his back out, causing all horse owners to panic. They'd found a replacement to shoe their horses, but nobody loved the new guy as much as old Hank.

"How about tomorrow I take you out to see all the new babies? There are four, to be exact. And there's one I think you'll really like. He's the spitting image of Mirage."

Turning to Portia, he noticed with a start that she had fallen asleep. When had that happened? He shook his head, realized he'd probably been talking to himself for the past few minutes, and gently got up, whispering to her sleeping form. "Sleep well, Peaches. I'll check on you soon."

Chapter 19

Boone, Dirk, and Anderson pored over the maps they spread on the kitchen table. They'd been discussing options for over an hour after the two men returned from dumping the truck in the pond. Boone had checked on Portia twice, and she was still curled in a ball, sleeping on the glider with both dogs snoring on the grass beneath her.

Daisy and Grace crouched over a laptop, sitting side by side on the couch. Grace announced their findings as they progressed.

"Found the town of Baraboo."

"Here are the obits—they're listed with photos in the Baraboo News Republic."

"Lots of people died this month. Wow."

"Mostly women, elderly."

She and Daisy exchanged disappointed glances, then stood and came to the table. "No luck so far. Either he's not dead, or no one's found him yet."

Dirk grimaced. "Looks like we need to make some phone calls, and if that doesn't work, we take a road trip."

Boone leaned his chair back, balancing on two legs. "We need to find out more about Murphy. First of all, how and why he chose Portia. Secondly, how much he knew about all of us. From what she said, he followed the case in the papers, it's gonna be really hard to just blend into the town as if we are passing through. Especially if we start asking a lot of questions. He might have friends up there who could tip him off."

Anderson chewed on the end of a pencil. "Unless we concoct some story about one of us being a journalist. Maybe I could be doing a piece on 'living off the grid,' or something like that? I could try to do it over the phone, and contact someone at The Baraboo News Republic."

Grace pulled out a chair and sank into it. "With your theater background, you'd be the best one to pull that off. You're a natural actor, honey."

Boone looked up. He'd forgotten Anderson taught drama classes. That was how he'd met Grace, when she had a part in one of his productions. "Good idea. You could try to dig up a list of names of folks who live out in the woods. There probably wouldn't be too many, especially those who live there year round."

Dirk's thoughts seemed to drift elsewhere. He stood, walked around the table a few times, and stopped at the window. "It just dawned on me. If he's alive, there are two ways he might have reacted to Portia's escape. Either he's pissed off and will want revenge, maybe to recapture her...or he's afraid she'll bring the cops down on him and might have disappeared even further into the woods to hide. After what happened to that guy Ariel Castro—he might be running scared."

Portia appeared in the doorway, the quilt and pillows in hand. "He'll be mad. He has a huge ego, and an even bigger temper. If he's alive, he'll come after me."

Daisy ran her hands through her short hair. "Well. If that's the case, you men sure can't desert us and head out to Wisconsin." Her brow furrowed. "What if he's already on his way here? Or somewhere out there, in the woods? Watching, waiting?"

Stillness came over the room.

"Right," Dirk said. "I'm getting my rifle."

Boone stood up and scanned the woods through the kitchen window. "Mine's in the truck. Might be better to keep it here, by the door." He turned to Dirk and Daisy. "Might also be a good idea for me to bunk in the groom's shed until we figure out what's going on."

Daisy shook her head. "No. You can sleep right here on the couch. It's much more comfortable and closer."

Dirk turned to him. "You sure your family can spare you, Boone? We've already taken terrible advantage of your kindness."

Boone shook his head. "They're doing fine. You folks are my second family, anyway. I'd never desert you at a time like this."

Dirk shook Boone's hand, pulling him into a bear hug. "If I'd had a boy, I'd have been proud for him to turn out just like you, son."

Portia tossed a grateful smile at Boone, then went toward the stairs. "Think I'll go up for a rest."

Grace jumped up to go with her. "It's my turn. Can I come with you?" She linked arms with her sister at the bottom of the stairs.

"Sure," Portia said with a soft sigh. She whistled to the dogs, who immediately followed the girls up to the bedroom.

Chapter 20

Grace climbed into the bed with her sister and snuggled closer to her, lying on her side facing Portia. "Just like when we were little, huh?"

Portia sighed. "Yeah. Except..."

Grace. "I know. A lot has happened."

"Too much."

"You too tired to talk?" Grace said, one hand stroking Portia's shoulder.

"I don't know. It is pretty exhausting. You know, reliving the whole thing."

"I can only imagine."

"I don't want you to. Nobody should have to know about that kind of evil."

Grace's eyes puddled. "He really hurt you."

"Uh huh."

"What did he do, exactly?"

Portia's eyes closed. "I think that's a story for another day. I..."

Grace's face fell. "I'm sorry. I shouldn't have asked."

"Tomorrow, maybe. Let me get my strength back. K?"

"Okay."

The dogs jumped onto the bed. Cupcake sat on Portia's pillow, licking her face, and Boomer wiggled up between the girls.

With eyes closed, Portia spoke in a soft, mumbling tone. "Dogs are the best."

Grace stroked Boomer's soft fur. "Yeah. They are."

In minutes, they were both asleep.

❧❦

Murphy came for her as always, big and hulking, naked, and glistening from the shower. His shoulders bunched and he leaned forward to touch her face. "Hey, sugar. You ready for a night of romance?"

She screamed a silent NO! and strained against the ropes that held her tight to the bedposts while he untied those holding her legs to the footboards. Kicking with all her might, she landed blow after blow on his tree trunk body, but nothing stopped him from moving closer.

Hovering over her, she tasted his salty lips on hers and cringed with all her soul, pulling away, shrinking as far inside herself as she could.

NO!

His rough hands pulled back the clothes, and he lowered his face to her breasts, suckling her like the child she'd never have. He hurt her, with his none-too-gentle teeth biting her tender flesh. Twisting and turning beneath him, she cried and groaned, but he wouldn't stop.

When he lifted her skirt to touch between her legs, she let loose and screamed, because for some odd reason, today the duct tape had been removed from her mouth and she was now gloriously, wondrously free to spew the terrified sound as loud and as far as possible.

❧❦

"Portia!" Grace shook her. "Wake up."

She woke in a cold sweat with fear clamped tightly around her heart, squeezing the breath from her. "Oh, God. It was *him*." Tumbling into her sister's arms, she sobbed against her, hearing her mother and father, Boone, and Anderson pounding up the stairs and queuing in the doorway.

"What happened?" Dirk shouted.

"Just a dream," Grace said, stroking Portia's back. "She's okay. It was just a bad dream."

Portia didn't open her eyes. She couldn't. She heard the crowd of family and friends dissipate, and when they were alone again, she uttered one last huge sob against Grace's chest, then pulled back, burrowing under the comforter.

"I'm sorry," she whispered. "It was *him*. He was coming at me again."

Grace surprised her with the sweet ministrations she offered. She'd never seen this side of her sister, and told her so. "You're so nice to me. Just like mom." She raised a tear-stained face to her sister. "Thank you."

Grace's face crumpled. "Well, after all I put you through in our childhood, I kinda owe you, Sis."

Portia shook her head. "Don't be silly. Everybody does dumb stuff when they're young. You weren't much different from other kids your age."

"Yes, I was. I didn't just dabble in drugs. I lived for drugs. I was…I am…an addict."

"Still?" Portia's eyes widened.

"Once an addict, always an addict," she said. "I don't use any more. But I always feel the pull. Especially when stuff goes wrong."

"You mean like when I was taken?"

Grace nodded. "That. And any other reason. But to tell the truth, when I saw mom fall apart after you disappeared, it made me stronger. I had to be there for her. So I resisted, mostly."

"Mostly?"

Grace hung her head. "Once in a while I screw up. I've done some bad things, Portia. I can't seem to resist a hunky guy. It makes me all crazy inside." She checked the doorway. "I've cheated on Anderson. Three times."

Portia tried not to show her surprise. What Grace didn't need was a preachy older sister right now. "Does he know?"

"I'm not sure. Maybe. We never talked about it. I just go away for a few days, then I finally come to my senses and call him." A few tears glistened in her eyes. "He never asks questions, he just comes to get me. And we go home. As if everything is normal."

She glanced toward the door again. "But it's not! I'm not normal, Portia. I've got issues. Serious fidelity issues."

It was Portia's turn to comfort her sister, and she stroked her hair, looking into Grace's worried eyes. "Listen. Everybody's got stuff they need to work on. But Anderson seems like an amazing man, like he has a heart of gold."

"I know. He loves me no matter what I do."

"Well, then. That's the sign of true love, right? Unconditional love?"

"Yeah." Grace's mouth trembled. "I guess we both have work to do, you and me. Huh?"

"I guess." Portia reached for her sister again, cuddling against her. "Maybe we can help each other."

"Count on it, sis."

Chapter 21

Portia woke the next morning after a restless night of playing tug-o-war with Grace and the comforter. She'd insisted on spending the night with her, and Portia hadn't argued. It felt good to have her sister close.

Now Grace stood on the other side of the room, looking out the window. Portia watched the sun play over her sister's freshly washed hair. The soft morning breeze rippled her thin bathrobe. It flapped in the freshening draft, and Portia was surprised to see Grace wore nothing beneath it.

Grace had worn sweats to bed the night before, and Portia realized that since her sister's hair was still wet, and she'd tossed a damp towel over the chair in the corner, she must've just wrapped herself in this flimsy housecoat after getting out of the shower.

Grace stared down at the yard, so intent on the object of her interest, she didn't hear Portia stir.

The girl dropped her robe and stood naked in the sunlight. Portia's immediate thought was how supple and healthy Grace looked, how she'd filled out in all the right places, and how different she looked from the drug-addicted girl two years ago.

Although surprised at her sister's casual behavior, she couldn't help but compare her own emaciated body with Grace's. Where her hips softly swelled beneath her waist, Portia's bones stuck out. Grace's golden hair hung softly on creamy-looking shoulders, where Portia's shoulders were...different.

Quietly, she got up and padded to her sister's side, following her gaze down to the barnyard.

Boone stood in the paddock, tossing hay to the mares crowding around him. It was barely seven in the morning, but it seemed he'd been at work for a while. His blue tee shirt was soaked along the back and under the arms. Both girls stood and watched him work, his muscles rippling beneath the shirt, his shaggy hair blowing in the breeze.

When he glanced up at the window, at first Grace didn't move away.

Portia inhaled sharply, grabbing her sister's arm. "Move back! He'll see you."

Grace's lips slid into a smile. "I know." She slowly moved back. "He's a real hunk, isn't he?"

Portia grimaced. She tightened Grace's robe around her, tying the belt into a bow. "For goodness sakes, Grace. Get a grip. You're a married woman."

Grace trilled a laugh. "I know. I'm not sleeping with Boone. I just like thinking about it."

"What?" Portia stifled a laugh. "That's horrible!"

"Oh, come on. Don't tell me you never fantasized in your old life. About some guy you saw, who was maybe already taken?"

"I—" Portia couldn't remember how she felt before it all happened. Before he took her, before he tied her to the bed, day after day, night after night. Before he took her soul.

"Don't tell me you *never* thought about it?"

Portia collapsed onto the side of the bed, running her fingers through her dark copper hair. "I honestly can't remember. My life before...it seems like it belonged to someone else. I can hardly remember college. Or high school. Or any of it."

"Do you remember me?"

"Of course I do. I remember how hard life was for you back then."

Grace slid onto the bed beside Portia, laying her wet head on the pillow and sighing. "You had no idea."

Portia tried to rise above her own self-pity and took Grace's hand. "What do you mean?"

"I did some horrible things back then. Stuff you guys never knew about." A panicked look came over her face. "I'm lucky I wasn't murdered or put in jail."

"You're exaggerating, right?"

"No." Grace slumped further against the pillow, her voice muffled. "I sold myself for money once. And another time, I stole drugs and money from a dealer."

Portia sat still, digesting her words.

"Do you hate me?" Grace asked, tugging on her sister's hand.

"Of course not. You just took me off guard, hon. I can't picture you doing that. I never knew it was *that* bad."

"Oh, it was. I was a real lost cause. I used to try to seduce Boone to get money."

"Really?" One of Portia's eyebrows lifted.

"Really. But he never gave me a penny. All he did was give me a ride to the rehab center, after he squealed to Dad about me."

Portia smiled. "He's a good man."

"Yeah. I guess. Gorgeous, too."

"I suppose."

"You may not see it now," Grace said. "But he's in love with you."

"What in God's name are you talking about?"

"It's the way he looks at you. And doesn't look at you. I have a sense about these things. He's got it bad."

Portia stood, shaking off her sister's hand. "You're delusional. I'm damaged goods. No man will ever look at me. And I'll never be able to stand being alone with a man ever again." She closed her eyes, feeling the walls closing in on her. "Maybe I'll just become a nun or something."

92

"A nun?"

"I don't know. Either that or an old spinster. The kind who rocks on her porch and scares little kids, she's so mean and ugly."

"Mean and ugly?" Grace laughed. "That's too hard for me to picture. Besides. You're not damaged goods to Boone. And I think he'd wait forever for you." She sat up, stretched, and walked over to her sister's side, taking both her hands in hers. "You know what else I think?"

Portia started to pull away, closing off the topic. "What?"

"Look at me, Portia."

She locked eyes with Grace. "What?"

"I think you and I are both going to be okay. We'll help each other. We'll get through this."

"You think it's possible?"

Grace smiled, pulling her sister into a close hug. "I do. I love you, sis. And I know you love me."

"I always thought you hated me."

"I did. For a while. Then I came to my senses and grew up. Sort of."

"You did. You're amazing now."

Grace's lips curled into a sad smile. "Wanna know what made me miss you the most?"

"Yes."

"I'd been missing you, searching for you, helping Mom through the whole thing, year after year." She took a deep breath. "But the worst was my wedding. I couldn't help but feel this horrible, big hole in my heart when you weren't my maid of honor."

Tears trickled down Portia's cheeks and her face crumpled. Grace gently wiped the tears away. "No, hon. Don't cry. We're together now. I'll show you my wedding dress and all the pictures. I'll tell you about every magical, bittersweet moment. Okay?"

Portia smiled through tears that wouldn't stop. "I'd like that very much," she said, and pulled her sister closer. "I love you, Gracie."

"Back atcha, Sweet Pea."

"You haven't called me that since we were little kids."

Grace grinned. "I know. Remember you used to call me Baby Cakes?"

Portia laughed through her tears. "Oh, gosh. I'd forgotten. Baby Cakes. Can I still call you that?"

"Long as I can call you Sweet Pea."

Grace laid her forehead against Portia's. "You've got a deal."

Chapter 22

Portia came out of the shower half an hour later, pulling her hair into a loose ponytail with a stray band she found in the medicine cabinet. *He'd* never let her wear her hair any way other than loose and long on her shoulders.

She found her parents waiting in the bedroom. Their tight-lipped expressions made her stop mid-stride.

"What's wrong?" she asked.

Her father stepped forward, looking nervously through the window and driveway below. "The Sheriff's here, honey. He wants to ask you some questions."

She froze, hot acid rising in her throat. "What the hell do I tell them, Dad?" She turned to her mother. "Mom?"

Her mother hurried toward her. She wrapped her arms around Portia's shoulders and searched her eyes. "You tell them the truth, but leave out the location and the truck. That way, if you did...er...kill Murphy, they won't be able to find him or charge you. And they won't be able to get you for the truck theft, either. Just tell them you escaped from a cabin in the woods."

Her father stepped forward. "You don't know where he kept you. Just that it was the woods somewhere in Wisconsin. You ran and ran, you hitched rides, and you got here by the skin of your teeth. We've all got the story down, princess. Just keep it simple."

She let out a long breath. "Okay. I escaped. I hitched home from somewhere in Wisconsin."

Her father nodded. "Yes. Keep it simple. I don't want you going to jail for murder. Not with this crazy legal system we've got now. Every time you turn around, the innocent are getting punished for shooting some intruder in their own homes, and the criminals are protected." He swiped a hand over his face. "Well. Not in my family. You're gonna be safe, princess."

Portia squared her shoulders. "Okay. I think I've got it."

Her mother linked arms with her. "Everyone's been briefed, including Boone. Just stick to the facts. No elaboration. You'll be okay."

᷇ᵛ᷇

Boone watched Portia and her parents descend the stairs. He'd already been questioned and kept his responses simple and short, just like the Lamonts suggested. No, he didn't know what had happened. Portia hadn't said much. She'd just shown up on the kitchen porch.

His heart squeezed when the frail girl entered the living room where Anderson sat with the Sheriff and his deputy. He'd been talking politics with them, and had shown an uncanny ability to get them off the topic of Portia. Anderson had played down her return with great skill.

"That President of ours is destroying this country!" Deputy Mills circled the living room with his hands waving in the air. "Do you know how much me and Miranda are paying for health care today? Almost a thousand dollars a month! And that's not counting all the copays we gotta fork over for prescriptions and hospital visits. If you'd told me ten years ago I'd be paying more than half my salary for health care, I woulda laughed in your face."

Boone watched the young man with the shock of red hair gesticulating and ranting. Anderson had really gotten him going.

Anderson stood with his arms around Grace, who'd just set a tray with coffee and cookies on the chest in front of the couch. He nodded to Portia and her parents. "Well, I agree, Deputy Mills. But looks like our dear Portia is ready to chat with you."

The Sheriff, who'd been sitting in the armchair staring at his notes, glanced up. "Ah. Miss Lamont. It's a real pleasure to see you back home. We've been looking for you for a long time."

Portia paled, wobbled against her father, and sank onto the couch between both parents, who draped their arms protectively across her shoulders. "Thank you, Sheriff. I'm just glad to be home."

Boone wondered about her ragged tone of voice. Could she pull off the story? Would they suspect her of anything? With all his might, he willed her to be strong. To stay safe. To keep out of jail.

Sheriff Dunne stood and came forward, tipping his hat and then offering a hand to her. "Welcome back."

She touched her limp fingers to his, releasing a long sigh. "Thank you. But I have to warn you, it's still really hard to talk about what happened. It's all too fresh."

He backed up and sat down again, pulling a pencil from his breast pocket. "Understandable. But if you want us to catch the guy who hurt you, you'll have to tell us everything you can."

Portia leaned back against the couch. "I'll try."

Daisy sat up, and Boone felt a tug of love for her, too. She was so brave. Such a great mother.

"Sheriff, my daughter's been through hell and back. She's a wreck. If we could keep this short and simple, it'd be best for her today. As more and more details come back to her, we can call you. We'll keep you up to date."

Sheriff Dunne wiped a handkerchief across his brow. "We'll try to make this as painless as possible. Let's start with the night of the abduction." He looked over the tops of his bifocals, his eyes riveted on Portia. "You *were* abducted, right? That's what Boone and your sister said."

Dirk interrupted with an angry outburst. "For crying out loud, Sheriff. We've told you—hell, I told you *for two years in a row*—that she was taken from us! Why do you still have to act so damned suspicious?"

"Sorry, Dirk. Didn't mean to doubt you." The Sheriff nodded to him, then around the room to the family. "I know it's been hard. And I realize we've had to ask questions that upset you. We've just been trying to do our job."

Grace stood beside Anderson, leaning against him with one arm around his waist. She suddenly straightened and huffed. "Your job? Your fucking job was to find her! And you didn't! You *stopped* looking for her, Sheriff. You told us you thought she ran away. That she didn't want to be found. And that *really* pissed us off."

Daisy's eyes flew toward her youngest daughter. "Grace, please!"

Boone smiled. "Grace's right, Sheriff. You kinda lost interest after a while."

Deputy Mills ran a hand through his short red hair. "Hey, let's calm down here. Maybe you folks have a point. Well, of course you do. But let's move forward. We'll ask our questions and be outta your hair soon. Right, Sheriff?"

Sheriff Dunne's shoulders dropped a quarter inch. "Of course. Let's get on with business." He turned to Portia. "Sorry, Miss Lamont. Can you describe the guy?"

She answered readily. Boone noticed her description wasn't as detailed as before. *Good. If he's dead, it'll be harder to link her to his murder. If he's not...well, later we can tell them more.*

"Why don't you just tell us what happened on the day you disappeared?" Sheriff Dunne said.

Portia handled this part well. She'd already told it to the whole family earlier, and the second time through, the words seemed to come more readily. She went through the events that led up to her abduction, then stopped for a breather, leaning against her father's shoulder.

The Sheriff scribbled for a while, then turned to her. "Good job. Now, did the man pay for his plants with cash or credit?"

She answered readily. "Cash."

The Sheriff noted it down. "Damn. No credit card to trace, I guess."

Portia nodded. "No."

"Where did he keep you?"

Portia paled, now it was getting tricky. "A cabin in the woods. Windows all boarded up. Doors always bolted. I think it was somewhere in northern Wisconsin."

"Town name? Street names?"

Portia faced him straight on, and it was at this point Boone knew she'd be able to hold her own. "I escaped in the middle of the night, Sheriff. I ran for my life through the woods, afraid he would follow me. I ended up on a lonely road. Hitched a ride with a fisherman, then went from truck stop to truck stop on the highway to make it home. It's all a blur. I just remember a few signs. One for Chicago. One for Milwaukee. I think."

"Maybe we can study a map later on, see if any of the towns jog your memory." The Sheriff added notes to his book. "At any time, did he mention his name? Did you see any mail? Hear him talking on the phone?"

"No." She lowered her eyes, and Boone saw her fingers tighten on her father's hand.

Daisy spoke up. "But we're worried, Sheriff. He's a real possessive sort. Portia's afraid he might try to come get her again. Exact some sort of revenge for her leaving him. You know?"

The Sheriff stood and paced, glancing out the window. "That so? Did he ever threaten you with that?"

Portia shrank into the couch. "Yes. He did." She closed her eyes as if reciting from memory. "He said if I ever left him, he'd

99

find me, and kill me slowly." She shuddered. "Those were his exact words."

Deputy Mills leaned forward. "He doesn't know where you live, does he?"

Portia's eyes filled with tears, and all Boone wanted to do was gather her in his arms and take her away, far away from it all.

"Yes. He followed the stories in the papers. Clipped the articles about it. He loved reading their accounts about how I disappeared." She crossed her arms in front of her chest. "And he'd laugh. Talk about how much smarter he was than the police."

Sheriff Dunne bristled. "Well, he may be smart, but we've got God on our side. We'll find this bastard, Miss Lamont. We'll find him, arrest him, and make him pay for what he's done to you and your family."

In spite of the fact that Boone was worried for Portia—seriously afraid she might have committed murder in self-defense—he realized he liked this guy. "Sheriff," he said. "Anything we can do to help, you just let us know. We want him behind bars more than you'll ever know."

Deputy Mills narrowed his eyes, doubting Boone's right to be there. "You part of the family, son?"

Boone stood his ground. "Hey. I've known Portia since she was a little kid. We used to ride the hills together. And my family's been friends with the Lamonts forever. They went through hell when she was taken. And if you need a hand, you can deputize me on the spot. I'm one helluva shot."

The Sheriff sent a nod in his direction. "Thank you, Boone. We'll keep that in mind. Now, Miss Lamont. How do you think this guy targeted you? Did he you watch you? Plan it for a long time? Or do you think it was on impulse?"

Portia looked him straight in the eye. "He told me he'd been trolling for the right woman, Sheriff. He kept the chloroform in his truck, and he'd been searching for the past few weeks, driving from state to state. He said—" Her voice broke and she stopped for a minute. "He said when he saw me, he knew I was 'the one.'"

Sheriff Dunne grimaced. "Crap. Sounds like a lunatic."

Portia's face tightened. "You've got that right."

Mills flipped a page in his notebook and interrupted. "What the hell did he do to you, anyway, Miss? Why couldn't you get away?"

Before Portia could answer—Doc Hardy entered the room, black bag in hand and a worried expression on his kindly face. "Mills, you're an idiot. Look at the scars on her wrists and ankles. The monster tied her up."

Deputy Mills stuttered, his eyes raking Portia's wounds. "Oh, I...er...sorry."

Doc pushed past them. "You need to give this girl some space. Portia's fragile right now. I'm here to see how she's coming along." He leaned down to lift Portia's chin, examining her eyes. "Think you guys could continue another day? The kid needs her rest."

Doc took her wrist in his hands, checking his watch to measure her heartbeat. "Haven't you got enough to go on yet?"

The Sheriff nodded and closed his notebook. "I think we're good for now. I'm sure we'll have more questions, but we can do this another day. The important thing is she's home and safe." He rose and turned to Dirk and Daisy. "I'd like to assign an officer to keep watch on your place. That okay with you folks?"

"Thanks, Sheriff." Dirk stood and peered out the window. "That's not a bad idea. Until we know what we're up against, anyway. God knows where this monster is. He could be watching us right now."

Boone glanced toward his rifle that stood by the door beside Dirk's. *No way is that guy getting to Portia. Not while I'm alive.*

Chapter 23

Boone slumped over the computer in the Lamonts' living room, staring at the screen. He'd been at it for hours after the family went to bed at nine o'clock. The couch beckoned with its soft pillow and comforter Daisy had laid out for him. She'd even tucked a fresh sheet into the cushions.

But he couldn't give up. He needed to find out as much as possible about this guy Murphy, and his quest unearthed more than he expected.

The archives of the Baraboo newspaper were mostly online, and his searches for things like school photos, town events, and related articles had borne fruit. The printer had been spitting pages for the past hour, and he'd laid them out on the table beside him.

Murphy was a football star in high school, and yes, he'd gone to Baraboo High. Some well-intentioned enthusiast had posted football photos in albums by year on the school website of all varsity teams going back to the fifties. It was a work of love, and Boone silently thanked the person who'd scanned photos, uploaded them, and meticulously labeled the players' names by row.

He found several photos of Murphy in 1995, captain of the team. He'd been a senior then, so Boone figured he was born in 1979 or thereabouts, which would make him about thirty-five now.

Charles C. Murphy. The name matched the scowling face of the brute in the fourth position of the top row.

He looked big all right. Massive shoulders, beefy face, taller than his teammates.

He'd also shown up in a newspaper photo of a fishing derby winner's circle two years ago.

There he was, smiling like a fool, holding up his giant pike.

Had he gone fishing while Portia was tied to his bed? Or was this before he'd gone mad and kidnapped her from the greenhouse parking lot?

Footsteps came down the stairs, slow and steady.

Boone glanced at the clock. Two A.M.

"Boone?" Anderson ran a hand through his sandy hair. "You still up?"

"Yeah. Doing some research."

Anderson shuffled toward him, yawning. "I've been trying to sleep, but kept dreaming about that monster who took Portia." He bent down to look at the computer screen. "We need facts. We've gotta know if he's dead or alive."

Boone stretched his arms over his head, leaning back in the chair. "Exactly. Which is why I'm doing this." He waved toward the photos. "Now we know what he looks like."

Anderson came fully awake and picked up the printout of Murphy in the fishing derby. "Great Scott. You did it." He peered at the face. "This is him, huh?"

Boone nodded. "I want to make the picture bigger. You know how to do that?"

Anderson seemed excited. "You bet I do. Shove over. Let me see if they have Photoshop on this beast."

Boone got up and stood behind Anderson, who searched for the program, found an old version of it, and uploaded the picture file saved on the desktop.

"There we go." He clicked on the photo, highlighted Murphy's face, and dragged a square around it. "Now, I just need to crop it, and..."

Murphy smiled at them from the screen.

Boone grimaced. "Mr. Charles C. Murphy, we're coming to get you."

Anderson shot him a grim smile. "You thinking what I'm thinking?"

Boone nodded. "Tomorrow morning okay with you? I printed out the directions on MapQuest. About eight hundred miles. Maybe twelve hours of driving. If we trade off, we could be there by dark, head out to find the cabin in the morning."

Anderson stood, his eyes burning with purpose. "We'll take care of this bastard."

Boone studied Anderson's eyes. He hadn't expected such murderous passion from a drama teacher. "You seen any action before? I mean, you're a college prof, right?"

Anderson smiled, his chest swelled. "Iraq. Two tours of duty."

Boone smiled broadly and shook his hand. "Afghanistan. Two years." He glanced upstairs. "Dirk's a good shot. He was a sniper in the army, long time ago, and he can hit a fly on a toad two miles away. The guy's amazing. He'll protect the ladies while we're gone."

Anderson paced the living room, thinking out loud. "I hate to leave him here alone, though." He turned to Boone. "What about your brother? Could you ask him to hang out here while we're gone? Keep an eye on things?"

Boone slid his phone out of his pocket and started to text. "Excellent idea. Let me send him a message. He's a light sleeper."

An hour later, Ned stood in the living room, dark hair tousled and rifle in hand. "I've got this, guys."

Boone quickly filled in his brother and gave him a copy of the blown-up photo of Murphy, while Anderson changed and threw together a backpack with clothing and supplies. Miraculously, the rest of the family hadn't awakened.

Boone slid into his jacket and gave his younger brother a hug. "Take good care of them for me, buddy. And tell Dirk I'm sorry I didn't wait. I just think the sooner we get up there, the better."

Anderson shouldered his pack, smiling. "Grace's gonna be mad. She didn't want me to go when we talked about it yesterday."

Ned shrugged. "I've seen her pissed off before. I was in her Spanish class in high school." He laughed. "She's a wildcat. But I can handle her."

A smile slid onto Boone's lips. "I know you can. Thanks." He headed for the door, then stopped and turned back to his brother. "Tell Portia we're gonna take care of this. And...tell her I'll see her soon."

Ned raised his rifle in a mock salute. "Will do. Now just go."

The men slipped into the dark night.

Chapter 24

At 2:30 PM in the afternoon, Anderson pulled into a MacDonald's in Madison, Wisconsin and shook Boone awake. "Boone. Almost there."

Instantly awake, Boone sat up and grabbed the map. "Where are we?"

"We just got off the beltway." Anderson pointed to U.S. Route 12 on the map. "South of Baraboo. Probably another half hour."

"Let's get some burgers," Boone said. "I'm starving."

Anderson nodded. "Me, too."

Over their meal of burgers and fries, the men plotted.

Boone demolished the first burger and started on his second. "When we get there, we find the newspaper office first. I'll wait in the car. Got your story straight?"

Anderson nodded. "Absolutely. I'm doing a story on aging football heroes. I think that's less telling than what we talked about before, checking out hermits living off the grid, don't you?"

"Yeah."

"I'll ask 'Where are they now? What happened to them over the years?' I'll show them the photo of Murphy's team."

"Right. And if they get suspicious, tell them you work for the Democrat and Chronicle, and that you're going cross-country to gather your material. If they ask for credentials, admit you're a freelance wannabe, and that you hope to sell this to the D&C when you get back."

"Got it."

"And pour on that charm. Find a gal you can wow with your big geeky smile."

Anderson chuckled and popped a fry into his mouth. "Sure. I'll just use my phantom of the opera voice."

"Huh?"

"I played that role in college, after I got back from the war. It was a blast. And it got me a number of...shall I say...adoring fans?"

Boone snorted a laugh. "Is that what you call them?"

"I didn't sleep with them all."

"Really?"

Anderson's smile widened. "No. None of them, actually. I had a girlfriend at the time. She would've killed me."

Boone nodded. "That sounds more like you." He wiped his mouth with a paper napkin. "Now, be cool about this. Show her photos from several years. You've got the new ones I printed out, right?"

"Right."

"Don't ask about Murphy specifically until she tells you he was the captain. Then go in for the kill and find out where that damned cabin is."

Anderson's eyes turned somber. "Consider it done."

࿔

Boone waited in the car while Anderson disappeared into the office of the Baraboo News Republic. He watched a few trucks pull into the loading docks in the back, and wondered if they were delivering rolls of blank newsprint or picking up papers to deliver. A few people came and went, and after about fifteen minutes of boredom, his mind began to wander back to Portia. He tapped her parents' phone number on his phone and waited for someone to pick up. Dirk answered on the first ring.

"Hello?"

"Hope you're not mad, Dirk," Boone said.

"Gosh darn it, Boone," Dirk practically shouted into the phone. "You didn't even give me a choice in the matter."

108

"Listen, I know. I'm sorry. But Portia said Murphy knows you, and somebody's gotta be there to protect the family. In case we're on a wild goose chase, you know?"

Dirk was quiet for a moment, and Boone pictured him walking in tight circles around the yard by the barn.

"I know. It's just..."

"You wanted to be part of this. I understand. I do."

"I wanted to kill the bastard, not just be part of it. That is, if he isn't already..."

"I know." Boone almost smiled. "But that's another good reason for you to stay home. We don't need more complications."

Dirk sighed. "I guess."

"Listen. We're here, anyway. Anderson's in the newspaper office right now, trying to get some info on the cabin. I'll let you know what we find out, okay?"

"Call me when you can. We're going crazy here, wondering. And Portia seems kinda worried about you."

"Yeah?"

"I'm still mad at you." Dirk suddenly barked a laugh. "Yeah. She's worried about you. But don't get too excited about it. She's still my little princess, and nobody's ever been good enough for her."

"I hear you. Portia's gonna need lots of help to get through this. I'd never..."

"I know."

"So, how did Grace take it?"

"She threw a hissy fit. Said she'd kill Anderson when he got home."

"That's kinda what he expected," Boone said. "We didn't want to hang around and fight about it. We just needed to get it done, you know?"

"I do. Even though I'm still kinda pissed off that you left me behind."

"Again, I'm sorry, Dirk."

"Yeah. So you say."

Boone sat up straighter. "Gotta go. Anderson's coming out."

"Boone?" Dirk's voice took on a more serious tone. "You come back in one piece, you hear?"

"Yes, sir. I'll do my best."

"We'll count on it, then."

Boone thumbed off his phone and watched Anderson hurry down the steps to the parking lot.

Chapter 25

Anderson slid into the passenger seat and motioned with a brisk wave of his hand. "Go."

Without hesitating, Boone pulled out of the parking lot. "Which way?"

"Take a left up here. We've gotta head south, back down to Devil's Lake."

Boone eased into light traffic and headed south again. "Okay. So spill. What'd they say?"

Anderson clipped his seatbelt closed and turned to Boone. "Well, first of all, I did find a lady to chat with."

"Yeah?" Boone smiled. "Did you use your Phantom charm?"

"I did. And it worked." Anderson's lips curled up. "On an eighty-four-year-old woman."

Boone pulled into the passing lane. "Hey. Whatever it takes, right?"

Anderson unrolled the printouts he clutched in his hand. "She was a sweetheart. Told me much more than I needed to know. She's been working for the paper since she was a teenager. You want to know anything about the town, you go see Hannah."

"We hit the jackpot, then?"

"We did. I've got directions to the cabin, but she said it gets pretty dicey when you enter the state land. Lots of little roads, no more than trails. She gave me directions to the edge of the park, then told me to work my way toward Devil's Lake and watch for the cabin with the boarded up windows."

"She knows it?"

"Vaguely. Has heard about it, hasn't actually been there."

"Did she know Murphy?"

111

"Yes. By name and reputation. Remembers him entering and winning the derby. But she hasn't really had much to do with him on a personal level."

"Okay. Let's do this."

Boone followed Anderson's directions to the edge of the state land, and after following a fairly well-traveled dirt trail for a while, the road forked into a Y.

"Hang on," Boone said. "Let me take a look at my GPS. I should know which general direction the lake is in."

Anderson examined both roads while Boone got out and tried to get a signal.

"Damn," Boone said, waving his phone around. "Signal's too low."

"That's okay. Let's try this side," he said, getting out and examining the right hand track. "Look. It's got some deep tire ruts. Could be from Murphy's truck. Looks a bit more worn than the other side, too."

Boone hopped back in the car, but first grabbed both rifles from the trunk. "Let's see how far we can drive in. Then we'll continue on foot."

It wasn't as easy as they'd hoped. They came to multiple forks in the road, and each time, Anderson examined them and chose the one he thought seemed more traveled. But seven times they came to a dead end, had to back up or do tight K turns, and ended up almost where they began.

"This is ridiculous," Anderson said, wiping sweat from his brow. "Come on. Let's go back to that last intersection."

Boone followed his directions, then stopped and pulled over. "Look."

Anderson glanced up from the map he'd drawn of the trails that nested throughout the forest. "What?"

A row of antlers were nailed to a tree, in a bizarre he-man showoff display of *I killed it.*

"Okay. That's what Portia told us about, right? Now you're talking, Boone old man. Let's take this one."

"How 'bout we just park it here and hoof it in. The cabin can't be too far."

"Good idea." Anderson grabbed his gun, took a swig of water from the bottle in the drink holder, and smiled. "Let's go find this creep."

They tromped through the greenery. Birds sang with abandon in the woods around them, as if they hadn't borne witness for the past two years to the torture of one very fragile young woman.

Boone's heartbeat quickened. He breathed deeply, calming himself. He needed to focus. "I see something," he whispered, throwing out an arm to stop Anderson.

"Right," Anderson whispered back. "Straight ahead."

Both men melted into the woods, off the trail, carrying their weapons low.

"Slow and easy," Boone said.

Without speaking, they made their way toward the cabin, stopping to listen every few minutes. No sounds came from within, no lights winked through the boarded up windows.

"Let's just wait and watch for a bit," Anderson suggested. "See if there's any movement."

They crouched behind a low hanging spruce bow, listening and waiting. The minutes dragged onward, and Boone's muscles ached to move again.

After fifteen minutes, they nodded to each other and moved forward. Boone motioned for Anderson to go around the back. He reached one side of the cabin and slowly peered into a crack between the planks blocking one window on the Devil's Lake side. His eyes raked the room within. Woodstove. Couch. Small dining room table and two chairs.

No Murphy.

Anderson met him at the back of the cabin. *Sotto voce*, he said. "Nothing on the porch. No movement. Can't see anyone inside."

Boone straightened and spoke in a more normal tone. "Okay, then. Let's go knock on the front door."

PART II
The Taking
(two years earlier)

Chapter 26

Portia thrashed against the foul rag pressed to her mouth and nose, but the man was strong and clamped it tighter. She held her breath, struggling to escape his arms, but he held her like a child gripping a doll against its chest, tightly and with no intention of letting go.

No luck.

Don't breathe, don't breathe, don't breathe!

What the hell was happening? Who was this guy who'd parked his truck behind the greenhouse? And why did he say she was "with him" now?

The dark night went darker. Her head swam.

She breathed.

Hours later she woke in the truck, arms tied together with rope and her head pounding. He'd parked around back of what looked like a gas station, and had left her in the truck alone. She wanted to scream, but something about the drug he'd used made her head stuffy, her throat muscles didn't respond to her brain's signals.

Yell! Scream! Shout!

Her brain demanded, but her lips just mumbled nothingness.

Get up! Run!

A figure emerged from the men's room, approaching the truck.

Help. Help me, please.

He came closer, opened her door. And it was then she realized it was him. The crazy guy who'd taken her.

"Awake, sugar?" His voice sounded odd, almost robotic.

With one hand, he pushed her helplessly back against the seat. With the other, he doused more of the foul smelling liquid onto the rag and raised it to her face.

"Sorry. Just a little longer, and we'll be home. You sleep now. Sleep."

She'd fought him weakly, but hadn't stopped his arm from forcing the acrid smell into her nose and mouth.

When she next awoke, the sun had risen and a pink horizon greeted her gritty eyes through the passenger side window. She noticed the red geranium for the first time on the floor by her feet.

They were crossing a river on a metal bridge, and the light winked on her face in repetitive flickering waves.

"You won't need this anymore, sugar." He leaned over to roll down her window and tossed her purse out into the open space. It sailed over the bridge railings and disappeared.

"No!" A weak gurgle escaped her lips. Hot tears scalded her cheeks. "My phone." It was all she could manage. And in spite of all the other essentials that flew past her and into the river below, all she could think of was her beloved iPhone. Gone. Wet. Useless.

"How will I call my parents?" she murmured, as if the crazy guy next to her would actually care or answer her.

He patted her leg, leaving his hand on her thigh.

She pulled away.

"Oh, don't worry. You won't need your folks anymore. You're with me, now, sugar."

"Stop calling me that!" With a sob, she drew herself closer to the open window, for one wild moment thinking maybe she could throw herself out of it, roll on the road, and scream for help.

But her muscles flagged and her arms were tied.

He leaned over her and rolled up the window. "No crazy ideas. Sugar."

She closed her eyes and let the tears stream down her face. "Why?" She opened them and turned toward the monster sitting beside her. He looked so normal. So much like every other guy on the street of small town USA.

"Because you're the one. You were meant for me. Now hush up and go back to sleep." He reached for the rag again.

"No! Please. I'm thirsty. Can I have a drink, please?"

He leaned down and opened a small cooler sitting on the floor between them. Uncapping a bottle of water, he handed it to her. "Drink up."

She drained the bottle, managing to hold it between her bound hands.

"What do you say?" he growled, lowering his eyebrows in her direction while turning onto another highway.

"Huh?" She turned blurry eyes toward him.

"What. Do. You. Say?"

Heart pounding, head aching, she leaned as far away from him as possible. "Um. Thank you?"

"Good girl. Now shut up and let me drive."

Chapter 27

When she next awoke it was to the truck bouncing over potholes and ruts. Her head bumped against the window, and her bleary eyes shot open.

Outside, tree branches swept past the truck. Beyond that, deep blackness.

The inside of the cab smelled like fast food. Portia realized she had eaten nothing since her capture, and suddenly her stomach rolled in hunger. "Is there any food left?" she asked, sounding to herself like a beggar child asking for a morsel at the king's table.

He seemed relaxed. Happy? As if she were a sudden annoyance, he tossed her a bag.

She dug into it, finding half a carton of cold fries and an apple pie. She slid the pastry out of its sleeve and bit into it, deciding it was the best thing she'd tasted in years. Later, she'd wished she'd eaten the fries, too. At least they had calories. Even cold, there had to be some nutrition in them. Better than nothing.

When she gobbled down the last bite, she reached for another bottle of water and drained that, too. Urgent pressure on her bladder came minutes later, when they jarred over another bump.

"I have to go," she said. "It's an emergency."

He grunted, looked at her as if she'd interrupted a pleasant daydream, and stopped the truck. "Well, don't go far. We're almost home." He gestured toward the door. "You can do your business in the woods. But there are bears and wildcats, so stay close."

She fumbled with the door handle, incredulous. He was going to let her go! She could pee in the woods, then turn to run. Anywhere would be better than here. Anywhere, even if there were bears waiting to pounce on her.

Slowly, she opened the creaking old door and slipped out.

He cranked down her window. "Make it snappy, sugar."

Sugar, again. Oh, how I already hate that nickname.

She backed away ten feet and crouched behind a bush, quickly emptying her bladder. When she stood to zip her jeans, the world spun.

Damn. That chloroform, or whatever it was, is still in my system.

"Come on. We're almost there, and I'm tired."

In spite of her muddy thoughts and the dizzying sensations coursing through her, she turned and ran as if chased by the hounds of Hell.

In the distance, now that her eyes had adjusted to the dark, something glimmered. Silvery in the moonlight, it beckoned. Salvation. Freedom. A lake! Could she swim across it to get away from him?

His heavy grunt met her ears, then a shout. "Hey! Where are you going?"

She pushed her rubbery legs as hard as she could manage, swinging under pine branches, almost falling, and stumbling through the underbrush. Thorns raked her skin. Her eyes began to tear, because although she tried to run as fast as she could, she realized she was actually lurching at a painfully slow pace, like a crazy drunkard, arms and legs moving, but making little or no progress.

His footfalls came heavy and loud behind her, punctuated by his mechanical, raspy breathing. "God damn you, girl. You'll pay for this."

She froze inside, panicking. The silvery sparkle, which she now thought of as her salvation, didn't seem any closer. With one last huge effort, she forced her legs to move forward. Stars blurred overhead. Trees loomed out of the darkness. She

120

slammed into a big oak tree, banging her head against its massive trunk.

Turning, she saw him, getting closer.

He was laughing.

"You're not getting very far. What's wrong? Lost your sense of direction? Feeling a little woozy, sugar?"

She spun, legs churning away from him.

Come on, Portia! Move! Do it for your family. Do it for your horses. Get away from this crazy bastard!

With a deep gulping breath, she poured on the speed, feeling hysterical pleasure in the long strides that took her away from him.

Go, go, go! Her mind chanted encouragement, and she felt her brain clear, just a little. There, to the right, a trail led to the water.

Pounding faster now that she had no obstructions, she flew down the trail, not daring to look over her shoulder.

"Sugar, you'll never get away from me."

He sounded closer than she'd expected.

Run!

She reached the lakeshore, and without stopping to take off her shoes or jacket, slogged into the cold water.

Too late.

His hand reached her arm and jerked her backwards.

"Are you stupid?"

She fell into the water, soaked to her neck.

Heavy breathing met her ears and she felt the world spinning again. "Let me go!" But her words sounded feeble, even to herself.

His arm reached around her neck, squeezing hard. "I said, *we're almost home.* Now, don't go spoiling everything. I've waited a long time for this."

121

His arm pressed harder against her throat, and when she could no longer breathe, she stopped struggling, and the world went black. Again.

Chapter 28

The man lay next to her on the double bed, curled away from her. He wore gray flannel pajama pants and no shirt. Blackish gray hair swirled over his chest, up his neck, and down beneath his waistband. He breathed evenly, snoring slightly through parted lips. Long gray hair lay flat against his skull, spilling onto the pillow.

She looked down at her body, covered in a sheet.

Oh, God. No.

Waking rapidly, she took stock of her situation, lifting the covers.

Relieved, she found she still wore her underclothes, but noticed her wet shirt and jeans on a chair by the boarded up window. Her sodden sneakers lay on the floor beneath the chair.

What had he done to her while she blacked out?

She moved on the bed, wiggling her legs and hips. She didn't feel sore, so she didn't think he'd forced himself on her. *Thank God.*

The room was simple, walled with rough boards whose chinks were filled with what looked like dry mud. One chair. A small table. A door leading to the bathroom. Closet, closed. And another larger room on the other side. Probably a living room, she figured.

She wiggled sideways, sliding her bare legs off the mattress and to the floorboards below. Slowly, carefully, she edged toward her clothes on the chair. They were still damp, but not wringing wet like they must've been when she was dragged out of the lake, unconscious.

She squirmed into them, slid on her still-wet sneakers and looked around the room. All windows were boarded up, even the little window in the rustic bathroom.

The man snored louder, snorting once and turning onto his side.

Barely breathing, she eased out of the bedroom into the living room, which she discovered was the only other room in the cabin. A mini-kitchen stood off to the right. A table and two chairs separated the kitchen space from the couch and chairs that faced a fireplace. Jackets and caps hung from a wooden peg by the door, which was firmly shut. She approached it, praying he couldn't lock it from inside, but her heart fell when she saw the four-inch steel padlock attached to a chain looping through the door handle and to a bolt on the wall.

She tried it, anyway, and with a sob of frustration, fell to her knees by the door.

Locked in.

Trapped.

Panicking, she shot to her feet and tried to pry one of the boards off the windows. Attached from the inside, she realized they were fastened with long, heavy screws, three on each side. The wood seemed almost petrified, it was so thick and heavy.

She looked around for a tool to pry one of the boards off.

There, by the fireplace. A long brass tool hung on a hook. She lunged for it, trying to be as quiet as possible in her squeaking sneakers. Slowly, carefully, with shaking fingers, she inserted the flat-tipped end of the tool beneath one board, pushing hard on it.

It didn't budge.

Again, she leaned her weight against the tool and pushed as hard as she could.

The board didn't move, not even a fraction of an inch.

Frustrated and exhausted, she collapsed on the floor in a heap.

What's he going to do with me? Kill me? Rape me? Keep me like a little wife to cook and clean and polish his boots?

Sobs overtook her, and still, the steady snoring came from the bedroom.

What should I do?

She glanced toward the bedroom again, thinking of ways she could immobilize him and steal the key. Maybe she could knock him out with the fireplace poker? Tie him up?

Could she overpower him?

No. He was too big. Too strong.

Her mind continued to race, but a sense of helplessness and fear descended on her. After another twenty minutes, her tears dried. Maybe she should just wait and see what the situation was. She might be able to slip out later in the day, or during the night. Once she knew where the key was, she—

Before she could finish her sentence, his voice interrupted her thoughts.

"Good, you're up." He lumbered into the living room and sat on the couch, watching her. "Trying to escape already? Well, aren't we the little wildcat, huh?"

She shook her head and looked away, leaning against the wall beneath the window.

"Fireplace poker didn't work for you?" He laughed, metallic and rough. "I don't think so, sugar."

Anger coursed through her. "Stop calling me that! I have a name."

He rose and approached her. "Looks like I'll have to teach you a lesson in respect." He grabbed a handful of her hair and yanked her toward the bedroom.

Chapter 29

It wasn't a punishment for the weak.

No food, no water, for one whole day.

He'd duct taped her mouth and shackled her to the bed like a dog on a chain, with only a chamber pot to use in an emergency.

She lay beside him the next morning, weak and ravenous, but seething with anger.

How dare he? How could he? Who does he think he is?

She turned to face away from him, but the restraint on her wrist wasn't made for comfort. Wiggling up on the bed, she managed to flip over and put one hand beneath her cheek, while the other remained tangled by rope.

She had to figure out how to play him. How to appeal to him.

It seemed he wanted obedience.

Well, I can fake it as well as anyone. I'll be his goddamned geisha girl if he'll just feed me.

Once she got her strength back and her head on straight, she'd come up with an escape plan.

Yes. That's it. Pretend to be respectful and sweet. Go along with him. Watch and wait.

But what if he wanted more than she could give?

What if he expected all the favors of a wife?

She shuddered, suddenly feeling cold all over. The last time she'd made love with a man had been almost a year ago, when her college boyfriend Ben and she parted. He, off to the Peace Corp in Africa; she, back home to Bittersweet Hollow.

The Hollow.

Oh, how she missed it, even now, even though it had just been a few days. The peaceful green fields. Her beloved horses. Her mom and dad. Her new puppy, Boomer.

Tears crept behind her eyes, tightening her throat.

NO.

I will not cry in front of him. I'll be strong.

With a deep shuddering sigh, she controlled herself.

I can do this. I can beat him.

As if he read her thoughts, he woke, sitting up on the side of the bed. Yawning, he grumbled the words at her. "Scheming again? Trying to figure out how to get away?" He ripped the tape from her mouth.

She turned toward him, masking her face in tranquility. "No."

"Learned your lesson yet?" He stood and yawned, stretching his arms over his head.

His movement was so human, so natural-looking that it cast her situation in an even more surreal light. How could such a monster look so normal? Act so normal? And yet be so absolutely abnormal?

"Yes. I'm sorry." She rubbed the sides of her mouth where the tape had reddened her skin.

He almost smiled. "Well. You should be. I went through a lot of trouble to bring you here."

She nodded meekly. "I know. Thank you."

In a flash, his face turned red. His bushy eyebrows shot down, his jaw tightened, and his eyes bore into hers, reminding her of a mad dog. He leaned forward and grabbed her hair again, yanking her toward him. "You'd better not be playing me, bitch."

The switch from mild-mannered psycho to raging bull surprised her. She realized maybe she'd laid it on too thick.

Maybe it wasn't believable. This time, she let the tears out. He'd expect that.

"No. I'm not playing you," she said, weeping openly now. "I'm...I'm just so hungry. But I miss my family a lot, too. I really want to go home."

He tossed her onto the bed, knocking her head against the headboard. "That part of your life is over. I'm your family now. Me." He growled at her.

The hairs on the back of her neck raised as a chill stole down her neck.

He leaned in so close she could smell his horrible morning breath. "Me. And me alone. Get it, sugar?"

She gulped, wiped her cheeks, and nodded. "Yes."

"All right. I'm untying you now. Go make us breakfast."

"I need the bathroom. May I?" She nodded toward the closed door.

"Yes. And empty that smelly pot while you're at it." He motioned toward the chamber pot on her side of the bed. "It's disgusting."

She wanted to scream at him, to tell him he made her use the gross thing, to tell him to shut the hell up and go screw himself.

But she didn't. Like a beaten slave, she shuffled to the pot, lifted it, and took it into the bathroom with eyes cast downward.

She didn't dare ask him if she could shower. He'd probably explode. So she did her business, washed her body as best she could with a facecloth, drank for a full minute from the faucet, and combed her hair with the black comb on the counter that had his gray hairs protruding from it. She'd cleaned it out, had run it under boiling hot water from the tap, and then after wetting her hair under the faucet, ran the comb through it. She'd managed to hang on to the hair tie from the other day, and pulled it back into a tight ponytail.

128

When she came out, she went straight to the kitchen. He talked to her while she made scrambled eggs, toast, and fried ham.

"Today you're going to start on a schedule. You'll wear the clothes I bought for you, they're in the closet. Get rid of those skanky jeans and that disgusting shirt. And you will not," he said, lunging toward her and pulling on the ponytail, "wear your hair like this. I want it loose. Flowing. On your shoulders."

With an apologetic nod, she quickly removed the hair tie. "Okay. I didn't know."

Grunting, he pulled out a kitchen chair and sat, waiting for her to serve him. "Now you do. Don't forget."

In a way, she realized that having her hair loose might be easier on her. He probably could get a lot more leverage from a ponytail, yank harder and throw her further across the room.

What a sick thought.

Her brain commented on the whole scene as if it were a critic watching a movie.

Really? You're going to obey him? Just like that?

She stirred the eggs, forcing herself not to gobble them hot from the pan. Her stomach hurt. Her throat was parched, even though she'd drunk from the bathroom spigot a few minutes ago.

She laid the table, sat primly in front of him, and waited for him to tell her to eat. When he gave her the signal, like a master to his dog, she controlled her gnawing need to shovel it into her mouth, and ate as if it were a normal breakfast.

Later, when she cleaned up, she secretly gobbled all the rest of the food she'd left in the frying pan.

Chapter 30

He pushed back his chair and belched. "Not bad, for your first day. Tomorrow, add more garlic powder to the eggs."

Portia cringed, and finished washing the pan in the tiny sink. It wasn't easy, and the water had started to go cold. "Okay."

He stood and watched her dry the pan, then sniffed the air like a hound. "You need to clean up. You stink."

She turned to him, ready to throw back a retort, but bit her lip. "The hot water's almost gone."

"Then you'd better hurry through your shower. Come on. I'll show you how to work it." He pulled her into the bedroom. "Take off your clothes."

She stared at him. "Now?"

He stared back, his face impassive. "Yes. How do you expect to shower without undressing?" He actually chuckled, turning toward the bathroom. "It's not as if I haven't seen you naked before."

She froze.

What?

When had he seen her?

She'd been in bed last night with her underwear on. Did he take them off her, then put them back on? Or was he thinking of another time, another woman?

A staggering thought hit her. *Were there others before me?*

She heard the water turning on in the shower.

He closed the curtain with a screech, then came out holding a towel. "This is the only one we've got that's clean. I need to get to the Laundromat."

She unbuttoned her shirt. "Okay. Thanks." Sliding past him, she peeled off her shirt and held it in front of her. "I've got it now." She accepted the towel and clutched it over her breasts.

"What? You're gonna be shy?" He roared with laughter. "Forget it. We're living together. You'll be giving me what I want, every night. Sometimes in the day. There's no room for bashfulness here."

He jerked the towel and her shirt from her in one swift motion. "Take it all off, now."

She stood, shivering before him, but couldn't move.

With a leer, he lunged for her hair again, twisted her around, and unfastened her bra. She tried to hold it in place, but he ripped it away and tossed it into the other room. "Are you deaf, sugar?"

"No." Shakily, she unsnapped her jeans. *He's insane. He's going to rape me. He just as good as told me.*

I need a plan. Now.

Nothing came to her.

Could she knee him in the balls? Would it incapacitate him long enough for her to find the key to the door?

Probably not. She needed to know where he kept the key, and that meant watching him next time he left and came back inside.

"You're losing your hot water."

Hurrying, she turned her back to him, slid out of the rest of her clothes, and got into the shower, pulling the curtain closed behind her. The water was lukewarm at best.

He dragged the curtain to the side and openly stared at her, his lower lip hanging as if he were a caveman seeing his first female.

Up and down, his eyes raked over her body. "Soap's on the shelf."

She turned away from the telltale bulge in his pants to pick up the huge bar of yellow soap. No shampoo. No body wash. Nothing she was used to. Fear made her hands shake and her breath come quickly.

What could she do? She needed an idea. Fast.

She started to soap up, and the water cooled even more.

"I told you to hurry."

Freezing, she stuck her soaped up hair under the spray and rinsed it clean. With a gasp, she backed out of the cold spray and shut it off. "It's ice cold!"

He laughed. "You'll get used to it. That's life in the woods. Now get out and dry off. Your new clothes are in the closet."

She squeezed past him to get the towel, but this time he laid a hand on her backside, caressing it as she passed. He ogled her again. "Nice and clean. Doesn't it feel good?"

With the towel tucked tightly around herself, she pasted on a fake smile and hurried into the bedroom toward the closet. Inside, she found a pile of new white cotton panties, old-fashioned nylons and a garter belt, and about a dozen 1950s nurses uniforms, complete with a few white caps on the top shelf and several pairs of old-fashioned white nurse shoes on the floor. No bras.

Stunned, she stared at the selection. *What the hell? Oh, God. He's sicker than I imagined.*

Now I have to pretend to be his nurse?

She hurried into the panties—two sizes too big—and then picked through the uniforms. Some were huge, size 3X. Others were closer to her own size eight. She found one that wasn't too far off and quickly put it on. The white fabric was almost sheer, and she realized without her bra, he'd see her nipples.

My God. This is insane.

"Do you have any bras or slips? I think this will be cold." She didn't turn toward him, but searched for some socks.

132

She found him in the chair by the door, lustfully watching her. "No bras. You don't need them. It's summer. And put on the garter belt and nylons."

With a shivery sigh, she did as he said, then slid into a pair of white size seven shoes that actually fit.

The previous woman must've been huge. The other pair looked like clown shoes.

What had he done to her? Killed her? Was she buried outside the cabin in the woods?

She finished tying her shoes. "Were there other girls before me?"

He ignored her. "Put on the cap."

She perched the cap on top of her head, but realized it wouldn't stay without pins.

"Bobby pins are in the top drawer of the dresser."

God, he thought of everything, didn't he?

She found them, clipped the cap to her hair, and turned to him. "I'm done."

He didn't respond, but instead unzipped his jeans and began to stroke himself. "Very nice. You'll do very nicely for me. Just stand still. Don't move."

She closed her eyes while he finished his business. Quaking inside, she held onto the bedpost for balance.

Maybe this is all he'll do?

Maybe he's a voyeur.

Maybe he won't touch me.

God, please. Let it be so.

Chapter 31

The days blurred and the weeks marched forward, filled with back-breaking work and humiliation.

It's not enough that he wants me to be his slave.

Portia moved forward another foot on the cold linoleum floor, scrubbing it with a stiff brush and a bucket of lukewarm water with borax cleaner.

No, more than anything, he's reveling in the power he holds over me. That's what he enjoys.

"No lollygagging there, missy." He laughed from his chair in the living room, cutting out yet another article about her disappearance to plaster on the wall beside him.

Lollygagging? She hadn't heard that term since her grandfather used it when she was little.

Her mind wandered as she fulfilled her Cinderella role, bare knees already sore from the constant rubbing on the floorboards.

Why is he like this? What turned him into such a Nazi?

Was it his childhood? Was he made to clean like this? Was he a slave, too?

Or maybe it was his mother? They always blame the mothers, don't they?

And who was the nurse that caused such a fetish in him?

Portia pulled down the horrible white dress to try to cover herself. She knew he was watching. Enjoying the show.

Was his mother a nurse?

Or was there some nurse in his past who'd cared for his mother or father in a hospital, and maybe screwed up? Maybe killed them because of a medical error?

It happened sometimes.

Was he bent on revenge and harbored an equally sick lust for nurses since then?

She really wanted to know, but there were so few personal items in the cabin she couldn't learn much about him. There must be another home. Somewhere where he grew up, where a real family had kept things like photo albums, tax records, and crocheted afghans.

And where did he get his money?

Clearly, he had enough cash to buy food and keep the generator filled with gas. He bought supplies on a weekly basis, he'd told her. And today he was planning to go out to do just that.

Where, she didn't know. For how long?

She had no idea.

But Portia couldn't wait to get rid of him. She'd learned to despise him so quickly, she didn't know she was capable of such strong, hateful emotions. It surprised her, frankly. But in her head, with all the analyzing that was going on full speed all day long, she didn't blame herself.

How could she?

Anyone would react like this. Wouldn't they?

Sure, she used to get furious at Grace, especially when she hurt her mother and father. But that was family. And beneath it all, she still loved her deeply.

But this guy. Oh, no. It was different.

She seethed with anger.

They'd eaten pretty well for the past few days, with her cooking for him. But the food was starting to run out, and if he didn't replenish the larder soon, they'd be eating pinecones.

She watched him using the scissors to carefully cut out the articles.

The scissors.

If only she could see where he hid them when he was done.

Maybe she could jump him when he came back. Hide behind the door. Surprise the hell out of him.

She smiled.

"What's so funny?" he growled, getting up and stomping toward her.

Pasting yet another fake smile on her face, she looked up at him, but didn't stop scrubbing. "Oh. Nothing. Just remembering a funny T.V. show."

"What show?" He nudged her with his foot. "You're lying. You were laughing at me, weren't you?"

"No, I swear. It was a Lucy episode. The one where she and Ricky—"

He kicked her hard in the stomach, knocking her sideways. "You're lying."

On the floor, she curled in a ball, away from him.

Three more swift kicks, this time to her back and legs.

Stop. Stop. Stop!

Crying, she tried to take herself out of the moment. Pictured Bittersweet Hollow. Her family. Her horses.

Just don't think about it.

"Get back to work, you whore."

Whore? Now she was a whore?

She painfully pulled herself back to her knees, afraid not to obey him. There, on the table by the chair, lay the scissors.

Could she do it? Could she actually stab another human being?

Damn right she could.

Out of the corner of her eye, she watched him shuffle back to the chair, sit heavily in it again.

"I'll be gone for a while, so make your food last, sugar."

She almost didn't ask, but found the courage. "How long?"

He smirked. "Why? You gonna miss me?"

She didn't say a word, just kept scrubbing, definitely *not* smiling. She'd have to watch that in the future. Now she could add paranoid to his list of problems.

He grunted when he tucked the scissors into his jacket pocket. "I don't know. Depends."

"Okay." Like the good little hearth maid, she kept moving the brush in steady circles. Around and around and around. Dip in the water. Slosh water on floor. Around and around and around.

I'm going mad.

He took out a set of keys, unlocked the chest he used for a coffee table, and stowed the scissors inside. Firmly, he locked the lid and pocketed the keys.

Damn. She should have noticed him opening it earlier, but she'd been cleaning the bathroom when he started.

I have to get those scissors.

Chapter 32

"I'm leaving now, sugar."

Portia sat back on her heels, the brush still in her hands. She didn't smile. Didn't say a word. Just sat there with lowered eyes like the obedient little beetle he wanted her to be.

"What? No goodbye kiss?" Laughing, he grabbed a knapsack and fished his key ring out of his pocket, where it seemed to stay all day, every day. "Okay. Maybe next time."

Portia watched as he pulled one big silver key from the ring and inserted it in the front door padlock.

Click.

Freedom beckoned.

She felt it in her gut, its call was primeval, almost, and it was all she could do to keep herself from surging toward him, screaming with arms flailing.

Let me out!

Her brain shrieked the words, but she sat still, her face impassive.

Bide your time, honey.

It was her father's voice she heard in her head. He counseled her, soft and steady. He loved her. He knew she could get out of here.

Didn't he?

For a moment, she crossed into a world of self-comfort that bordered on crazy. Nervous, she shook her head and tried to focus.

Would she go insane? Was it nuts to hear her father giving her advice?

No.

No, it was okay.

Whatever it took to get her through this, she would use it.

The monster left the house, and she heard a click on the outside.

Another padlock, just like the one on the inside? Same key?

Her mind raced. She jumped up from the floor and ran to the windows, peeking through the crack.

There he went. The old truck tires spit dirt as he bumped onto the trail and drove away.

He's gone.

She felt oddly elated, as if him leaving gave her freedom. But of course, she was still locked inside the damned cabin.

Maybe she could get those scissors out now, work at that lock on the chest. Or pry at the window boards some more.

With renewed energy, she stood, pulling down the hem on the ridiculous 1950's nurse uniform.

She still wondered about his obsession with nurses. And why such a clownish costume?

Wait. Could it be a Halloween costume? It felt like it had been designed to titillate, not for utilitarian service. That's probably why the hem was so short and the neckline plunged. He'd bought the damn outfits at a party store, she was sure of it.

But why were there so many different sizes in the closet? They went from her size all the way up to plus sizes. It didn't make any sense.

Shrugging, she stepped away from the chink in the boarded up window, where she had been staring at the sparkle of the lake through the trees.

Oh, to be able to step into that cool liquid. To immerse herself in the velvety softness of lake water. To swim, stroke after stroke, away. Away, away, away. To land on a far shore and run for help.

She wondered what the lake was called. Lake Serene? Lake Pleasant? Silver Lake?

And now, an aching urge hit her. She wanted home, yearned to go home to The Hollow, to her quiet, comfortable pink-curtained room, to her family's big kitchen that always had food in the cupboards, and to see her favorite horses.

She thought about Mirage, the black Morgan stallion who had been producing prize-winning colts for three years straight. He was unusually gentle for a stallion. She'd even ridden him out into the foothills of the Green Mountains without concern. She was certain it was that steadfast Morgan bloodline, the calm and serene personality bred through his ancestors for decades that produced the beautiful, strong, gentle horses.

Unpinning the nurse's cap from her hair, she combed her fingers through it, luxuriating in the feel of being freer, but trying to ignore the stickiness of yellow soap residue that she never could get rid of because the hot water ran out so darned fast.

She placed the pin and cap on the sink in the bathroom. When she heard him drive in, she'd run into the room and pin it on her head again.

So, now to business.

Walking with purpose, she approached the coffee table chest and knelt before it. Feeling giddy suddenly, she almost wanted to clasp her hands together and pray for success, as if it were an altar.

She laughed out loud, glad he couldn't hear her, and leaned over to examine the lock. The thing was old fashioned, like the kind of locks in doors that used skeleton keys. It reminded her of the lock on her mother's grandfather clock. She peered inside, wishing she had a flashlight. Or some little tools, like those dentists used. Sharp. Pointy. Curvy? Anything to pry around in there.

How did they do it in the movies? They used one tool to hold some thingamajig away, while the other pried and twisted some other part.

She sighed, speaking aloud. "Goddamn it. I don't know how to pick locks. I just need one humongous sledgehammer. Then I could smash the window and break out."

She almost cried, but didn't.

"Then again, if I had a sledgehammer, I could hit him with it. Really hard, right when he walked in the door."

She lingered over that thought for a while, enjoying the image of herself bashing in his head. The realization sent her mind whirling. "Did I really just think that? And like the idea?"

Honestly. Who am I? Has he turned me into an enthusiastic murderer?

She turned to the mirror on the wall, watching her shadowy eyes focus on themselves.

Is that really me?

God, I look like hell.

For the next hour, she tried to find tools to unscrew the boards on the windows. Most of the screws wouldn't budge no matter what she tried, although after twenty minutes on one screw, she worked it loose with the tip of a butter knife.

Somehow, this small victory gave her courage. If she could do this with every screw, a little every day, and carefully re-screw them loosely in place so he wouldn't notice, then eventually she might be able to loosen one whole board and break the glass behind it. Then she could wiggle through the opening.

Yes.

She had a plan.

Now, to make sure he wouldn't notice, she had to come up with something clever.

Curtains? Maybe she could offer to make curtains, and thus hide her scratches in the wood and the loose screws.

She'd try that, too.

I'm gonna get out of here. Soon.

With her heart singing, she walked boldly into the bathroom and filled the tub with hot water. Without worrying about him seeing her lying there, she sank into the tub and refined her plan.

Chapter 33

Six days. Six days of gnawing hunger, each day worse than the last.

Portia looked in the cupboards, even though she knew there wasn't much there. The fridge was empty. Totally. And all she had left was some Crisco, sugar, and a little flour.

With a shrug, she thought about pancakes. Could she make them with those ingredients? No milk. No eggs. No oil. No syrup. But water could substitute for milk. And the Crisco might melt down into oil.

It could work.

She took down the last of the ingredients and wondered if he'd ever come back.

With her knuckles raw from banging them against the window boards, trying every possible way to break out, working for hours on the padlock with her bobby pins to no avail...she felt exhausted.

I want fruit. An apple. Some juice.

I want scrambled eggs.

I want...food.

Weak, she knew that drinking was the most important part of this whole thing. At least the faucet worked and cool, sweet water came from it.

What was it they said about people lost in the desert? They could last maybe a week without food, but just days without water.

With a sigh, she held her hair back and leaned over and drank from the spigot for a long time.

It was good, and it filled her stomach a little bit.

She mixed up the flour, a little melted Crisco, and water, and beat it so it seemed almost like pancake batter.

What about shortcake? Could it be made into that?

Since the batter seemed pretty thick, she formed it into little mounds and laid them on a baking tin.

They were ready in fifteen minutes, and to her surprise, they tasted pretty good. A little butter or jam would have made them almost heavenly.

But of course, she didn't have that.

She ate them hot and dry, slaking her thirst with cold water from the well. This time, she set up the table as if it were a real meal.

Plate, utensils, napkins, and a pretty flowered glass.

Maybe when she broke out of here, she'd bring that glass home, as a reminder of how strong she was.

In her whole life, she never imagined having to go hungry. Most of the time she was more worried about eating too much, getting fat. But now, she thought of the big, hearty meals her mother and father would prepare for her every day, and salivated.

Oh, to have a big slab of roast turkey and some stuffing.

Or a bite of mashed potatoes and gravy.

Or, better yet, a piece of Mom's pie. Portia loved the strawberry rhubarb the best, and she'd readily go out and pick the berries and rhubarb at any time of day to get a slice of that heaven on her plate with some vanilla ice cream.

She took another dry bite of shortcake. It wasn't terrible. And there were three more little cakes to make last.

She finished her sparse meal and did up the dishes.

Now what?

The place was as clean as it could be. No excuse for him to punish her when he got home.

Another hot bath? One more time, before he could watch her undress again?

No. She'd done that just this morning, and who knew if the water had heated enough yet, anyway. It seemed to take forever and the tank had to be tiny since it barely filled the tub and then went cold.

She wandered over to the pegboard on the wall, where he had pinned copies of the newspaper articles about her disappearance. In one article, her parents and sister were shown at a press conference, holding hands and looking brave.

How she longed to speak to them, to embrace them. Even her little sister, the perennial trouble maker.

She wondered if this whole kidnapping thing would make Gracie go crazy, force her to fall back on her bad habits. She prayed out loud. "God, let her be strong for Mom and Dad." Kissing her fingertips, she pressed them against the picture, coming away with black newsprint.

Oh God. Would he see the smudge? Would he flip out on her?

There was nothing she could do now.

And then she spotted them.

Pushpins. Several blue-headed pushpins sat clustered in the corner of the board, waiting for more clippings to post. Maybe she could use one as a weapon?

They were pathetically small, of course. But sharp. What if she raked one across his face? His eyes?

Shuddering, she tried to imagine having just enough time to distract him with the pain so she could slip out the door. But it would have to be the minute he returned, so he didn't have time to relock it.

The sound of his returning truck galvanized her to action. She grabbed one of the pins and shoved it into her dress pocket, shaking.

She watched through the crack in the boards. He got out, arms loaded with grocery bags and one large bag from

145

McDonalds. Hunger swarmed over her, and she felt her resolve melting.

The door unlocked. "I've got more in the truck. Take these," he said.

She ran to the door, reaching for the food.

Oh, it smelled so good. Burgers. Fries. Ice cold soda. She even thought she smelled an apple pie. Maybe she could eat first, attack him when she was stronger?

Horrified at her own thoughts, she walked like a zombie to the table and put the food down.

I have to get out. I can't give in.

But before she had turned to remake her plan, he stood glowering at her. "Where's your cap? Are you trying to piss me off?"

She reached frantically for her hair. Oh, God. She'd forgotten it. Rushing madly, she ran to the bathroom and quickly pinned it on.

Then she looked in the mirror.

You're a coward.

A weak, sniveling coward.

She knew it was true, and realized she needed to screw up her courage for next time. She needed to be ready. Really ready.

Patting the pin in her pocket, she sighed.

Next time.

"Come on, it's getting cold, sugar."

She hurried to the kitchen table and sat when he gestured to the chair.

"Bet you're hungry, huh?"

Like a robot, she nodded. "Yes."

"Sorry I took so long."

She realized with a start that he wore pants and a shirt she'd never seen. Green khaki's and a black and white plaid shirt.

Where had those come from?

Where had he been?

"Where did you go?" she asked meekly, waiting for him to tell her to start eating.

He laughed. "Go ahead, open the bag. It's all for you." He got up to lock the door, pocketing the keys. "Why do you want to know?"

She took a huge bite of her hamburger, then a handful of fries. They were still hot. *So there had to be a little town not too far from here.*

"Just making conversation," she said, drinking the sweet orange soda from the extra large cup.

"I got a place up north," he said noncommittally. "I fish there sometimes."

"What about this lake?" she asked. "Does it have good fish, too?"

"Devil's Lake?" he said. "Oh, sure. But sometimes a man needs a change, you know?" He stared at her with that sick, lustful expression she'd come to hate. "A man needs variety."

"Uh huh." She continued to eat, trying to slow herself down so she wouldn't get sick.

"What did you catch?"

He smiled at her. "You're a regular Chatty Cathy today, aren't you?" He got up and moved toward her, playing with her hair. "You really missed me, didn't you?"

She nodded, looking down. "Of course."

"When you finish, put the food away. Then come into the bedroom."

Chapter 34

"**S**tand in the corner," he growled from the bathroom. The closet door stood open, and she couldn't see him.

In the bedroom, Portia's knees shook and her heart banged beneath her ribs.

Is this it? Is he finally going to force himself on me?

Every time she'd been afraid in the past, he'd just made her stand in the corner with the damned nurse costume on while he took care of business on a chair on the opposite side of the room.

That had suited her just fine. As long as he didn't touch her.

Of course, he had touched her in other ways. So far, it had been to hit, kick, or drag her by her hair. Not that she liked that, but it was better than him assaulting her sexually.

"Put that around your neck," he called again, from the bathroom.

She noticed the plastic stethoscope on the bed. "This?" With a shrug, she put it on. Another prop. Another sick addition to his fantasy.

"Now, sit on the bed."

This was different. She'd never had to sit on the bed before. Nerves fluttered in her stomach.

Oh, no. Please, no.

"Close your eyes." His voice sounded weird, kind of sing-song.

She closed her eyes, and through tiny slits in the lashes noticed a figure coming toward her.

"Okay. Open them." He towered over her, and a grin split his ugly, pitted face.

It was all she could do to stifle her hysterical laughter, for he stood before her in one of the nurse uniforms, his hairy chest and legs open to the air and to her ridicule.

"Oh," was all she could manage. She didn't let her mouth twitch. Didn't let the laugh bubble out from her throat.

Now we're twins, she thought.

Twins.

What the hell was this guy playing at, anyway? Now he wanted to be a nurse, too?

Well, this answers the question about the plus size uniforms in the closet.

To her horror, he slid onto the bed beside her.

"Check my heartbeat," he said, with a coquettish tone.

Now her stomach turned, and she was afraid she'd lose her much-needed food if he got any weirder.

I won't throw up. I won't.

When she hesitated, he roared at her in his usual gruff voice. "Check it, I said!"

She inserted the plastic tabs in her ears and leaned toward him, pressing the plastic disk against his open chest, where he'd left all the buttons undone. "Okay. Breathe deeply."

He grabbed her wrist and squeezed it hard. "No talking."

She nodded, and kept moving the stupid toy around his chest as if listening.

He flipped up his dress, exposing himself beneath it.

Of course. He's naked.

Dread filled her throat. Oh, God, what's next?

He lay back on the pillows and began to stroke himself. "The other girls knew what to do. Why are you so shy?"

The other girls?

She shrank from him, but couldn't help answering. "I'm not shy."

149

"Then sing to me."

"What?"

"Sing to me. I want a lullaby."

"Um. Okay." In a thin, warbling voice, she began to sing the only lullaby she could think of, "Hush Little Baby." She couldn't remember the words to all the verses, and was sure she mixed them up, but she just kept singing with her eyes closed until he moaned, shuddered, and sighed. She felt the bed shift as he got up.

"Enough," he said. "That was good. Now you know what to do."

She watched as he lumbered into the bathroom, where he started the shower.

I've gotta get out of here.

The thought repeated in her mind, over and over again. And then she realized that when he'd changed into his starchy white uniform, he'd left his clothes in the bathroom. Which meant the keys were unattended for a few minutes.

She began to plan again.

As she lay on the bed waiting for him to emerge, a thought slammed into her brain.

Oh, God. There were other girls.

Other girls. Girls with an 's.'

So where are they? What did he do with them? Are they all buried around me in the woods?

What if I sneak in the bathroom right now and get the keys?

Without stopping to judge the risks, she darted into the bathroom and noticed the shower curtain was fully closed.

Working on pure adrenaline, she grabbed his pants, reached into the pockets, and pulled out the ring of keys.

He hadn't heard her over the water of the shower.

RUN.

Her heart drummed rapidly as she flew to the front door. She knew which key she needed, she'd memorized it. Big, silver, slightly tarnished.

Here it is.

Hands shaking, she inserted it into the giant padlock and turned.

Click.

The lock opened, and the shower turned off.

"Get me a towel," he roared from the bathroom.

"Rot in hell," she whispered, and ran into the cool summer air.

Chapter 35

He bellowed behind her like a wounded bear, shouting from the cabin. "Sugar! God damn it, come back here."

RUN. RUN. RUN.

Don't stop.

With feet churning through leaves and over clumps of moss, Portia headed for the lake and didn't look back.

There it was. Devil's Lake. At least now she knew the name, and for some reason, it made her laugh.

Running from the Devil to his very own lake. *Devil's Lake. Devil's Lake. Devil's Lake.* The repetition of the name matched her footsteps.

But in spite of the name that didn't seem to match its serene beauty, she wanted it. She wanted to reach the dock, jump in, and swim like hell.

Behind her, more yelling.

"Sugar!"

Oh God, he's getting closer.

Redoubling her efforts, ducking through pine boughs and over clumps of brush, she flew through the woods toward the water. It grew closer, and she could even see a few fishing boats in the distance.

If only she could get their attention.

She broke into the clearing where the shore met water, felt the hot sun on her skin, and began to scream, waving her arms. She pounded across the dock, past the rowboat, and at the end, she braced her legs and dove into the cool blue water. When she broke into the air, she heard his footfalls pounding along the pier.

I made it.

Giggling hysterically inside, she threw arm over arm and stroked away from him. Away from the cabin. The humiliation. The fear.

Use your fear. Move!

Go, go, go!

The voices in her head encouraged her as if she were in a race and they were cheering alongside her route. She focused on breathing and swimming, and tried to ignore the sound of a small motor starting up.

No!

Harder, she threw her arms far and wide, long, powerful strokes, surely enough to distance her from her monster.

"Sugar!"

His voice sounded impossibly closer, and she dared to turn to see the boat chugging up behind her. Why was the shore so close? Why hadn't she made more progress?

Oh, please, God. Please don't let him catch me.

Laughing, he moved the craft up beside her.

She glanced sideways. "No!" Screaming, she treaded water and yelled for help as loud as she could.

The engine puttered softly, and he simply watched her struggle. A huge smile bloomed across his ugly face. "Time to come home now, sugar."

"No!" She screamed again, tiring suddenly, feeling as if she couldn't move another foot in the water.

"They can't hear you. They're too far away," he said, as if to a child.

She considered letting herself sink to the bottom. Wouldn't that be better than facing him again?

NO.

Next time, she would have to incapacitate him. Knock him out.

153

Kill him.

Next time.

Her mind let go, and when he caught her around the neck with the fishing gaff, she barely struggled.

"There you go," he said, as if he were drying a wet puppy after a rainstorm. He hauled her into the boat and turned the boat around, churning back to the cabin.

She lay on the floor of the wooden craft, soaking wet and exhausted.

"Now, sugar." His metallic voice rasped, even more pronounced out here on the lake. "You're gonna have to learn some manners. That was very rude. Trying to leave me after all I did for you."

She closed her eyes and breathed deeply.

Next time.

Chapter 36

When they reached the shore again, she'd regained some strength, and one more time, she tried screaming.

"Help! Anybody? Please, help me!"

She twisted away from him and started toward the woods, but this time he caught her in seconds, pouncing on her from behind. His heavy body slammed her to the moist sand.

"Now, stop that, sugar. There's no hope for you. Nobody can hear you."

Anger built inside her, billowing into a volcanic head of emotion. "Stop it! Get off me. And stop calling me sugar! My name is Portia." She curled sideways and hammered at him, hands slamming his face and feet kicking his knees. "I don't even know your name, you big, filthy monster." Sobbing, she tried yelling again, but could barely hear her own voice. "Help!"

"Now, stop that. You know the drill. I'm bringing you back inside." He grabbed her hair and began to drag her like a caveman to his stony enclave.

Twisting and turning, she grabbed his wrist to lessen the force on her scalp. "No!"

He kept right on, as if she were nothing more than a rabbit he'd shot in the woods. Just bringing home dinner on a quiet Sunday afternoon.

"Stop!" she screamed again, louder this time. "I don't want to be locked up anymore."

"Oh, you'll be locked up, all right. Tighter 'n a titmouse's tree house. I'm tying you to the damned bed again." He sneered over his shoulder, still dragging her toward the cabin.

"Please..." she whimpered. "I'll do anything. Just let me go."

With an irritated groan, he jerked her hard. "You stop. You crazy bitch. You're my woman, and you belong in the house with me. End. Of. Story."

The filter on her mouth didn't work anymore. And she didn't care. Still struggling, pulling away and yanking his wrists, she yelled at him. "I'm not your woman! And what about all the others? Do you have more out there, wherever the hell you disappeared to last week? Are they nurses, too? Do they sing lullabies to you?"

Now she'd done it.

He turned, his face dark red. "Shut up," he growled. With a shout, he punched the side of her head. "Just shut the fuck up."

She saw stars, and suddenly her arms and legs went all floppy. She knew she'd pissed him off this time. But she didn't care. It had felt good to yell at him. And damn the consequences.

Barely aware of what was happening, her ears ringing and eyes unfocused, she realized he'd picked her up and slung her over his shoulder.

I don't care anymore. Give me your best shot.

He must've hit her pretty damned hard, because when he reached the porch, she felt the hamburger and fries rolling in her stomach.

Screw you.

With a hysterical laugh, she promptly threw up on him.

"Mother of God!" He dumped her on the porch, kicking her away from him. "Look what you did, you filthy bitch!"

Out of bleary eyes, she saw him peel off his shirt and hurl it toward the woods. "Get inside!" He had lost all control, and his face screwed up with fury. "I'm gonna kill you!"

She couldn't move, her legs and stomach hurt so badly from being kicked. Curling on her stomach, she whispered, "Can't."

"You'd better move it, girlie. Get up!"

Another kick, this time to her hip.

"Get up! Get up! Get up!"

Three more kicks, timed with his words, and she felt the blackness descending. Sweet oblivion filled her mind, and she drifted off to a place where no one could hurt her anymore.

Chapter 37

She woke feeling cold and shivery, coughing and spitting water. Naked, she lay on her back in the bathtub. The shower relentlessly rained frigid water onto her.

"Well, look who's awake," he chuckled, looming over her, big and dark and sinister. "You ready for your punishment?"

She sputtered some more, turning her head sideways and trying to get up. "Enough. Please. Let me up."

He shoved her back with one massive hand. "No. You stay there until I say you can get up."

She woke fully, and wanted to leap at the monster, tear at his eyes, kick him where it counts. She wanted to rake her nails over his body and scratch him to death.

But he was stronger than she was. At least right now. She had to act smart. Play the part again. Get him to lower his defenses, and then she'd do what she had to when the time came. Which had better be soon, or she'd go stark raving mad.

Like a docile dog, she relaxed and lay there, curling onto her side.

Try to conserve your energy.

If you don't fight him, he'll have nothing to push against.

She controlled the whimper that threatened to rush from her lips, pressing them tightly together.

You can do this.

Shivering hard, she lay as still as possible, then said in a meek voice, "I'm sorry."

He leered over the tub, his eyes focusing on her bare skin. "What's that you said?"

"I'm sorry." She didn't look at him. Didn't move.

"Okay." He turned off the water. "Now, dry off, put these on, and get on the bed."

He watched her every move. The wet uniform she'd worn into Devil's Lake hung on the towel rack, still dripping onto a rag on the floor. It occurred to her that it couldn't have been too long since her failed escape attempt. The dress was still soaked. Maybe only a few minutes?

With her back to him, she pulled on the underwear he'd laid out for her. All that lay on the chair was a white nurse's cap, a dry one from his collection. She towel-dried her hair and combed it with her fingers, then pinned the hat to her damp hair, and covered her breasts with folded arms.

"Nice," he said, eyeing her body. "I like this look on you." He reached up, pulled her arms away. "And aren't you just a perfect little specimen of womanhood. My, my."

She left her arms at her side, much as they wanted to spring up again to hide herself from his lustful gaze. She stayed as calm as possible, remembering that he'd never forced himself on her. He'd always stopped when he got too close.

This time, however, he seemed bolder. He reached up and caressed one breast, circling it. "Very pretty." He leaned forward and kissed it.

NO! It took every ounce of her strength not to resist, not to turn away. Oh, how she wanted to slug him, to wipe that horrid smile off his face.

Get your slimy hands off me.

Her brain screamed the words, but she didn't move.

"On the bed," he said, wiping his mouth with the back of his hand. "Now." His arm shot out and pointed.

She realized she hadn't moved, then hurried—still shivering—to the mattress. "I'm cold," she said, hoping he'd give her more clothing.

"Too bad," he sneered. "Hey, want me to warm you up?" He crawled after her to the bed, fastening her wrists with the ropes he'd used on the first day of her capture. "Hold still, damn you."

She knew, once again, that she'd been struggling involuntarily. Forcing herself to relax, she let him restrain her. "Please. Can I have a blanket? I'm really sorry."

"How sorry are you, sugar? Somehow, I don't believe you anymore. You've lost all credibility, girlie."

"I just lost it back there. I was so lonely when you were gone. It was awful. It made me crazy, I think."

He stopped and looked at her. "Really?" A broad smile crept over his lips. "Good. Maybe you'll appreciate me more now."

"I do. But I need to ask you a question."

He lay near her and leaned over her breasts, tracing his fingers across both nipples. "What's that, sugar?"

"What's your name? You never told me."

Surprised, he dropped his hand and locked eyes with her. "Really? You want to know my name?"

"Uh-huh." She didn't exactly flutter her eyes at him, but it was close. "I do."

He sat back, thinking out loud. "I guess it wouldn't hurt. You can call me Murphy."

"Murphy?" she echoed. "That's nice. Is that your first or last name?"

Wrong tact.

His face darkened and red crept onto his ears. "Why do you need to know that, for crying out loud."

She tried to back peddle. "Oh, no reason. I was just curious. Murphy's good. I'll call you that if I may."

He nodded, brought his hand back to her breasts. "Okay. Now hold still."

She closed her eyes while he kneaded her flesh. The sound of his zipper being opened made her wince inside, but she lay perfectly still, ignoring the sounds of his hand sliding over his flesh.

Stay where you are, please don't come closer.

She summoned songs in her head, trying to block out his moans. The Beatles, first album. Yes. There they were, singing "Please, Please Me" to her. She brought up the voices of Paul and John, and focused on them.

It was working.

Now Murphy's sounds were gone and she sat in an auditorium, watching the band performing their first hits on The Ed Sullivan Show. Her mother had been a huge fan, and she had grown up on all the sixties music Mom loved. Each record was scribed in her brain.

Now, "Love Me Do" rang through her brain, and she heard John's harmonica wailing throughout the hall. She imagined herself jumping in the air, screaming for Paul, her favorite. Now he winked at her, and her heart swelled.

Keep it up. This is a good fantasy.

She added bits and pieces to the vision, including the smell of her mother's perfume she imagined pinching just before she got ready for the show. She pictured herself in an old-fashioned getup, with a woolen skirt and sweater, a pink headband, with her hair in bangs.

When she got to "P.S. I Love You," the soft haunting sound of Paul's voice made her cry inside. She pictured tears of joy and yearning streaming down her cheeks, her heart melted, wanting someone to love so badly.

"Hey. Why are you crying?"

He shook her roughly, and she pulled herself out of the reverie, opening her eyes. "I'm not..." But she touched her cheeks and realized the tears had been real. Her cheeks were soaked. "I...I don't know."

"Listen. I'm treating you good. You need to behave, okay?"

She glanced over. Thank God he'd zipped up. She didn't want to see *that*. "I don't know. I think I'm just tired. Or hungry." Maybe if she mentioned food, he'd want her to start cooking. It had worked before.

"Huh. Okay. Well, you'll have to wait for your outfit to dry."

"Couldn't I wear my old clothes? Just for now?"

He glanced sideways at her and curled his lip. "They're disgusting. But if you want for now. I guess."

Hmm. Sex made him more mellow. That was a good thing to remember.

"Thanks." She lifted her wrists. "Can you please untie me?"

He did as she asked and she scrambled to the closet, where her jeans and tee shirt lay in a crumpled heap on the floor. She couldn't believe he hadn't thrown them out. Thank God.

Even though they didn't smell really fresh, they felt so good to her. She actually smiled and turned to him. "Hungry?"

He got up, grunted, and went into the living room to stare at the pegboard. "Yeah."

She went through the food he'd bought, picked out some ingredients, and went back to her obsequious role. "How about chicken tonight, Murphy?"

He waved a hand in her direction, focused on the news clippings. "Yeah. Whatever."

Humming "Please, Please Me," she went to work.

Chapter 38

Months passed. Seasons came and went. And the rhythm of the captivity didn't change. Slavery. Abandonment. Hunger. Duct tape on her mouth when he got sick of her. Triumphant return to the weak little servant who begged for crumbs.

Portia lost all track of time. She'd tried to keep up with it for a while, but now she didn't care any more. She felt lackluster, dead inside. The more he did to her, the further she retreated into her little worlds.

One day in summer—she didn't know what month, but knew it was in her second year—Murphy left her alone again to pick up gas for the generator. Without the gas, they had no power. Without the power, they had no lights, no cook top, no refrigerator, and no water. He took the truck into town, saying he'd be back soon.

As usual, he tied her up, this time surprising her with a kiss to her forehead. She lay on her back on the bed, still clad in her jeans and tee shirt, grateful for small favors. At least her breasts weren't hanging out from that obscene nurse's outfit, and her legs were covered.

Hairy legs, she thought, curling up and reaching down to feel the soft fuzz on her calf. I haven't shaved in... how long? And I'm just now thinking about it?

What does that say about me?

God. Oh, God. Please help me.

She hadn't let him see her cry since the first year. But now she let the tears roll down her cheeks, and sobs wracked her body. Shuddering, she let the hopeless feelings wash through her, and let herself fully see what she'd tried so hard to block out.

I'll never get out of here.

Oh, my God. I'll be here until the day he tires of me, until I push him just that little bit too far, and he kills me.

And then he can bring home a new girl, see what uniform fits them, and start all over again.

Where were the bodies? Sunk to the bottom of the lake with cement blocks tied to their feet?

She shook and wept harder.

I don't want to die.

She lay like that for two hours, forlorn and forgotten. The tears finally stopped, and she wondered if he'd ever come back.

Five minutes later, she heard the truck. With a sick realization, she caught herself being relieved. Almost happy? How had she turned into such a mess? Such a pitiful little slave?

The sound of the padlock being opened met her ears, but there was something else, too.

It sounded like someone whining, almost animal-like.

"Sugar? I've got a surprise for you." His deep voice rumbled from the porch. "You ready?"

Her heart fell. What kind of surprise now? Another fun time on the bed with him pleasuring himself?

Please, no.

There it was again. Almost a whimper.

"She's in the car. I'll go get her."

Murphy hadn't untied her yet, so she couldn't see what he was doing. But she heard the door shut, the padlock click.

All safe and secure, just like always.

He stood in the doorway with something wiggling in his arms.

A dog?

Yes! A cute little scruffy mutt, who wiggled with joy to see her.

164

He put the creature on the bed, and it scrambled to her side, licking her face.

"I found her in the woods, she's got no collar. Seen her a few times over the past week." He actually leaned over to pat the animal. "I think she's hungry."

"Untie me, please." She pulled on the restraints, smiling at the creature who stood on her hind legs on the bed, as if she were dancing in a circus. "Please!"

Murphy grunted and released her. "Okay, okay. Don't get too excited. It's just a mongrel."

Portia embraced the creature with tears of joy. "Oh, she's beautiful!" She cuddled and stroked her soft fur. "Where do you belong, little one?"

The dog licked her hands, nosed into her arms, and settled on her lap as if that was where she belonged all along.

"Oh, she's so sweet. She's lying in my lap, just like a little cupcake."

"That's what you should name her, then."

"Cupcake?" Portia genuinely smiled for the first time since he'd taken her. "Yes. That's what I'm going to call her. My little Cupcake."

Chapter 39

On a warm day in mid summer, Portia won a battle with Murphy. It was a small accomplishment, but she felt ridiculously victorious.

He worked outside, chopping wood near the cabin. She'd asked to sit on the porch, and he surprisingly agreed. Of course, he tied her to the porch railing. Tight. With only a foot of slack.

The cycle of starvation and abandonment had continued, and she wondered more and more about the other girl or girls he kept.

Where were they?

She had no idea. The only clues she got were his returning with different clothes than he'd left in.

And she wondered how she'd endured her second winter in that cabin. It had been freezing for so long, in spite of the woodstove in the living room that made that room toasty, but hardly heated the bedroom. And the baths had been so cold...only once a week now. Spring had never felt so good, and now, summer had come, warming her face and body through the cracks in the windows where the mud had fallen out leaving little holes for sunlight to come inside.

Murphy didn't relent one bit. When she wasn't cooking or cleaning, she was restrained on the bed, even though now she had the little dog to lie beside her, and that made it so much better. When he showered, he tied her up. And he always hung the keys in the shower with him, on a hook he installed for just that purpose.

Portia had lost so much weight that she wondered if anyone would recognize her these days. She'd shared her food with Cupcake, always making sure the sweet little dog had enough to eat.

Thankfully, the jerk had relaxed a little as far as the required "dress code" went. He even let her wash her jeans and tee shirt every few days in the bathtub. She wore them all the time now, except when he needed his special attention.

So far, she'd been lucky. He hadn't pressed her for more yet. He'd been happy to touch her in various places while satisfying himself on the bed next to her, or sometimes on the couch. He had violated her in so many ways, taken her freedom, humiliated her, touched her where she shouldn't, forced her to lie still while he did disgusting things to himself, and all of that had made her sick to her stomach, but still, she was relieved he hadn't raped her. She didn't think she could have survived that.

Thank God.

She didn't think she could survive if he actually tried to go further. Could she?

Could a person live like this forever?

Would she have to be here until she died? Would he tire of her, abandon her for good one day?

She sat in the beam of sunlight that kissed her forehead, rocking back and forth in the porch chair, cuddling Cupcake on her lap. The fresh air felt so good, so tempting, but it also was a painful reminder of what she'd come to expect in life. The inner walls. The constant humiliation. The fear and pain and need to escape.

She escaped in her mind all the time. It really helped. The scenes she imagined were colorful, filled with music and laughter. She pictured herself readying Mirage for a ride, mounting him, and heading off for the hills. She drew every trail, tree, and rock from memory in these dream-like scenes, and she enhanced the visions each time she drew on them. She pictured her family's kitchen, her father making pancakes. Her mother's lasagna and fresh bread. She even imagined the smell of the bread in the oven.

Oh, how she longed for home.

Something inside her snapped.

Wait. What's happening to me?

Why have I become so passive? So subservient? Why am I so damned appreciative of every little thing he gives me?

Maybe I'm brainwashed.

A surge of anger flushed through her, and in an instant, she knew what her next move would be.

She watched him, waving once in a while to make him feel safe and secure. Maybe he even felt loved by her, in his strange and bizarre heart? If he had a heart, that is. Slowly, she lowered the mutt to the porch floor. "Shh, now, baby. Don't give me away."

She waited until he was almost done, then began to moan. Softly at first, then louder.

"What's wrong with you, sugar?" he said, setting his axe on the ground. "You sick?"

The ash bucket sat in the corner beside her, its square black shovel tucked into a clasp on the side of the pail.

She lowered her head to her chest, slumping in the chair so she slid down to the floor, her hands still restrained above. Her wrists hurt, but she figured maybe he'd come to her, maybe he'd untie her and...

Footsteps came up the porch steps. "What the hell's wrong with you, girl?" He poked her with one foot, but she didn't respond. Cupcake licked her hands and face.

He pulled her head up with her hair, and the dog began to bark, snarling around his ankles.

Damn, that hurt.

She didn't flutter an eyelid, let her face stay slack and droopy.

"Oh, cripes." He untied her arms and she fell onto the porch, huddled near the bucket.

When he leaned down to lift her, she grabbed the shovel and jabbed him in the crotch with it, as hard as she could.

It wasn't sharp enough to cut him, of course, but she hoped it put him down for a long time.

He howled in pain, fell to the ground, and released her, cupping his injured parts.

Like a gazelle, she leapt over the porch railing and for the second time in her long captivity, she began to run toward the lake with Cupcake racing behind her.

Chapter 40

At the woodpile, she stopped and stared.

There was the hatchet, and beside it, a heavy sledgehammer.

Should I?

Thoughts raced through her mind like tumbleweeds in a tornado, completely twisted and crazy and running wild with murderous intent.

Murphy moaned on the porch, and before long, he'd get up and chase her. Again. And he'd probably catch her, unless she did something different this time.

She stopped mid-flight, grabbed the sledgehammer, and returned to the porch where the monster lay, groaning and swearing at her. Cupcake stopped and sat on the grass at the bottom of the porch, looking confused.

"God damned loony woman," Murphy moaned again. "You'll...pay...for...this, bitch."

"Never again," she said, the words hissing from her lips in a near scream.

The sledgehammer was so heavy, she could barely lift it. But anger surged through her, giving her power she'd never known possible, and she swung it wide and high, three times.

Three times it thudded against his skull. Three times she felt the sick, sweet feeling of revenge coursing through her veins. Three times she saw him shudder as it slammed his temple.

And then he was still.

And there was blood. Not a lot, but enough to send chills of fear racing down her back.

Oh, God. Oh, God! What have I done?

She leaned down to feel his pulse, but couldn't find it and was afraid to check for too long. He might get up. He might be faking. He might grab her.

Her father's voice came into her head again, offering steady council. *You've done what was necessary to survive. Now get out of there.*

With a start, she realized she should hurry. *What if he isn't dead? What if he wakes up and recaptures me?*

Quickly, with shaking hands, she tied the ropes he'd used for her onto his hairy wrists. At least if he woke up, he wouldn't get free right away.

She streaked back into the cabin.

What do I need?

The pegboard! Get rid of the articles. If he's dead, they won't be able to connect her to the murder. She ripped the articles off the board and jammed them crumpled into her jeans pockets.

What else?

She'd only come with the clothes on her back, and had nothing personal to reclaim. Except maybe her fingerprints, which would be impossible to wipe down. They were on every glass, every counter, every surface.

Screw that.

Get the keys. Get the dog. And get out.

The keys were in his jacket pocket, and by shoving and rolling Murphy until his pockets were accessible, she finally fished them out. He flopped onto his side with arms loose and mouth agape. Blood trickled down his forehead, and she felt nausea creeping up inside her. She couldn't see his chest rising.

Did that mean...

NO. Don't think about it.

Should I drag him inside? Lock the door?

No, if he were only stunned, he might wake up and grab her.

She noticed his wallet bulging in his back pocket, and carefully slid it out. Inside was over two hundred dollars in tens and twenties.

She took it, folding the money into her jeans pocket. "You owe me a lot more than that," she said, surprised at the harshness of her tone. "Bastard." She almost kicked him for good measure, but the dog was watching, and for some reason, she didn't want Cupcake to see her perform any more violent acts.

"Come on, honey," she said, cuddling Cupcake in her arms. "We're going home."

PART III
Revenge

Chapter 41

Boone took a deep breath and knocked on the cabin door.

Silence.

"Hello?" He called a second time, then knocked again.

Anderson pointed to the ropes tied to the porch railing. "Crap. That's where Portia said she tied him up after she hit him with the sledgehammer."

Boone frowned. "Yeah, also where he tied her to the rails the day she escaped."

Anderson fingered the ropes. "She's one brave lady."

"Damn right she is. Now. Where's the sledgehammer she hit him with?" Boone asked, poking around the porch. "There. On the woodpile."

Anderson followed his gaze. "That's not where Portia left it. She said she just dropped it right here."

"Which means...he's probably alive." Boone's face pulled into a worried frown.

"Let's check out the cabin," Anderson said.

Boone pushed on the door, frowning when he noticed the padlock. "It's locked."

"Not for long." Anderson smashed the lock once with the butt of his rifle, then glanced over his shoulder at Boone. "What?"

Boone smiled. "Nothin', go right ahead. You just beat me to it."

After four more tries, the lock hasp broke away, and the door swung open.

Boone entered first. "Let's just do a quick check, and get out of here."

The interior matched Portia's description, right down to the pegboard on the wall. Boone headed over to it, picking up a crumpled piece of newspaper that had landed in one corner of the room. He unfurled it and saw Portia's face staring up at him. "Guess she missed this one when she ripped all those clippings off the board."

Anderson opened all the cupboards and refrigerator. "No food left, just a little salt, vinegar, and ketchup." He motioned toward the bedroom, taking pictures as he went on his cell phone. "Look at this." He opened the closet door. "Empty."

Boone noticed the ropes on the headboard and cringed. "That's where he restrained her, man." His voice caught, and anger surged through him. *"Bastard."*

Anderson stood on his toes and reached to the very back of the closet shelf. "What's this?" He pulled a white object from the top and blew dust off it. "Guess he left one of his toys behind."

Boone stared at the nurse's cap. "Jesus. What a sicko." When Anderson started to put it back, he held up one hand. "Wait. Is that a hair on that bobby pin?"

Anderson squinted at it, holding it up in the light. "Crap. You're right. And it's reddish. Might be Portia's."

"Let's take a picture of where we found it and bag it. Just in case we need some kind of DNA proof or something."

"Well, we've probably destroyed the evidence by messing with it already, but hell, you and I could testify to where we found it, right?"

"Right."

Anderson took a few more pictures inside and out, then checked his cell phone. "No signal. And crap, it's getting late."

They left the cabin, closing the door as best as they could by tying one of the ropes to the handle and then to the chair arm beside it. "At least the animals won't get in," Boone said, leading the way back to the Jeep. "Come on. We've gotta get a signal and warn Dirk. If Murphy's not here, then he's gotta be alive. And if he's alive..."

"He could be in Vermont." Anderson nodded. "Let's hurry. We need to get home."

"Amen to that," Boone said, jumping into the Jeep. He pounded the roof with one hand. "Move it, Jeeves. We've got a job to do."

∾∾

When they reached the Baraboo town limits, Boone's phone suddenly showed three bars. He dialed the Lamont's home number, and waited while it rang several times.

"Hello?" Dirk answered warily, then when he recognized Boone's voice, he choked with relief. "Oh, thank God it's you. We've been getting calls all afternoon from reporters. Somebody leaked that she's home."

"Damn," Boone said, rolling up his window to cut down on the road noise. "Listen. We found the cabin."

"And?"

"And he wasn't there. Nothing on the porch except the ropes he was tied with. And nothing inside. He took the collection of uniforms. No food. Looks pretty deserted, Dirk."

"What about the sledgehammer? Was there blood on it?"

"We didn't check, but he must've moved it back to the wood pile, because it wasn't where she left it. He's either alive, or someone found him and kept it quiet."

Dirk sighed. "He's alive all right. I can feel it in my bones."

"Listen, we're heading home. Should get there by morning. Tell my brother to hang tight and plan on staying the night, okay? We might need an extra gun there if he shows up."

Dirk agreed. "He's a good boy, your brother. Nice kid."

"More important, he's a helluva shot, Dirk. I trust his hand-eye coordination better 'n my own."

"Nice to know. He's been out back, target practicing on cans all afternoon."

"Good. I want anyone who's watching to be worried about the manpower, or gun power, I should say. I don't want him to think Portia will be an easy mark."

"Good point."

Anderson spoke up. "Tell him to keep all the lights on in the house and barn. And to alert the cops. I think it's safe enough now to fill them in on the details, since she unfortunately didn't kill the creep."

Boone switched the phone to his other ear. "Did you hear that, Dirk?"

"Got it. We're on it. Um, there's somebody here who wants to talk to you."

"Okay," Boone said, expecting it to be his brother. When Portia came on the phone, it took him off guard.

"Boone?" she said, hesitantly at first. "Are you there?"

"Right here," he said, surprised at the intensity of the emotion flaring through him. "It's good to hear your voice, Peaches."

"You, too. Are you okay?"

"We're fine, hon. And I'm sure you heard your dad, but we didn't find Murphy. No body. And it looks like somebody cleaned out the house. Everything's gone and it was locked up."

"Oh, God. That means…"

"He's either done a runner, or he's coming after you. Either way, we'll find him. And when we do," he said softly, "I'm gonna kick his sorry ass."

A surprised laugh escaped her lips. "Boone!"

"I mean it. I can't tell you how pissed I am at this guy. I really want a shot at him."

She was silent for a moment. "Um. Thank you. But you might have to wait in line behind me. I want the first punch."

177

"Good for you," he said with a grin. "You keep up that attitude, and we'll bring him down. Guaranteed."

They hung up, and Boone focused on the striped highway that stretched for miles ahead of them.

By sunrise, we'll be home again.

And good luck to anyone who tried to hurt Portia. As God was his witness, he wouldn't let that happen, ever again.

Chapter 42

Anderson and Boone pulled into the barnyard and parked beside Dirk's pickup. The place was surprisingly quiet, except for the muted sound of dogs barking in the house.

"That's weird," Anderson said. "I thought I'd get a big hug from Grace."

"Or maybe a slap," Boone said. "Remember, you didn't tell her you were going until after we left."

"True," he said.

They lifted their backpacks out of the car and headed up the porch steps.

Although he'd felt his heart creeping into to his throat with every mile that passed, Boone had just called Dirk ten minutes ago, and knew everything was fine. No need to be nervous now. He'd had enough of that on the long ride home, switching off driving and sleeping every three hours, wondering where Murphy was, and picturing him hiding out in the woods near Bittersweet Hollow.

I need to stop my mind from going into overdrive. This is ridiculous.

With an inner sigh of relief, Boone saw Dirk open the kitchen door and wave to them.

Boomer and Cupcake tumbled down the steps, raced toward them, and jumped up on them, whining and kissing the men's hands. Cupcake even did her circus dance for them, making Anderson laugh.

"She missed us, I guess," he said.

Boone crouched down and gave them both some attention, then straightened and headed for the porch.

"Welcome back, men."

"Thanks, Dirk." After a round of hugging and backslapping, Boone followed Anderson and Dirk into the living room, where the whole family waited, including his brother.

Ned stepped up and pulled him into a quick hug. "All's quiet on the home front."

Boone nodded surreptitiously toward Portia. "Everyone okay?"

Ned shrugged and headed for the coffee pot. "Best as can be expected. Don't think they've been sleeping much. Everyone's kinda jumpy." He poured a cup and offered it to Boone. "Want some?"

Boone passed. "No thanks, I'm all coffee'd out."

Grace flew down the stairs and jumped into Anderson's arms, wrapping her legs around his waist. "You son of a gun!" she screamed, hugging him. "I'm really mad at you." She alternately kissed him and pounded his chest.

He hugged her back, laughing. "Well, I'm glad to see you, too."

Portia stood in the corner by the computer, a shy smile on her face.

Boone headed for her side. "Hey, Portia."

She offered a hand to him, an action that made his heart pound like a bull's hooves thundering toward his matador. He took her hand in his, pressed it, and realized she must've had a breakthrough. She no longer seemed to fear him, or shrink from his touch.

"Hi, Boone."

They stood awkwardly for a minute, before Boone realized he still held her hand in his. "Oh, s-sorry." He felt like a schoolboy, flushing and stammering.

"Want to go see the horses?" she asked. "I haven't been given much free rein since you left. Too hard to protect all us lil' women folk, you know?"

180

She actually smiled, and he noticed a light in her eyes that had been missing before.

"That'd be great," he said. "Let me hit the facilities, then get my gun from the truck, just in case."

"Okay. I'll cut up some apples. Meet you on the porch?"

Minutes later, side by side, with the rifle tucked under his left arm, they wandered into the barn.

"Looks like Pookie is ready to pop," she said, motioning to the pregnant steel gray mare nosing into her hay bag.

"She's due any day now," Boone said.

Portia clucked to Pookie, who came to the door and pushed against her chest. "Oh, you're just a beggar, you are." She fished in her pockets for the apple she'd diced before they came out. "Here you go, honey."

The horse chomped on the apple pieces and asked for more by gently pushing her head against Portia.

"Okay, okay. I guess you're eating for two. You deserve seconds."

"By the way, what's Pookie's official name again?" he asked.

"Bittersweet Silver Sun Frosty," she said. "But that was too much of a mouthful. So we nicknamed her Pookie."

"That's right." He smiled. "Fits her."

The horse's dappled gray coat glowed in the sun streaming through her stall door. Boone watched Portia work her magic with the mare, whispering, and combing her fingers through Pookie's black mane.

She really has a way with the animals.

He watched her, standing back to give her time with the mare, and his heart suddenly squeezed with affection. It dawned on him how much this woman meant to him, and how angry it made him that Murphy had just plucked her from their lives as if she were a flower to steal from someone's garden.

How could he do that?

And how did Portia survive for two long years? She must be made of strong stuff. With a sudden gushing inner realization, it hit him.

I want to be with this woman. Forever.

I want to raise horses with her. Have a passel of kids. Surround ourselves with dogs and cats and rabbits and whatever else the kids wanted. Maybe some goats?

An involuntary laugh escaped him.

Portia glanced up from kissing Pookie on the muzzle. "What?"

He noticed today her hair seemed fuller, healthier. It glistened copper in the sun and fell on her shoulders in pretty waves.

"Boone?" she said. "What's so funny? You look like you're in a daze."

He laughed again, trying to cover his embarrassment. "Uh. Yeah. I don't know. For some reason I was picturing you and me and a barn full of animals."

"We are in a barn full of animals," she said with a grin. "What's so funny about that?"

"No, I mean, all kinds. I pictured horses, rabbits, cats, and goats."

"Goats?"

"Yeah. The kind with the floppy long ears. You know?"

She pursed her mouth for a minute. "Um, Nubians?"

"Yeah. I think that's what they're called. They're pretty neat. What do you think of making goat cheese some day?"

"With you?" she asked, now quieter, seeming to withdraw a little.

"Only if you want to," he said.

What the hell were they talking about? It almost had sounded like a proposal, and he sure as hell wouldn't put this frail creature under that kind of pressure.

"I like goat cheese," she said, turning back to the mare.

"Well, maybe some day we can try it," he said, relieved that she hadn't gone all spooky on him again. "It could be fun."

"Right," she said, backing up. "Let's go check on Mirage. I'll bet he missed us."

Chapter 43

When they came in from the barn, Portia watched Boone interacting with her family. There was something about his easy smile, the way he grabbed her father and his brother in big bear hugs, and how he approached her so gently, as if she were a skittish colt, that made her heart and mind soften.

She realized with a start that in spite of all the terror of the past two years, in spite of her trauma, her fears, her debilitating mental state, she was falling for him. That school girl crush of long ago had blossomed, grown, and now it felt real. It felt...possible.

He crouched on the ground with both dogs making a fuss over him, licking his hands and face, and she really felt the tug of a grin trying to break through.

It felt simply amazing, that urge to smile—that hint of happiness. She'd missed it for so long, she barely recognized the sensations it stirred up in her.

A few yards away, Grace sat on Anderson's lap on the couch, kissing him nonstop.

Portia shook her head and almost laughed out loud. *Where does she think she is, up at Make-out Point?*

Occasionally her sister's eyes would flit to Boone and back as she wiggled rather provocatively on Anderson's legs.

No way.

Is she honestly trying to make Boone want her?

Portia breathed out a long-held breath. *No. I'm thinking crazy thoughts.*

Poor Anderson looked overwhelmed. He tried to slow her down, and gently disengage himself. When it seemed as if she were going to unbutton his shirt and have sex with him right on the family couch, he stood up abruptly, dumping her onto the cushions beside him. With slightly pink cheeks, he kissed her forehead, whispering, "Tonight, baby. Not in front of your whole family in the middle of the day."

Grace's eyes flared. "Hey!" She righted herself and stood, smoothing her pretty pink skirt over her hips. "That wasn't very nice."

Anderson gave her a dimpled smile, shrugged, and offered his hands palms out in an excuse. "Sorry, sweetie."

Portia excused herself from Boone, who gallantly pretended not to watch the show Grace put on. She encircled her sister's shoulders from behind the couch and leaned over to whisper in her ear. "Down, girl. What the hell's gotten into you?"

Grace made a face and harrumphed like an old lady. "Geez. I was just glad to see him."

"Well, be glad to see him in the bedroom. Tonight. You're getting *that way* again."

Grace stuck her tongue out. "So what?" She pouted and patted the couch. "Come sit with me. We can watch those Neanderthals from here."

Portia skirted the couch and sank beside her sister, slipping an arm into hers. Leaning close to Grace, she said, "I'm worried about Mom."

"I know, me too. She looked like a ghost this morning."

"You noticed, too?" Portia tried to keep her voice low, so her father wouldn't hear her. "Dad seemed a little worried when she went up for a nap so early in the morning." She glanced up the stairs, wondering when her mother would wake. "We should bring her some lunch, maybe. What do you think?"

Grace nodded. "Good idea. How about chicken salad?"

Anderson had wandered over to talk with Dirk, Ned and Boone. Their low, urgent discussion included hand waving toward the mountains and grave expressions. Portia wondered if they were planning some sort of trap for Murphy, but then shook off her concerns.

We don't know Murphy's in the area. He could be in Timbuktu by now, for all we know.

Grace took out some cold chicken legs from last night's supper, three stalks of celery, and a large jar of Miracle Whip. "Okay, Sweet Pea. Wanna chop?"

"Sure." As if she hadn't been gone for two whole years, Portia found the cutting board and her father's favorite knife without even thinking about it, and settled at the table beside Grace, who rounded up the spices and a big bowl to mix everything in.

Grace reached for the bread and set it on the counter by the toaster, then sat beside Portia, who diligently chopped.

"Sorry about that scene on the couch."

Portia rinsed the celery under the faucet, then sat down to cut it into small pieces the way her mother always did. "Hey. I know you've got some issues to work on. How 'bout next time I see you acting up, I just dump a bucket of cold water on your head, Baby Cakes?"

Grace snorted a laugh. "Dear sister, how I've missed you."

੭ఞ⌒ఄ

Dirk stood with his arms crossed, tossing around ideas about Murphy with the guys. Boone had come up with some good ideas for security, like installing wireless video cameras out by the barn and above all the doors to the house. Anderson thought some booby traps might come in handy, and they'd thought up a few good ones.

But he couldn't get his mind off Daisy.

She'd looked too pale this morning, and hadn't smiled as readily as yesterday.

Afraid to face the awful truth, he'd pushed it out of his mind, worrying instead about some crazy-ass demon lurking in the woods or hiding in the barn. He'd focused all his worry and attention on this immediate danger, and tried not to think about Daisy's cancer.

But when she excused herself for a nap at ten in the morning, his heart had exploded with worry. She'd shushed him and waved him off, saying it was just all the excitement that had tired her out.

His gut told him that the experimental pills they gave her weren't doing the same job as the IV they'd hooked her up to at the hospital.

Maybe the tablets weren't as strong? Maybe there was a difference in how this new medicine worked when you just swallowed a few pills instead of getting it infused directly into your bloodstream?

He knew he had to call Dr. Kareem.

And he knew what they'd say.

Bring her back to New York City.

So, now he'd have to make an impossible decision.

Bring Daisy back to New York? Or stay home to protect his first-born child?

He couldn't do both.

With a deep sigh, he nodded at something Boone just said, but he had no idea what he was agreeing to.

Chapter 44

Portia woke with a start at five the next morning. She hadn't slept well; her night had been filled with screams.

In the endless nightmares she'd stood over her mother's grave, sobbing, shaking, and collapsing into a dark, dirty hole in search of something that wasn't there.

She slipped out of bed quietly, careful not to disturb Gracie, who'd come in during the night to comfort her. Her sister lay on her pillow, hair strewn about in a messy tangle, lips drooping like a child. So innocent. And yet...

To her surprise, both dogs stayed asleep on the bed, their eyes closed, breathing softly.

Softly, she tiptoed into her parents' room.

Daisy lay in Dirk's arms, head nestled against his bare chest. In the pale light of dawn, she watched her mother's chest rise and fall and listened to her father's soft snoring. With love surging in her heart, she stood quietly in the doorway for a few more seconds, willing her mother to recover, to get some color in her cheeks today, to feel a bounce in her step.

The sound of a truck in the driveway made her freeze, heart pounding. She ran to the window and experienced a rush of relief when she saw it was Ned, who'd gone home last night to help his father with a difficult calf delivery. As promised, he came back at the crack of dawn.

She quickly showered and dressed into her comfortable, clean jeans and a white blouse, tossing on a gray hoodie to keep away the morning chill. Sliding into her old sneakers, she tied them in neat knots. Smiling, glad she wasn't wearing 1950s white nurse shoes, she walked to the bathroom and ran a brush through her hair, pulling it back into one braid that hung down her back. It felt so darned good to wear what she wanted, when she wanted. And to be so clean, to enjoy fresh shampoo, to use her Oil of Olay soap. She smiled at herself in the mirror.

I won.

I survived. I beat him.

She wouldn't let herself think of what might come next.

No.

Pushing away the worries, she glanced at the soft pinkish-orange slit of light on the horizon. Boone would be getting up soon from his makeshift bed on the couch, and she wanted to make coffee for him.

I want to make coffee for a man?

I never thought I'd feel that way again.

She actually chuckled and headed downstairs, descending carefully so as not to wake him with her footfalls.

He lay spread-eagled on his back on the couch, one foot over the back cushion and the other hanging over the armrest. The red and white apple quilt her grandmother had made lay draped over his chest, but his green boxers showed, with his long, lean legs stretching out forever.

Tempted to avert her eyes, she resisted the urge and looked. For a moment, she forgot the last two years and her newfound fears, and let herself admire his body from the safety of the alcove between the kitchen and living room.

He breathed steadily, deep and quiet, like one of her horses. His lips hung slack, and occasionally a soft snore escaped them.

Again, for just one second, she felt the desire to run her fingers over his mouth, his cheeks, his eyebrows.

Good old Boone.

Or was he a new Boone?

He'd been such an integral part of her childhood, she had trouble merging this rugged man with that tall, thoughtful boy who'd led her on such fun adventures on horseback.

189

One eye opened and he grinned at her. "You gonna make the coffee, or just stand there all morning?"

With a start, she jumped and almost fell over. "Boone!" She whispered his name with a hiss, but couldn't help the slow smile that came after. "You scared me."

"What time is it?"

"A little after five."

"Thought so. I almost overslept."

"I'll make the coffee. You want a shower first?"

He sat up and rubbed his hands over his eyes. "Yeah. I'll hop into the downstairs bath. I think your mom washed my clothes yesterday and actually laid them out for me. Time to change, I've been wearing the same thing for two days."

"Good idea, you don't want those pants to start walking on their own." Portia laughed and turned to the kitchen. "Okay. Coffee will be ready when you are."

She busied herself in the kitchen, listening to the sounds of Ned opening the sliding barn doors. Out the window over the sink, she saw him tossing flakes of hay into the paddocks.

Both brothers astounded her. Ned had taken over where Boone left off, feeding the horses without even asking if Dirk needed a break. He just showed up and went to work.

Amazing.

She rinsed out the coffee carafe and smiled. This was almost like having two strong brothers in the family.

Almost.

Then again, Anderson made three. Three big brothers.

She would have liked to have had brothers to look up to, to defend her in high school, to teach her how to fish or hunt. Dirk hadn't been much of a fisherman or hunter, but he had taught her how to handle a rifle.

Boone emerged with wet hair, rubbing it with a towel. "Is Ned here already?"

190

On cue, the kitchen door opened and Ned burst inside. His eyes flicked to Boone, filled with dread. "I...uh...I think you need to come outside and see something."

Boone's face tightened, and Portia set the carafe into the coffee maker and flicked on the switch, watching silent messages shoot back and forth between the brothers.

Boone dashed toward the door. "Stay here."

Portia frowned and followed the brothers to the top of the porch steps. "No. I want to know what's going on. Are my horses okay?"

Ned had grabbed the rifles from the kitchen, and tossed Boone's to him. "Um. Yeah. They're okay."

Boone stopped, turning to her. "I thought I told you—"

"I'm not waiting inside," she said. Boomer and Cupcake appeared at her side, following them outside as if ready for a romp in the fields.

"Cripes, Portia." He took her arm and hurried after Ned to the far side of the barn. Boone was barefoot, and his feet had already turned dusty.

Ned stopped and looked up, then glanced toward the woods.

Portia froze, staring at the spray-painted words scrawled on her barn.

Hey, Sugar. Miss me?

"I..." Her throat tightened and she wobbled in place, but she didn't faint or slump to the ground. Murphy could be watching, and damn it, she wouldn't give him the satisfaction. She steeled herself and touched Boone's hand. "It's him."

"Okay. This has gone far enough." Boone grabbed her and dragged her toward the house, frowning at Ned. "You should have told me. She shouldn't be outside. He could be watching."

A distant rumble of thunder made Boone jump. Fat raindrops began to pelt him, and where the water hit the ground, puffs of dust bloomed upward.

A shot rang out and pinged the ground near his bare feet. "Shit!" He lifted Portia in his arms and barreled toward the house, flying up the porch steps.

A bullet zinged past her ear and lodged in the side of the house.

They ducked inside the kitchen, slamming the door shut behind them, already dripping from the rain that had turned heavy. Thunder boomed again in the distance.

Boone grabbed the phone and began to lock all the doors and windows, pulling down shades and closing curtains. "I'm calling Sheriff Dunne. We need reinforcements."

Portia slumped onto the couch, her heart pounding. "Are you going to tell him the whole story?"

"Not everything." Boone said. "But he needs to know that we've identified Murphy, where he comes from, and what he's after. He can't help us if we don't give the facts."

Portia nodded. "Okay. Do what you have to do."

Chapter 45

Dirk stumbled down the stairs, rubbing his eyes and feeling dazed. The thunder had woken him, almost sounding like gunfire, and he glanced outside to see a black wall of water pouring onto the land. Lightning arced across the dark sky, which looked more like night than morning.

He'd been up most of the night with Daisy, who was restless, weak, and going downhill fast. He needed to call Dr. Kareem at the clinic, but he wouldn't be able to reach his office until nine, when they opened. He lurched unsteadily toward the kitchen, longing for a strong cup of coffee. "What's going on?"

His daughter sat stiffly on the couch, all color drained from her cheeks. Boone and Ned carried their guns and ran around checking locks on the doors. Boone held the portable phone to his ear, speaking into the receiver with forceful confidence.

Speaking about an intruder.

About Murphy.

Heart banging beneath his ribs, Dirk ran to join them and pulled back the kitchen window curtain to look outside.

Boone jerked him back. "No! He's out there. He shot at us already."

"What?"

"Sheriff Dunne's on his way with reinforcements."

Dirk stiffened. "We need to get Anderson down here."

Ned nodded and ran toward the stairs. "I'm on it."

Boone paced, talking fast. "Listen, Dirk. I told the Sheriff most of what we learned up at Devil's Lake, but I didn't mention the truck. I didn't want to give them an excuse to arrest any of us for stealing or hiding stolen property. Even though it was probably already stolen by Murphy before Portia took it."

Dirk grimaced. "Okay, good." He went to the corner for his own rifle and paced back and forth behind the front door. "Where's he shooting from?"

Boone sat down on a stuffed chair opposite Portia to put his boots on. "Up on the ridge. Behind the stand of twisted spruce trees, I think. He wrote a message on the side of the barn to get us out there." His face twisted. "Cripes. Portia was with us when we went to check it out."

Dirk glanced over at Portia, who sat still. "Honey?" He strode to her side and sat beside her, one arm around her shoulders and one arm still cradling his gun. "Are you okay?"

"I'm fine, Dad." She sounded a little wooden, but her eyes narrowed and her voice was steady as a rock. "I knew he'd come for me." Her fists clenched on her lap. "But I'm not letting him get to me this time. "

"Good girl," he said, pride and worry vying inside him. "We'll get this prick."

"He thinks I'm his victim. That I'll be scared, crying, running away." She turned a steely gaze at him. "No more. Never again. I want to teach him a lesson he'll never forget."

This switch in her persona almost scared him as much as the thought of that sicko taking pot shots at her. What was she saying? "Listen," he said, stroking her arm. "You let us take care of him. The cops are coming, baby. They'll find him. They'll arrest him."

"I've been thinking about this a lot, Dad. And I'm pretty sure he's got other women stashed away somewhere." She turned in the direction of the door, gesturing for Boone to come closer. "Boone, we need to capture Murphy, and make him tell us about the other girls he's taken. Someone's got to save them."

Boone nodded. "I'm with you there, Peaches. If the cops ferret him out of the woods, he can be questioned by the experts."

She spat the next words. "I'd like to question him."

Dirk stood. "Listen, Portia. I don't want you getting any weird ideas, okay? You just do what we tell you to. We know how to keep you safe. Okay?"

She didn't answer.

"Okay?"

She rose and walked to Boone's side. "How many officers are coming?"

Boone shrugged. "I'm not sure. Sheriff Dunne and Deputy Mills, I think. Maybe more."

She pulled the curtain aside and peeked out. "It's not enough."

Anderson, Grace, and Daisy came down the stairs. Anderson went for his weapon hanging in a holster on the coat rack. Gracie stumbled toward the coffee machine. And Daisy stopped at the kitchen table, taking in the closed curtains and shades.

"What's going on?" she said, her voice trembling. "Dirk?"

Chapter 46

Daisy felt exhaustion ripple through her body. She toppled forward, as if her legs had lost their muscles, as if they'd been pulled right out from under her.

She landed in a heap on the kitchen floor, her cheek and shoulder jarred by the impact, throbbing painfully.

Around her, the family erupted into shouts and a flurry of movements that dizzied her.

She closed her eyes. Everything hurt.

"Daisy!" Dirk's voice came from far away, urgent, compelling her to answer. "Daisy, can you hear me?"

In spite of the muddiness in her brain, she recognized his tone of voice. Beneath the deep rumble, she sensed his fear.

What was he afraid of?

"Mom?" Portia and Grace both called to her, and someone lifted her from the floor to place on the couch.

Dirk's voice sounded stronger this time. "Call 911."

Someone in the background, maybe Boone, said he'd already called the police.

"We need an ambulance," Dirk said.

Who got hurt?

In a flash she realized they thought she needed to go to the hospital, but she didn't want to. She just wanted to be in her own bed, in her own bedroom, with her family around her.

Am I dying?

She shook herself mentally, with all the farm-wife strength she'd cultivated over the years.

No. I'm strong. I'm not giving in. Dirk, Portia, and Grace need me.

I'm not going anywhere.

Something flashed outside, and the rumble of thunder shook the house. She heard the sweet rain hitting the roof, dripping down the gutter spouts.

Summer storm, she thought. "We need the rain," she mumbled, then drifted away.

⚜

Boone punched in Sheriff Dunne's cell phone, glad Dunne had given it to him before he headed out to Bittersweet Hollow.

Dunne picked up immediately. "Dunne here."

"Sheriff? It's Boone Hawke. We've got another problem here."

"What's up, Boone?"

"It's Mrs. Lamont, Daisy. She's collapsed. Dirk thinks it's her cancer again. We need an ambulance."

Outside, the storm raged, the winds wild. Boone wondered if they were getting some kind of freak tornado or hurricane, because he saw a wheelbarrow topple over and one of the doors on the barn slammed open and shut, over and over again.

"Well, we've got another problem, Boone." The Sheriff sounded muffled, as if he were outside, holding the phone under his coat or something. "Wait a minute. Let me get back in the cruiser."

Boone stiffened. What else could go wrong? He heard the sound of a car door shutting, then the buzz of a radio and loud chatter.

"Okay, you there Boone? We've got an obstacle. The Bittersweet Hollow sign's come down. You know those two trees that it's strung between, the one with all the grape vines overhead?"

"Yeah, sure. Can't you just move it?"

"No. One of the trees has fallen across the road. It's a honking big one, Boone. We'll need a heavy-duty chainsaw. I've called for a truck, but it's about a half hour out. Trees are down everywhere. The Peterson's barn roof flew off. Looks like we had some kind of mini-tornado come through here. It's crazy."

Boone's insides tightened. "What about a helicopter? Do you think they could fly one in? We need help fast. Daisy's down for the count, and that bastard's shooting at anyone who goes outside."

"I'll call for a chopper. But I don't think they could fly in this. Not yet, anyway. And I've got more men coming by car."

Boone heard the sound of sirens through Dunne's phone. "I hear them."

"We'll come in on foot. The farm's about two miles from here. Should take us twenty or thirty minutes if we jog."

"Some of your guys need to circle up behind the twisted spruce trees on the ridge. You know where I mean?"

"I think so. Where the lightning hit in '07?"

"Right."

"That's where he's shooting from?"

"Best as I can tell. Unless he's moved."

"Okay. Keep everyone inside and don't let them stand near the windows. I'll call an ambulance and tell them to pick up a chainsaw on the way. That might be the fastest."

"Better yet," Boone said. "Let me call my father. He's closer and has a big Husqvarna that'll do the trick. He can clear it for the EMTs."

"Good idea."

"Call me when you're close, so we don't shoot any of your men by mistake. We're all armed and pretty trigger happy here, Sheriff."

"It's a promise. Talk to you soon."

They hung up, and Boone returned to the family crowded by Daisy's side.

"Ambulance is called and—"

The lights snapped off and darkness filled the living room.

Grace screamed.

Anderson shushed her. "Baby. Quiet." He ran to the kitchen door and listened, then pulled back the curtain in the window a fraction of an inch and looked outside. "I don't see anything. I think it's just the storm."

Portia knelt by her mother, whispering to her and holding her hand. "It's okay, Mom. It's just the storm. We're safe."

Daisy lay unresponsive on the couch beside her.

Boone punched in the number for his family farm, relieved his father answered on the first ring.

"Son?"

"Yeah, Dad. It's me."

"You okay?"

"No. We've got some big trouble here. And I need you. You and your chainsaw, Dad."

He filled in his father, who was out the door before he finished the conversation, heading to the barn to grab his chainsaw.

Quickly Boone told Dirk, Anderson, Ned, Portia, and Grace what to expect, then hurried upstairs with his rifle to Portia's bedroom window, the best vantage point to watch for Murphy and the officers who slogged through the downpour.

Chapter 47

Portia crouched beside her mother, stroking her hand and murmuring words of comfort, even though she still lay unresponsive. "It'll be okay, Mom. We're getting you help."

Dirk paced behind the couch, back and forth, on the phone with Dr. Kareem in New York City. "Okay. Yes. I understand, doctor. We'll get her airlifted as soon as the winds die down."

Grace—in spite of the warning not to look out the window—trotted to the kitchen and peered outside, waving to get her father's attention. "I think it's letting up, Dad."

Dirk nodded his thanks and relayed the information to the doctor.

Anderson scooped her away from the window. "What's wrong with you, woman? Do you want to get shot?"

Ned kept vigil at the back window in the small bathroom, in case Murphy tried to get in through the back of the house.

Portia sat in shock beside her mother, wondering how in the world so much could have happened in such a short time.

I hope Murphy's getting drenched.

Even better, I hope he gets struck by lightning.

Something felt wrong, but she couldn't put her finger on it.

Something even more wrong than her mother lying comatose on the couch, than Murphy lurking in the woods, than the power being out.

Something was off.

It hit her in a flash. *The dogs! Where are they?*

"Where are Boomer and Cupcake?" she said, straightening and running to the stairs. "Boone?"

Boone appeared at the top of the stairs, his face stamped with worry. "What's wrong?"

"Are my dogs up there with you?"

"I don't think so. Let me check the bedrooms." In less than a minute, he was back, trotting down the stairs. "They must still be outside. Let me check."

Portia almost beat him to the kitchen door, but he caught her before she could turn the handle.

"No." He turned her toward him. "He's still out there. He's waiting to get another shot at you."

"But my dogs," she said, tears springing to her eyes.

"I know." He gentled his voice, steering her to a kitchen chair. "Sit while I check." He locked eyes with her. "Please, Peaches?"

"Okay." She nodded and sat still, but didn't want to be manhandled like that. It reminded her too much of Murphy. But a tiny part of her knew he had her best interest at heart. It wasn't controlling, it was protecting. There was a vast difference, and she had to start realizing that if she was going to live her life without bristling every time someone touched her or tried to help her.

Boone sidled up to the kitchen door, and moved the curtain back a half inch. "Rain's letting up. But I don't see the dogs on the porch."

"I know they came out with us, Boone. Just before he fired at us."

"Right. I know. But I don't remember them coming back in, do you?"

"Since we were getting shot at, I'm embarrassed to say all I could think of was getting inside when you scooped me up and carried me. I left my poor babies out there." She felt tears welling again, but this time, she was able to stop them. Wiping them away fiercely, she stood. "Open the door a crack and let me call them."

201

Boone nodded. "Okay. Maybe they took cover in the barn."

"No. They'd be scratching at the door. Woofing to come in. That's their way. You know they never leave my side. Not if they can help it."

Boone motioned her over to the side of the door. He turned the knob and opened it an inch, keeping her back from it with his muscled forearm.

She leaned toward the opening, and whistled. "Come on, guys. Boomer! Cupcake! Come to mama."

Grace glanced up from the chair across from her mother, where Anderson had plunked her after she looked out the window. "The dogs are missing?" She sprang up and joined them at the door, leaning forward to do her own calling. "Boomer! Come on boy! Cupcake. Come get a treat."

After five minutes of calling, Boone closed the door.

Portia walked toward the coat rack for a slicker. "I'm going out to look for them. I don't care what you say, or how dangerous it is. I'm going out."

She could tell Boone was about to launch into an argument with her, but his cell phone beeped.

He picked up the call. "Sheriff Dunne? Yes. Good. Okay." He peered out the window again. "I see you. Stay on this side of the barn if you can. Right. I'll cover you."

With one wide sweep of his arm, Boone moved both women back into the center of the kitchen. "Stay. Put." He lowered his brow. "I mean it. I've gotta cover the sheriff and his men while they're out in the open, coming to the porch. Just stay there. Please." This time his words were fierce, definitely not gentle anymore.

Portia sighed, dropped the slicker on the rack, and gave in. "Okay. But we're looking for the dogs as soon as we can."

"Of course," he said, sliding the door open again and sticking his rifle through the crack. "We'll find them. Now stay back, out of the way."

Chapter 48

In five minutes, the house was full of dripping policemen. Portia busied herself making pot after pot of coffee, liking the feeling of having something to do, anything to do. She needed to keep busy to keep from thinking about her mother, Murphy, and her dogs. But of course, all she could do was think about them.

Dunne held the phone to his ear, manning the center of activity from the kitchen. "Okay. Good. We'll expect you in ten minutes." He turned to Portia, Boone, and her father, who stood near him. "Mercy Flight is coming, they'll be here soon."

She saw him glance toward the hills, where ten of his men swarmed over the muddy ground. The sun shown on the wet trees, and they'd opened the curtains to keep a better eye on their surroundings.

Since Murphy shot at them earlier, he hadn't tried again.

Portia handed another cup to Dunne and glanced outside. "They haven't found him yet?"

"Not yet. But don't worry. He shouldn't be hard to track in this mud. We found evidence of his stand up there in the spruces. He was there, all right."

Boone pointed to the side of the house. "And that bullet in the siding should be enough evidence that he's after Portia, Sheriff."

Dunne's eyes turned to her, narrowing. "Have you told me everything, now, young lady?"

She lowered her eyes, backing up. "Um, yeah. Pretty much."

"You know, if we'd had the whole truth when you first came home, we might've caught him at his cabin where you knocked him out. He might be in jail as we speak, instead of wreaking havoc on your family."

"I'm sorry, Sheriff." She sank onto a kitchen chair. "I thought I'd killed him. I was afraid you'd arrest me."

Dunne snorted a laugh. "For self-defense? No charges would've stuck."

She stiffened. "But you hear about it all the time on television. You know, where innocent women are put in prison for killing their abusers."

"Well, maybe. But in real life, when a woman's been kidnapped like you, and kept in bondage for years...there wouldn't be much doubt about your doing it to protect yourself. Least that's how I see it." He waved his hands as if getting rid of a pesky fly. "But that's in the past. Right now we've gotta keep you safe."

Her father stepped toward her and put his hands on her shoulders. "I want you to come to New York with me."

A shock wave ran through her. "What?"

"You'll be safer there," Boone said. "It's you Murphy wants. And it'd be easier to protect you in a big hotel with secure entry."

Portia stood and faced her father. "Dad. Listen. Much as I want to be there for Mom, I can't leave. I can't run anymore. I need to be here, I need to find my dogs, I need to be sure the horses are okay."

Her father didn't look surprised. He knew her too well. "I thought I'd try."

"I know." She leaned in to hug him. "But the Sheriff here will take care of us. And I've got three strong men to help protect me."

Sheriff Dunne turned to them. "We'll catch the sicko. You can bet on that."

"But, Portia." Boone's shoulders sank a half-inch. "You're not safe here. Look how close he came to killing you today."

"I know. I do. But I can't run anymore, Boone. I just can't."

His lips tightened. "Okay. Well, if that's the way it is, I'll be here for you. I won't leave your side until we catch the bastard."

"Me, neither," Ned added from the living room.

Portia smiled at Boone, feeling a sense of warmth invade her for his support. "Thank you, Boone." She called to Ned, too. "Thank you."

"You watch my girls for me, men. You take good care of them. Don't let that filthy bastard near them." Her father nodded to Boone, Ned, and Anderson, and the rest of the officers in the room. The sound of the helicopter came over the hills, and he hurried to Daisy's side. "They're here, baby. We're bringing you back to Dr. Kareem."

Chapter 49

She woke at three thirty in the morning to the sound of dogs barking. With a start, she sat bolt upright in bed.

Cupcake. Boomer.

Did I dream it?

Grace snored softly beside her, mouth open and one arm thrown over her head. She'd insisted on sleeping with Portia, and had left poor Anderson alone in the guest room.

Racing to the window, she drew back the curtains and peered into the dark, throwing open the window to feel the cool night air on her face. The barking came again, and it sounded like it was coming from the barn.

She slid into her sneakers and was down the steps in a flash, pulling on her bathrobe over her pajamas.

Heavy footsteps came behind her, and she turned to see Boone in his cutoffs. She'd forgotten he was sleeping in her parents' bedroom.

"Did you hear that?" she said. "It's the dogs."

He touched her arm when they got to the bottom of the steps. "Wait. It could be a trap."

She whirled on him, sick of him trying to order her around. "There's a policeman outside, sitting in his car. We'll get him to go with us if you're afraid."

His eyes widened. "Afraid?" He snorted, then faced her, almost nose-to-nose. "I'm trying to save your damned life, Portia. Get with the program."

She stood taller, ready to argue with him, then noticed the empty spot on the couch where Ned had been sleeping. "Where's your brother?"

He swung his gaze to the couch. "Ned?" Four long paces took him to the back of the room, where he glanced into the bathroom. "Buddy?"

Portia checked the kitchen. "He's not in here. Maybe he already went out to check on the barking."

Boone grabbed his rifle and picked up his phone, dialing Ned's number. He waited, watching outside. "No answer. Let's get the cop's attention. He told me to flick the lights if we wanted him."

Portia ran to the porch light fixture and turned them on and off three times.

Nothing.

"Maybe he fell asleep?" she said, worry creeping into her voice.

"Maybe."

Anderson came down the stairs, rubbing his eyes. "What's going on?" He wore his pajama bottoms and slippers.

"Dogs sound like they're out in the barn, barking up a storm," Boone said. "I can't rouse the cop. And Ned's missing."

Anderson came to full alert. "Oh, shit. Did you call Dunne?"

"Not yet. I just want to be sure it's not a false alarm. Ned could be right outside. Let's head outside together, lights off. We won't make a target that way."

Anderson grabbed his rifle and shrugged into a shirt hanging on the coat rack. "Okay. Portia, you stay inside."

Portia followed them to the door. "No way in hell. I'm coming with you."

Both men heaved sighs.

"I want to see my dogs. I need to know they're okay."

Boone didn't argue this time. "Stand between us, and put on this sweatshirt, and pull the hood up." He grabbed Ned's navy blue sweatshirt from the back of a kitchen chair. "Tuck your hair inside. Don't say a word. Maybe he'll think you're one of us guys."

"If he's still out there," Anderson said. "The cops think he's taken off." He flicked off the kitchen and porch lights and they slipped out onto the porch.

Silence.

Boone motioned to Anderson. "Check the officer in the car. We'll look in the barn."

Anderson disappeared into the darkness.

With his arm through Portia's, Boone led her to the barn. He didn't enter through the main door, but around the side, through a smaller access door. Barely audible, he whispered, "He'd expect us to come through the big door. If he's in there, that is."

Portia shivered, finally realizing how foolish she'd been. Boone was right. It could be a trap. And she might've made him walk right into it.

They reached the door and slid inside.

Horses nickered and stuck their heads out the stall doors. Mirage kicked his stall door and snorted.

Inch by inch, they worked their way down the aisle, patting horses heads and checking inside each stall.

"The tack room," she whispered. "I hear scratching at the door."

When they reached the door, he motioned her back. "Stay flat against this wall. Don't move."

He pulled the door open and aimed his rifle inside, swinging it right to left. "Oh, shit."

Before she could react to his words, Boomer and Cupcake leapt outside, whining and heading straight for Portia. She sank to the ground and welcomed them into her arms, letting them lick her and cuddle their wiggling bodies against her. "Oh, my poor babies. My poor little doggies. Are you okay?" They covered her in dog-kisses, telling her their story.

"Portia. Come here."

She leapt to her feet and hurried to Boone's side, where she found him inside the tack room, leaning over Ned's prone body.

"Call 911." He thrust his phone into her hands and rolled his brother over.

"Oh my God. Is he okay?"

"He's out cold. But he's breathing. And where the hell is Anderson?"

A chill ran down Portia's spine. "Oh, no."

Boone still whispered. "Make the call."

She punched in the numbers and summoned the cavalry.

Chapter 50

When Portia hung up, Boone took her by the shoulders and locked eyes with her. "I'm shutting you in here with Ned and the dogs. No arguments this time." He picked up his brother's rifle, which lay on the floor beside him. "Take this. And wait for me."

Portia nodded. "Okay."

Boone worried that she was just placating him, and that she'd burst out of the barn at just the wrong time to be shot by Murphy. "I'm serious, Portia. Murphy's out here. He's already put one of us out of commission."

"I understand. I'll wait until the sheriff gets here."

"Promise?"

"Promise," she whispered, glancing down at Ned. "Will he be okay?"

"I sure as hell hope so."

Boone shut the door behind him, leaving Portia hunkered against the wall with both dogs on her lap and the rifle propped beside her. He slid out the side door again and flattened himself against the outer wall.

Wait. Count to ten, then slide around the corner.

It was still pitch black outside, and he hoped he blended into the night. Breathing steadily, he held his rifle firmly at his side.

Slipping around the barn corner, he stopped and listened. Was that a moan? Someone nearby? He hurried closer to the patrol car, and noticed the back door hung wide open, and the dome light shone dully on a body on the ground.

Boone's heart sprang to life, banging hard beneath his ribs. He ran to the car, noticing at once that the cop was also lying sideways on the front seat. Anderson groaned, then tried to say something.

Boone leaned over him. "What is it, buddy? Are you okay?"

"Trap," Anderson spluttered. "Behind you."

Boone whirled in time to see the heavy club swinging toward his face.

The world turned black.

❧

Portia waited a full fifteen minutes.

Still no police.

Still no Boone.

What the hell was happening out there?

She picked up the rifle and cracked open the door to the tack room. "Boone?"

The dogs followed her, inches from her legs, as if they'd been separated for years instead of hours. She was grateful for their company, and patted them with her free hand. "It's okay, pups. We're just gonna see what's going on."

Carefully, she inched out the doorway, listening hard. "Boone?" She hissed the words. "Where are you?"

She heard a door slam in the house, and a vehicle start up. The patrol car?

Hurrying, she peeked out the barn door to see the patrol car skid past her, turn in a circle, and speed down the dirt road, away from the house.

Had the cop seen someone? Was he giving chase?

Her heart jumped when she made out three figures on the ground.

Three bodies.

Fear clenched her, sending shivers down her spine. She raced out to the driveway, realizing in seconds that the police officer, Anderson, and Boone lay unconscious on the cold gravel.

How had he done it? How could he disable four men in such a short time?

The dogs sniffed and licked the men, tails wagging, but whines emitted from both of them as if they knew something was terribly wrong.

"Are they alive?" she croaked, feeling for Boone's pulse first.

There it was, strong and steady.

Anderson was next. His heartbeat throbbed beneath her fingers, but as her eyes adjusted to the darkness, she noticed a big bloody gash on his head.

The cop lay unresponsive, too, she saw his chest rise and fall. Then she caught the whiff of chloroform.

Oh, God. He'd used it again, just like he did with her.

"They're alive," she said, grabbing Boone's phone that she still had in her robe pocket. "I'm calling for help." She picked up her rifle and glanced wildly at the road.

This time she punched in Dunne's cell that Boone had programmed onto his favorites. He answered on the first ring.

"Boone? We're almost there. What's happening?"

Portia spilled her words fast. "This is Portia, Sheriff Dunne. Murphy came back. He knocked out your officer, Ned, Anderson, and Boone." She waited for a second, then her voice became shrill. "I'm not kidding."

Dunne barked his questions to her. "Where are you? Are you safe?"

"I'm outside, I..."

"Get into the house. Now."

"Okay. I..."

"Where's Murphy? Can you see anything? Hear anything?"

"No. I think he just stole your police car."

"Wait a minute." There were sounds of shouts and radios blasting in the background. Confusion. Yelling. The squeal of tires and a crash. After what seemed like eons, she heard him talking into his radio. "Christ almighty. The bastard just knocked us off the road." She heard fumbling, as if he were reaching for the phone. "Portia? You still there?"

"Yes. Are you okay?"

"Hold on. I've gotta call for reinforcements. Maybe they can head him off at the highway. And I think I need a tow truck to get us out of this ditch. Go inside and wait. Lock your doors. Okay?"

"Okay."

She hung up and dropped to her knees beside Boone, tearing off the duct tape that bound his hands and feet. He stirred, and she laid his head on her lap, feeling as if her heart would break. "Shh. It's okay."

Anderson lay still, but she heard him breathing. Murphy hadn't bothered to restrain him or the cop. He'd probably chloroformed them both. And poor Ned still lay alone in the barn.

With a start, she looked back at the house. "I need help. We need Grace. Come on." She settled Boone back on the ground and jumped up. "Boomer, Cupcake. Let's go get her."

She ran to the house and burst into the kitchen, calling her sister's name. *How the hell had she slept through all this?*

"Grace, we've got trouble. Anderson's hurt. Come on. I need you."

She pounded up the steps, getting angrier with every step. "Grace! For crying out loud, wake up."

She's such a damned heavy sleeper. Always was.

"Grace!"

214

Finally in the hallway, she skidded around the corner and entered the bedroom, fuming. "I need you, for crying out loud. Get up."

She stopped. Inhaled a deep breath. Her hand flew to her mouth.

The bed was empty.

"Maybe she's in the bathroom?" Portia said to the dogs, who sniffed and growled at the bedclothes.

"Grace? Baby Cakes? You in there?"

She knew. She knew before she looked into the empty bathroom that she wouldn't find her little sister.

No, Grace wasn't in the bathroom.

No, she wasn't anywhere in the house.

Murphy had stolen her.

Chapter 51

When Dunne answered the phone this time, he sounded pissed off. "Dunne here."

Portia hesitated for a split second, then croaked out the words. "He's got her, Dunne. He's got Grace."

"What? Portia, is this you? You mean Murphy took her?"

"Yes. Please. He took her in the police car. I'm sure of it."

"Okay, hold on a sec. Let me report this. Just hang on the line."

She heard him barking instructions into the radio for three long minutes. Finally, he came back on the line. "Portia?"

"Yes. Listen, Sheriff, we need ambulances. I think Murphy drugged your officer and Anderson. I smelled the chloroform. And he must've hit them over their heads first. Anderson's got a bad injury on his head."

"Already called the whole fleet out to your place. They're on their way. And I see my tow truck coming."

She heard sirens in the background.

"And there are my reinforcements. I'm commandeering one of these cars and I'll be there in just a few minutes, okay?"

Portia kept the phone to her ear, but ran outside to check on the men again. "Okay. See you in a few."

She tried calling her father, but got no answer.

Ned still lay in the tack room. She knelt beside him. His breathing seemed regular. She tried to rouse him. "Ned? Are you okay?"

He moaned and slowly turned his head. "I feel like I've been kicked in the head by a horse." He pushed himself up slowly and leaned against the door. "What happened?"

Portia ran to the sink and wet a wad of paper towels with cold water. "Murphy happened. Here. Take this and press it against that bump on your forehead."

"Just give me a second." He took a minute to orient himself, then stood up shakily. "Where are the others?"

She motioned outside. "He got them, too. They're all out cold."

"What?"

Ned came to life now, grappling on the floor for his weapon. "Where's my gun?"

With a guilty start, Portia realized she'd left it in the house. "I've got it. I'm sorry, we can grab it in a sec. But Murphy's gone, Ned."

Still holding the makeshift compress to his head, he turned his eyes to hers. "How do you know?"

"He stole the police car."

"How'd he..."

"I don't know. But there's more."

"More?"

"Yes. He took my sister, too."

Ned's color drained to pale white. "Oh, God. He took Grace?"

"The Sheriff's got men chasing him. But I haven't heard yet..."

She helped Ned up and he hobbled outside with her, gaining strength as he moved. "Boone and the others are over here," she said.

The dogs followed close on her heels, and when they neared the downed men again, they once again began to try to lick them alive.

Ned fell to his brother's side, and she checked on the others. The policeman was quiet, lying on his back. This time, she noticed he was snoring.

217

Alive, and hopefully well.

Anderson's head wound scared her. "I'm going in to wet a towel for his head," she said. "It looks pretty bad."

"Okay." Ned finished checking Boone's pulse. "And grab a few blankets. It's kind of cold on the ground here."

"Will do."

When Portia reappeared on the porch, she saw the Sheriff and several other officers jump out of two vehicles and trot toward the men on the ground.

"Portia." Dunne called. "Ambulance is just thirty seconds out."

She nodded and fell to Anderson's side, dabbing at his wound gently with a warm, wet towel. "Thanks, Sheriff."

He crouched beside her, feeling for Anderson's pulse. "They lost him."

Portia's heart slammed beneath her ribs. She turned to Dunne, whose serious eyes drilled into hers. "He got away?"

"I'm sorry. They found the squad car abandoned out on the access road leading to your woods. It's got an electronic retrieval signaler, or else we wouldn't have found it so fast. Tracks there showed another vehicle had been parked before the rainstorm started, then left just recently."

"So he's in a car we can't track?" she said solemnly.

"Right. We're getting the tire tracks analyzed. We might know at least the class and size of vehicle. It looked like a truck or SUV to me."

"You know where he's headed, don't you?" she said, holding in the tears.

"Where?" Dunne said.

"Devil's Lake."

Chapter 52

An hour and a half later, the sun finally rose over the eastern hills, infusing the clouds with bright taffy pink and warming the air. With Boone and Ned awake and drinking coffee on her couch, Portia ferried cups to Sheriff Dunne and his men. After the ambulance took Anderson and the police officer to the hospital, they'd been piecing together the "Murphy" situation and reconstructing his clever attack.

Four men down in the middle of the night. One attacker, who apparently never drew his gun. One bludgeon, and that damned bottle of chloroform was all it took.

How could that be, she thought.

The bastard owns one stealthy set of skills.

How did he sneak up on each man, one by one, disable him, and then move up to the next one with such calm purpose?

He'd surprised them. And somehow, he'd weathered the thunderstorms without getting caught or injured.

Portia settled on the couch between Boone and Ned. Ned was in deep conversation with the Sheriff, so she turned to Boone. "How's the head?"

He moved the ice pack to be able to see her better. "Getting numb." A half smile slid onto his lips. "Are you okay?"

"No."

"Grace is one tough girl," he said, reading her mind.

"I know. She'll probably give him a helluva fight."

He smiled again. "Yeah."

"Do you think he's headed out west? Toward Devil's Lake?"

"Maybe. But he probably won't return to the cabin for a while. Not until things cool down."

She got up and paced, suddenly realizing how close she'd been sitting to Boone. And hell, she hadn't even cared. In fact, it had felt pretty darned good.

Maybe with all that had happened, her stupid fears and panicked ways would finally go away for real?

She paced around the room, looking outside.

Portia didn't know where she should be, she felt pulled in a dozen different directions.

She should be with Grace, first and foremost.

But no one knew where Murphy had taken her.

Dunne had alerted the local Baraboo authorities, and they'd already staked out the cabin. Maybe he'd return to it, but after thinking about it, she figured he'd avoid the place.

She should also be with Anderson, who'd been whisked away to the hospital, with what the EMTs thought was a concussion. He'd need stitches in his scalp wound. For Grace's sake, she should be at his side.

She wanted to be with her mother, too, in spite of the fact that she'd stayed behind to face Murphy. She still hadn't roused her father on the cell phone. But it was early, and she'd try again.

No. Here she was. Useless and fretting over something out of her control.

What good had it done to stay home?

All she'd done is to get her sister kidnapped.

Why had he taken Grace, and not her?

Did he think Grace was me?

It was dark in the house when he'd come inside. Maybe he'd confused them?

Her mind kept returning to Devil's Lake. Murphy loved that place. His fishing Nirvana. He'd be lured back there, Portia was sure of it.

And she knew he'd had a place not far away where he kept other girls.

Another cabin he'd commandeered? A house? Some deserted building?

"Sheriff?" She approached Dunne, who'd just thumbed off his cell phone, looking frustrated.

"Hey, Portia. You holding up okay?"

"I'm fine," she lied. "But I want to talk to you more about Murphy."

"Shoot," he said. "Let's go sit at the kitchen table. It's quieter there."

Boone followed them. "I'm part of this, too. Don't leave me out, just because I look like Frankenstein." When he lowered the ice pack, the ugly wound bulged from his forehead.

Portia pulled out a chair for him. "You do look pretty scary. But we'll let you listen in.'"

Boone shot a surprised glance at her. "You're making a joke."

"So?" she said. "What if I am?" She tossed him a smile and grabbed a set of maps from the cabinet, settling at the table.

"That's a good sign. You're one strong woman, Portia Lamont."

"Damned right I am," she said. "I'm from good Vermont stock, you know."

Dunne smiled, but he wanted to get right to business, which was fine with Portia. She had an idea.

She spread out the map of Devil's Lake and its surrounding areas. "I think he'd go back here, guys."

Dunne leaned forward to study the map.

Boone nodded. "It's so remote. There'd be a million places he could crash. Lots of camping spots and cabins."

Portia nodded. "He knows these woods like the back of his hand. And I'm positive he had another site where he kept at least one other woman."

Dunne looked at her with interest. "What makes you think that?"

She took a deep breath. "When he got tired of me, he'd disappear for a while. He'd come back with fresh clothes, pants and shirts I'd never seem him wear before. He'd be kind of...sated. That's the only way I can describe it. And he told me..." she hesitated for a minute. "He told me a man needs variety. That he gets tired of the same old thing."

"Whoa." Dunne questioned her about the timeline again, trying to hone in on specifics. When they were done, Boone pointed to the map he'd been studying.

"What's this place?"

All three leaned forward to study the markings more closely. Portia sat up straight. "Wait. It just came back to me. On the trip up there, even though I was groggy, I remember seeing signs for an old munitions plant somewhere up in the woods. It's not far from the cabin."

Dunne punched it in on his cell phone. "Baraboo, right?"

She nodded. "Yes."

"Okay. It's an abandoned site. Partially demolished."

Boone and Portia exchanged glances, and he stood, locking eyes with Dunne. "I think we should check it out."

Dunne raised one hand. "Wait a minute. 'We?'"

"Hell, yeah. I know how to get there. Ned could come up with us. You ready for a road trip, Sheriff?"

Dunne shook his head. "This isn't television, Boone. You can't just grab your guns and go in shooting. You're a civilian. This is police business."

Portia exploded. "Who cares whose business it is? My sister's been taken! And Murphy might be on his way right now up to Devil's Lake. You need to do something, or we will."

Dunne spread his hands wide. "Whoa, little lady. Hold your horses."

"Hold my horses?" she said. "Is that all you can say, Sheriff?"

He ducked his head. "Sorry. It's just I don't want you two going off half-cocked and getting yourselves killed. Or getting your sister killed, for that matter."

Portia calmed down, taking a deep breath. "I understand. But the longer we wait to do something, the longer he's got her."

Dunne's phone rang. He answered it, grunted, and hung up. "We've got a lead."

PART IV
Payback

Chapter 53

Murphy dumped the sister onto his bed in the old Army munitions plant where he used to work. He knew the place inside and out, and although many buildings had already been demolished, he knew about them, too, because he'd been part of the crew that worked on it. There wasn't a building or trail in this massive complex that he didn't know by heart. And this particular old building, tucked way off in the corner of the seventy-five hundred acre campus, had been a refuge for him for many years.

He'd taken other girls here, and it worked great. Nobody from the public was allowed on the grounds, not yet anyway. Somebody wanted to turn it into an RV park. Another group lobbied for a bird watching haven. But so far, no decisions had been made except to allow turkey hunters in during April and May. Since that was over, there was little activity in the area except off on one far corner where they'd begun cleaning up the trails. It was well away from him and his little nest. And he'd stayed hidden just fine.

His generator made a little noise when he needed to use it for power, but it wasn't too bad and he had camouflaged it after rigging it up to the old electric and water systems. In fact, it could be quite cozy in his little corner of the building.

He had a mini-refrigerator, a Coleman stove, a space heater for winter, and lots of blankets. Plus he'd even figured out a way to get his old television to work with a converter box and rabbit ears.

He could figure out anything, anywhere. His mother always said that about him.

He was smart.

Smarter than all those girls.

And sure as hell smarter than the cops.

He'd almost laughed at how easy it had been to trick the cop in the patrol car. He'd been nodding off for a while, anyway. Murphy brought the dogs down from the woods and stuck them in the tack room with a cat, letting them bark a little. The cop had started to come out of his car to investigate, and when he opened the car door, Murphy had sprung at him and knocked him out in seconds. A little chloroform kept him quiet.

When the kid came out of the house to investigate, he'd done the same with him, hiding with the dogs in the tack room.

Those dogs were nice. They liked him and had kept him company up in the woods. He'd miss them. Maybe he'd go back and take them again. They were friendly and didn't talk back to him like the voices in his head.

They didn't yell at him, like his mom had.

No, they were great little pals.

He thought back to his success this morning, the way he'd taken down that tall blond man.

All he'd done was hide in the back seat of the cop car. That big guy had leaned over to check on the cop, and whammo! He'd gotten him good, right upside the head.

He smiled at the memory.

The fourth guy, the tall cowboy type who had seemed to be trying to protect Portia the other day when he played with them by shooting from the hill, had been a little tougher. He'd turned and fought for a few minutes. He'd even landed a pretty good punch.

He rubbed his chin. Still sore.

But I bludgeoned him good and he fell like a little girl.

When he'd taken care of all the big, bad men who supposedly guarded Portia, he'd gone inside to get her. To take back what was rightfully his.

But who had he found instead?

226

A gorgeous little pouty-lipped sexy number. The sister, he thought. Portia's baby sister, the one he'd seen on the news, pleading with him to return Portia to her family.

He pulled up a chair and watched her sleep, stroking her fine gold hair.

She was plumper than Portia, who'd lost too much weight and had started looking a little too skinny, anyway. But plump in a good way, with soft, rounded hips, nice full breasts, and a face you'd see on television commercials. Pretty lips.

Oh, she was really fine. She might even be *the one.*

He ran his fingers along her shoulder, down to her hips and thighs, then back to her breasts. They felt soft beneath her pajama top.

He'd have to get her some clothes. The nurse's uniform in the wardrobe would probably fit her, but she'd need some clothes for when he didn't want her that way.

With a start, he sat up, as if struck by an epiphany.

This one might even be pure enough to become his wife. Not a whore, like all the others. All those dirty, nasty girls his mother would never approve of.

No. This one might be just perfect.

He smiled and reached for the tie-wrap to secure her wrists.

No sense letting her get away.

Chapter 54

Grace woke with a start. Confused, she tried to turn from her back to her left side, but her wrist was caught by something and she couldn't get it loose.

What the hell?

A dank smell wafted up from the strange bed she lay on, and when she opened her eyes, it all came flooding back to her.

That bastard, Murphy, had dragged her right out of Portia's bed and had clamped a foul-smelling rag over her face. Before she could utter one feeble shout, he'd slung her over his back and carried her away.

She'd woken once or twice in the car. It had been dark, and when he noticed her moving, he'd slapped that damn cloth over her face again. Too weak to fight him, she'd fallen back into a drugged stupor.

Where am I? Is this the cabin where he kept Portia?

And where is he?

Wait. *Portia.*

Did he kill her?

He wanted revenge, right? Because she'd escaped him, and kicked him in the balls?

A soft moan escaped her as she curled onto her side where her right wrist was secured to the frame of the bed with a plastic tie-wrap. She could see the room in murky darkness. And there, off to the other side, was another twin bed with a figure sleeping on it, facing away from her.

It's him. Murphy.

A shudder ran through her.

I've been taken by the same bastard who took Portia. It's real.

Something inside her almost snapped, but she shook it off and found her center.

Breathe.

Just breathe.

She forced herself to think.

How can I outsmart this bastard? What does he want? A sex partner?

She almost cackled out loud.

I'll give him what he wants. And then, when he's sleeping, I'll cripple him.

She waited another fifteen minutes, but the pressure on her bladder was too hard to ignore.

"Hey!" she yelled. "You."

Murphy rolled toward her and groaned. "Five more minutes."

"I'm not your freaking mother, moron. I have to pee. Get up."

Murphy opened one eye. "What did you say?"

"I have to pee. Unless you want this place to stink, you'd better get me to a bathroom."

She smiled inwardly. So much for giving him what he wants. She never could control her mouth.

He sat up and rubbed his eyes.

She studied him.

Yep. It was Murphy all right. Just like Portia had described him. Stringy gray hair, pitted skin. He was tall, too. Big and brawny.

A shiver of worry ran through her. "Wait a minute. Did you hurt my sister? My husband?"

Murphy heaved himself to his feet. "Portia's fine. I didn't even see her. Which one was your husband?"

She paled. Maybe he'd killed him after all. And that mechanical voice…God, that was creepy. What the hell was that all about? "The tall blond."

"Oh, him." Murphy grinned. "I just knocked him out. He'll be fine." He slid a knife out of his boot. "Hold still."

Her heart did a flip. *My God! He's going to cut me already? I just got here. Did I piss him off that badly?*

"Wait!" She struggled and shrank toward the wall. "I'm sorry. Don't. *Please.*"

He leaned down to her wrist. "Shut up and hold still. I'm just cutting off the tie." He slid the knife between her skin and the plastic tie and freed her. "There. Now, don't try anything."

She breathed a sigh of relief and stood up on shaky legs. *Get a grip. For God's sake. Don't show your fear.*

"Come on." He grabbed her shoulders and started to propel her toward a door. "Bathroom's in here. You gotta dump the bucket to flush the john."

She wobbled, reaching for the bedpost to steady herself. "Wait a sec. I'm dizzy."

He grabbed her elbow. "It'll pass."

She grimaced. "So, you've drugged a lot of girls?"

He didn't smile this time. "Yes."

She turned her face up to him. "Why?"

He forced her toward the door. "Don't ask so many questions. You're starting to annoy me."

She stumbled toward the door, wondering why all her joints ached. "I can't help it. Curious minds want to know."

He stopped, turned her toward him, and leaned down into her face. "Listen, missy."

"My name's Grace."

"Okay, listen, Grace. I was thinking maybe you were gonna be the one. But now you're starting to make me wonder. You might be just as skanky as all the rest."

"Skanky?" She snorted a laugh. "Do you even know what that word means?"

He frowned. "You might be a whore. Just like all of them."

She shoved his chest before she knew what her hands were doing. "Wait just one minute!" She walked toward him, and he actually stepped back. "You think I'm a whore? You think my sweet sister Portia was a whore?" Her face darkened in anger. "You're full of shit, you big, stinking, ugly bastard."

He stood as if dazed.

"My sister is the kindest, purest girl you'd ever know. She hardly had any boyfriends her whole life, you idiot." She roared the next words. "And I might've done some things with guys I'm not proud of...but I'm no whore."

Before he could react, she stomped to the bathroom and slammed the door.

Chapter 55

While Grace used the facilities, she analyzed everything in the room and took inventory.

Toilet. Toilet lid. (heavy, could be used to knock him out)

Sink. Soap.

Mirror. (crack it, use it as a knife)

No window.

Shower stall. Shower rod. (could I dismantle it and use it as a weapon?)

Plenty of possibilities. I just have to figure out when to go for it.

At night? When he's groggy? Maybe I can fake him out. Pretend to be really sick.

She finished up, poured part of the bucket into the toilet, and watched it flush. There was a trickle of water coming out the sink and she used it to wet and finger comb her hair, then rubbed wet fingers on her teeth to try to clean them. She figured he had jury-rigged the plumbing from the original building somehow to make this little half-functioning bathroom work.

With a confidant flourish, she shoved open the door and walked up to him. "I'm going to need some things, Murphy."

He glowered at her. "You're pretty pushy, lady."

She walked to a chair and sat. "Yes. I am. But you're stuck with me now, so you'd better get used to it."

He just stared.

"I need a toothbrush, toothpaste, fresh towels, shampoo and conditioner. I'll need some feminine products as well." She gave him a hard stare. "Do you know what I mean by that?"

He gulped and nodded. "Kotex?"

She crossed her legs. "That'll do."

As if he finally came to his senses, he rushed toward her and jerked her to her feet. "Listen. I'm the boss here. I make the rules. You can't demand stuff from me." He dragged her to the bed and shoved her onto the mattress.

"You don't need to tie me up," she said casually. "I kind of like this little hideaway. It's mysterious."

"What?" He studied her eyes. "Sure you do. I know you're lying." He grabbed a new tie-wrap from a pile on the table and secured her wrist again.

"Don't make it too tight," she said. "It'll cut off my circulation."

He stopped before cinching it, and left a little room for her blood to move. "This'll hold you."

"Why don't you just use rope?" she asked, conversationally.

He stood back and rubbed his eyes in frustration. "Because your damned sister got out of ropes. I've improved my methods."

As if she didn't hear him, she pointed to the mini-fridge. "What's for breakfast? I'm starving."

He sighed. "You don't stop talking, do you?"

She smirked. "No. Why? Does it bother you?"

He shook his head. "Just not used to it. Your sister didn't say much at all."

"My sister and I are worlds apart. We're like opposite sides of the same coin. She's quiet. I'm loud. She's private. I'm a social butterfly. She's focused. I'm scattered all over the place."

"You're prettier."

That stopped her. She hesitated, then kept talking. "No. I'm not. You just messed her up by starving her. You gonna do that to me, too, Murphy?" She narrowed her eyes at him, showing no fear. What he didn't know—she hoped—was that fear boiled in her gut right now and it was all she could do to keep up her sassy attitude. "Or are we gonna work on this relationship so we can have a future together?"

Murphy slumped into a chair, looking dazed.

Good, she was confusing him.

"What?" he said.

"I thought you said I could be *the one*. Didn't you?"

"Um. Yeah." He started to sweat.

"Well, if I'm going to like you, we have to dream together. Plan for things. Do you want children?" She shifted and smiled, as if pleased with the idea. "I do. And we need good food, not that junk you brought to my sister. All that fried food is no good for you. What's your cholesterol, anyway?"

"What? Cholesterol?"

"Yeah. When's the last time you had it checked? It's dangerous to eat food high in fat all the time. Don't you know that?"

He stood and threw his hands in the air. "Stop."

"Stop what? Asking you about your health?"

He scowled. "You're messing with my mind. I need time to think."

"Go for a drive, then, dear. And don't forget to come back with groceries. I'm starving. Bring back some eggs, bread, butter, cheese..."

He stomped to the door and turned. "Just shut the hell up, woman."

She smiled. She was getting to him.

He slammed the door and locked it. In five minutes, she heard a car peeling out.

She let the sobs out then, but planned to stop them well before he returned.

Portia. Anderson. Come find me. Please.

Chapter 56

Murphy returned with three bags full of groceries. She watched quietly while he put away the perishables, and started cooking eggs and bacon. He looked different to Grace, somehow more humble? More at peace?

When he turned to finally face her, she flashed him a small smile.

He flushed, turning beet red.

"Smells good," she said. "But I can't help you tied up over here like a prisoner."

He slammed the spatula down on the table. "Damn you."

She opened her eyes wide, and almost fluttered her lashes at him. "That's not very nice."

He lowered his eyebrows and stared at her, marched right up to her, and towered over her menacingly. "You need to shut up now. I'm not letting you go."

Tucking her legs up beside her on the bed, she pouted. "I'm sure as hell not trying to escape, honey. But you're making it really hard for us to get to know each other." She patted a space beside her. "Why don't you sit for a minute?"

Looking at her with utter frustration, he tensed, then dropped to the bed beside her. "Why?"

"Because you haven't even told me your first name yet. How can I go around calling you Murphy? That's just not right."

He almost growled, and she noticed the conflicting emotions playing over his face. *Good. Maybe I'm messing him up some more.*

"It's Charles. But I'm not stupid, woman. I can't be tricked. I know you're trying to trick me."

"Charles? I like that. May I call you Charlie?"

He stiffened. "No. That's what my mother called me. Only her."

Grace pulled back a little. "Oh. Okay. But I really like Charlie."

He clamped her free wrist in his big hand. "I said NO."

With a Scarlett O'Hara eye roll and sigh, she pretended to give in. "All right, then. Charles it is."

He grunted. "Jesus. Let me finish breakfast."

She lay back on the bed, stretching her toes out and yawning. "Oh, good. I'm really hungry."

He returned to the stove and flipped the eggs.

"Did you get coffee, Charles?"

He shook his head. "No."

"Why not?"

"Don't have a coffee maker."

"Well, you'd best get us one. I need my coffee in the morning, Charles."

He shrugged. "They have instant at the market. You drink that?"

She sighed and pouted again. Waited for him to turn around for her answer. "Oh, honey. That's the worst. I can't drink that stuff. We need a good brew. Why don't you go to a Walmart or something and get us a coffee maker? They're only like twenty bucks for the cheap ones. And then stop by Dunkin Donuts and get me a pound of their original blend. I would die for a cup of that right about now."

He rolled his eyes. "You don't ask for much, do you?"

She laughed, letting the notes trill into the sky with a lovely tinkling sound. "Oh, Charles. You know you want to please me." This time she did flutter her eyelashes. "Don't you, babe?"

He scraped the food onto two paper plates and dragged a small card table and one chair over to the bed. Setting it up so
236

they were facing each other, he motioned for her to eat. "Go on."

She looked helplessly at her bound wrist. "I can't eat like this. Please just clip off this awful plastic thing. My God, it's barbaric, Charles."

With a huge sigh, he drew his knife from his boot and sliced at the plastic. "Fine. Just for a while. But no funny business."

She sat up and rubbed her red wrist. "Ah. Much better. Thank you, dear."

He began to shovel the food into his mouth.

"Wait," she said, with a disapproving frown. "Let's say a little prayer first, okay?"

"I don't believe in God."

"Well, I do. And I like to bless my meals. After all, my name is Grace. It's fitting, don't you think?"

Fuming, he put down his fork. "Fine. Just do it."

She made a show of preparing, folding her hands, bowing her head, waiting a few seconds to start. "Dear Lord. Thank you for this food today. You are so bountiful and generous with your children. And help Charles know that I'm here for him and want to get to know him so we can become closer. And Lord? Please encourage him to buy me that coffee maker."

He actually sputtered a laugh.

She raised her eyes and smiled. "There we go. Now we can eat, Charles."

He picked up his fork. "You'll get your damned coffee maker. Geez."

She grinned at him, and inside, felt the first flash of hope.

Maybe it was working. Maybe she'd get out of this hellhole. She ate everything on her plate and asked for seconds. She'd need her strength in the days to come.

237

Chapter 57

She'd figured out Murphy's routine by dinnertime.

Each time he left, he locked the steel door leading into their little apartment. The keys went into his right pants pocket. The high, narrow windows were sealed shut, probably for the past hundred years. She thought perhaps she could squeeze out of the bathroom window, but she'd have to break it and be careful to remove all shards of glass.

The longer she played with him, the more she wanted revenge for Portia.

Not so much for herself, no. She could handle this. She'd lived in worse places and been treated worse when she was on drugs. But she kept picturing her delicate sister, willow-like and pretty, cowering in front of this man's blustering, powerful rage. He had a lot of anger pent up inside, and she was pretty sure it had something to do with his mother.

What had happened to him?

His mother had called him Charlie, that much she knew. Now she wanted to know if the mother was a nurse. That cabinet was stocked full of nurse costumes that creeped her out. Had they shared an unnatural relationship? Had he slept with her or something gross like that?

Portia told her she'd had to wear those ridiculous get ups all the time while he'd taken care of his own sick needs beside her. But he'd never had sex with Portia the normal way.

Thank God.

She hoped she didn't have to do anything like that. But if she had to, she could. She'd done it with worse people just to get a fix. She shuddered at the memories, pushed them away.

She'd kept Murphy busy with her constant prattle and silly little demands so far. But what would happen tonight?

Grace stilled her shaking hands and pulled into herself. She was a good actress, but there were aspects of this whole show she was putting on that were harder than others. It was starting to wear on her, and she'd have to really use her smarts to get the best of him.

Will I have to kill him?

Could I do it?

There was something else that was starting to bother her, and it was hard for her to face.

I'm starting to feel a little sorry for him.

How was that possible? The creep preyed on women, probably murdered them when he was done with them.

She needed to find out more.

What if Portia was right? What if there were more women out there, stashed away in different barracks in this old facility? What if they were hungry right now? Tied to beds like her?

She needed to get him drunk. Make him talk to her.

Then she'd make her move.

"Charles?" she said, the minute he came in the door with the coffee maker under his arm.

He locked the door behind him and came toward her. "What? What more do you want? I got your damned machine."

"Oh, lovely. Thank you. But I was thinking..."

He rolled his eyes and made a guttural sound. "What?"

"Wouldn't it be nice to have a few bottles of wine with dinner at night?"

He stared at her. "Are you serious? I just came in the door."

She pouted. "Well. I was just thinking it could be romantic. You know?" She let her lower lip tremble a little and pretended to wipe away a tear.

Would this ploy work on him? Or would he get too much pleasure from the power it gave him?

"Hey," she said, when he turned his back. "You didn't buy that coffee maker. Where'd you get it?"

"Another building. There's an office they still use once in a while for the renovations crew. They won't miss it. They're not coming in for another week."

"Did you get supplies, too? Filter and coffee?"

He pulled them out of a cardboard box. "Right here."

"Good." She watched him set it up. "And the wine?"

"I'll go out later. Now just shut up and give me some peace for a few minutes."

She sat quietly for a few minutes, then started in on him again. "My wrist hurts, Charles."

He growled, turning on his heels toward her. "Jesus, Mary, and Joseph. You're enough to drive a man to drink."

"Good! I am craving a good Pinot, you know? What kind of wine do you like? And what are we having for dinner? If it's beef, you should get us a red. If it's chicken—"

"I said shut the hell up!" He kicked the chair across the room. "Don't you ever stop talking, woman?"

With a steely glance, she let her anger show this time. "My name is Grace. I don't like being called 'woman.' Now you can either be nice, or call me nothing at all. My. Name. Is. Grace."

How would he react? Would he hit her? Or would he submit?

He threw his hands in the air, hissing through his teeth, then walked into the bathroom and slammed the door.

She smiled.

She was getting somewhere. Now she could go in for the kill.

Tonight.

Tonight she'd make her move on him.

Chapter 58

Murphy spent a long time in the bathroom, but when he emerged, he secured her to the bed again and nodded, heading for the door. "Be back soon."

"Okay, Charles." She tried to make her voice sweet and seductive. "I'll be waiting for you."

She sorted through her plans carefully while he was gone, analyzing one after the other.

Which would work on him?

Could she try to seduce him? Or would that make her a "whore" in his mind?

How could she tempt him and still seem innocent?

She thought about it for a while, then decided on her plan.

When he returned forty minutes later, she flashed him a smile full of gratitude. "Oh, honey. You got the wine!"

He grunted again, which seemed to be his favorite response, and put the wine in the mini-fridge.

"Is it white or red?" she asked. "I really like both."

"White. We're having chicken."

"Oh, goodie. I love chicken." She paused, watching him for a minute. "Charles?"

He turned, glowering at her. "What is it now?"

"I need to take a shower. Or at least a birdbath. Can you set me up in the bathroom?"

Rolling his eyes, he muttered under his breath. "You're a lot of trouble."

"Grace," she said. "Call me by my name, okay?"

"Grace," he said, standing straighter and looking into her eyes. "You are a lot of trouble, Grace."

"I know," she said. "But I'm worth it, aren't I?"

He bent down to get his knife from his boot, then cut her loose. "Come on. There's soap and a towel in the bathroom."

"Thank you, Charles." She stood and pretended to lose her balance, falling against him with her breasts pressed to his chest. "Oh, gosh. I'm still a bit dizzy." She made sure she clung to him for a long minute, then backed off. "Sorry about that."

He flushed, then helped her to the bathroom. "I got those things you asked for."

"Really?"

He handed her a bag of toiletries. "Here."

"Oh, perfect!" She dug into the bag and let an expression of joy creep over her face. "Oh, Charles. These are wonderful." She reached up and pecked his cheek. "Thank you."

"I'll start the supper while you clean up."

He's starting to sound like a real husband.

She closed the bathroom door and took off her pajamas and underthings. Filling the sink with tepid water, she splashed and washed using the bar of soap and a face towel, sure to make plenty of noise. When her body was clean, she refilled the basin and washed her hair, then filled it one more time to rinse. It wasn't perfect, but she felt worlds better.

She took the bath towel and pressed it to her chest, letting it drape over her torso. Then she opened the door a crack and peeked out.

"Charles?"

He turned from the stove and stared.

"Honey, I need something clean to wear. I can't enjoy a romantic dinner in dirty old pajamas."

He stared some more, and she made sure to reveal a bit when the towel accidentally slipped. "Oops. Don't look, now." Readjusting it, she asked again. "Do you have some clean clothes I could wear?"

243

He set the spatula down. "I have something. Hold on." He opened the makeshift wardrobe and sorted through the uniforms. "What size are you?"

She laughed. "I don't like to tell. But if you have something in a size eight, it'll probably fit me." Normally a size ten, she figured *tight* would be good tonight.

He carried a white uniform on its hanger to her, his eyes raking over her body. "This'll do."

She accepted it with one hand. "Do you have undergarments? I need to wash mine out."

He stopped, went back to the wardrobe, and rummaged for a while. "No. I guess I need to get you some."

"Okay. Well, if you don't mind, I'm going to wash out my little things and hang them on the shower rod. Darn. I wish that shower worked. Can you get it going for me?"

He returned to her and looked thoughtful. "I guess I could rig up something."

"Perfect, Charles. Thank you." She swiveled to look at the shower, letting him see her backside. "Oops. No peeking now." She laughed and closed the door softly, leaning on it.

Her heart beat fast against the wooden panel.

I can do this.

She hitched a sob, then forced it down.

I can do this.

Chapter 59

"Are you ready for me?" Grace peeked out the bathroom door and giggled. "I feel a little funny wearing this with no underwear. You sure you won't think less of me?"

His big head swiveled in her direction, his eyes full of anticipation. "It's okay. Just come out. Dinner's ready."

She'd buttoned the uniform up as far as it went, but her breasts still bulged from the low cut bodice. "It's a little risqué, I think." Easing herself out of the doorway, she held her hands over her chest. "I don't want you to think..."

He approached her, eyes devouring her. "You look good." He took her hands away from her chest and stared at her cleavage. "You look real good."

She noticed a telltale swelling in his pants and smiled.

"Come on, sit over here."

He'd set the little table up again, but this time, he'd arranged two chairs in the middle of the room. The wine sat on the table, and he'd poured some into chipped mugs.

"Very nice." She floated toward the table, trying to look impressed.

"Sorry I don't have wine glasses."

"That's okay. You can get some, right? We'll just have to imagine them."

She glanced at the sheet he'd thrown over the card table like a tablecloth, and the tiny bouquet of daisies he'd picked and set in a glass in the center. "Flowers." She let her eyes mist over and reached for his hand. "Oh, Charles. It's beautiful."

He stopped and stared at her, then dropped his eyes to his feet. "You're different from the others."

She smiled and sat at the table. "Of course I am. I'm me. My own person. I never met anyone like me before, either."

He actually chuckled. "Dinner's ready." He filled their plates with pan fried chicken breasts, heated baked beans, and canned corn, then slid them onto the table.

"Mmm. Smells so good." She took a sip of wine from her mug. "I'm starving." Widening her eyes, she gazed at him in what she hoped was an innocent, but provocative, expression. "Sit, Charles."

He sat and took a long swig of wine.

She smiled, took a bite of chicken. "You're a good cook, honey."

His cheeks reddened. "Not really."

"Oh, yes. You are. Now, tell me all about yourself. I want to know everything."

An hour later, Murphy's eyes had glazed over. He slumped in his seat, still talking. She couldn't believe she'd gotten him to open up. He told her about his high school football career. About being in the army. About working at the munitions plant. About fishing, and the derbies he'd won.

But he never mentioned his mother, and she didn't push it. Yet.

"Did you have any brothers or sisters, Charles?" She tried to use his name as often as possible. Anything to increase the familiarity, to make him think they were a couple. She fluttered her eyelashes again and looked at him as if she really cared about him and his stupid family.

"No. It was just me."

"You and your parents, right?"

"Just my mother."

"Was she a nurse?"

He glowered at her, slammed a fist on the table. "No questions about my mother."

With a placating touch to his hand, she pouted. "I'm sorry. I didn't know."

246

He picked at the last of the corn on his plate.

It was time for her to make her move.

"Let's go sit on the bed. I'm so full, and this wine has made me feel a little funny." She leaned forward, touching his hand again. "Does it do that to you?" She'd made sure to fill his cup until the bottle was empty. His eyes looked glazed, and the tops of his ears were red.

"No. I'm fine."

"Should we open the second bottle?" she asked. Again, the picture of innocence.

He pushed back from the table. "Okay."

She got up and leaned down to open the door of the mini-fridge, knowing perfectly well that the uniform would ride up in the back and expose her nakedness.

It was all part of the plan.

She tugged on the dress and shot him a chagrined smile over her shoulder. "Oops. This thing is a little short. Don't look, now."

His eyes grew big with desire.

She reached in for the wine, uncapped it, and walked back to pour more into his empty cup, leaning down so his face was practically nuzzling her breasts. He swayed toward her, reaching a hand up to touch them. "Soft," he said, his words slurring. "So soft."

She giggled and pulled away. "Now, Charles."

He took another swig of wine, emptying half the cup. "I like you in that outfit. It suits you."

"Does it?" She twirled and posed for him. "I never thought white was my color, though."

"Oh, it's a good color on you."

Slowly, she approached him, noting the permanent bulge that had been pressing at his crotch since they began. She leaned down and kissed his lips, softly, gently. "Thank you."

He looked up, confused. "For what?"

"For bringing me here. For cooking this lovely dinner. For the flowers and wine." She kissed him again. "For everything."

Suddenly, as if he had woken from an impossible dream, his face darkened. "You're lying. You're a lying bitch." He jumped up from the table and backed away. "You're tricking me. Laughing at me."

She stood stock-still.

Crap. She hadn't expected this.

He reached for a plastic tie wrap. "Get over here."

She cowered back against the wall. "Why are you so angry? I thought we were having a good time."

He stormed toward her. "I don't trust you."

"Wait!" She caught his eyes with hers, letting her temper show. "What the hell is wrong with you, Murphy?" She slapped his face hard, bearing down on him.

He lifted a hand to his cheek, staring at her.

"I've done everything to make you happy. I prettied myself up. I'm wearing this uniform for you." She pushed his chest, shoving him back a few steps. "I was ready to make love to you tonight, you stupid ass."

"I—"

"And what do you do? You ruin everything. The mood. The romance. You just stomped all over it."

He slumped to the bed. The tie wrap fell to the floor. "I'm...sorry."

Chapter 60

"**W**ell, you *should* be sorry," Grace said, flopping onto the bed beside Murphy. "But you can make it up to me."

Murphy opened one eye. "What do you want now, Grace?"

"A foot rub." She flashed him a brilliant smile and sat back against the wall, lifting her foot a few inches and wiggling her toes. "My feet hurt."

"Why? You've just been sitting."

She frowned at him. "Don't get me mad again. Don't you want to make it better?"

He shrugged and lowered his head. "Give it here."

"Wait. I need a pillow for my head. This wall is hard. Go get that extra one from your bed." When he didn't move, she smiled again. "Please?"

He shoved himself off the bed and trundled to the other side of the room. She leaned down, grabbed the tie wrap, and stuffed it under the edge of the mattress.

He returned with his own pillow, and she slid it between her head and the wall. "Much better. Hey, take off your boots. Stay a while."

He kicked them off, then scooted up closer to her and pulled her feet onto his lap, taking one in his hands and gently massaging it.

Grace wondered if he used to do this for his mother. He was pretty good at it. "You have strong fingers, Charles. Big hands, too." With her free foot, she rubbed her toes against his bulge. "You know what they say about that. Should I be worried?"

He laughed. "You're married. You're not a virgin."

"I *was* married. And anyway, I'm going to divorce him. Besides, he had a really tiny one." She giggled. "So. Should I be worried?" Grace said a silent apology to Anderson, who was more than adequate in that department.

He actually laughed. "Maybe. I was bigger than all the other guys in the locker room in high school."

"Well, don't think I'm too forward, or anything, but..." she rubbed her toes against him again, "...I am curious about it."

Murphy moaned and clutched his crotch. "Jesus, woman."

"Grace," she corrected.

"Grace. Right." He closed his eyes and started to unzip his pants.

This was not what she wanted. She didn't want him just jacking off on his own; she needed to be in control. She needed to weaken him.

"Wait." She slid up beside him lengthwise on the bed, propping his pillow beneath her head. "Let me."

His eyes snapped open, as if horrified at the idea. "No."

She purred in his ear, kissing it lightly. "Honey. If we're going to be together, we need to get closer. And I'm willing to do this for you. Only you." She took his hand and placed it on her bare thigh. The stupid undersized uniform had ridden up on her, practically exposing her nakedness. She purposefully worked it up even further by shifting a little on the mattress. "You can touch me, too. It's okay. I trust you."

He seemed to relax, searching her eyes. "Really?"

"Really. Now. Where were we?" She reached down, suppressed an urge to vomit, and unzipped his fly. "There we go. Now just slide out of these."

He wiggled out of his pants, and she realized when she saw him in his boxers that he wasn't kidding. Everything about this creep was big.

I've done worse things before. I even gave that disgusting dealer in Toronto a blowjob on the sidewalk when I was desperate for a fix. I can do this.

250

I can do this.

She moved his hand up to the Y between her legs and opened her thighs. "Go ahead, honey. Touch me."

He moaned and reached two fingers into her private area, moving the tips deeper inside her. She pretended to like it, arching her back a little. "Oh, Charles."

Taking a deep breath, she reached into his boxers and released his organ. It sprang to life before her, waving in her direction. Trying not to retch, she leaned over and touched her tongue to its tip. "Take these things off, Charles."

"Oh, God. Grace." He shrugged out of his boxers, then reached right back inside her, probing and rubbing with one finger.

Would he notice she wasn't aroused? Could she fake that, too?

She grasped him at the base and ran her fingers up and down the shaft rhythmically. His hips rose and fell as she stimulated him, and from sounds coming from him, she was afraid he'd explode before she could get him in the right position.

"Wait." She rolled over onto his legs, straddling him. "Do you have any lubricant?"

He looked at her as if she were nuts. "What?"

"You're so big, Charles. I need a little help." She glanced over at the table, noting the vegetable oil. It would have to do. "Hold on."

She got off him, grabbed the oil, and returned to straddle him, pouring the oil into one palm. "See how this feels."

He moaned again and from his position, she was sure he was about to explode. She needed to distract him, hold him off, just a little. "Now you do me."

She took his limp hand and poured oil into his palm. "Come on, now. Don't be shy."

251

He cupped his hand beneath her, smearing it into her.

"That's good. Now work it in." She moved against his fingers as he slid them up and down the slick canal. "Good. That's perfect."

With a deep breath, she lifted herself over him. "Just lay back now, Charles. I'm going to take you inside me." She slid over him, groaning a little when he pushed his giant organ inside her. It was huge.

His left hand held her bottom. His right hand yanked down the uniform and freed her breasts. He leaned up and licked her, moving his head from side to side as if he couldn't decide which breast he liked the best. She took his right arm and lay it straight back, running her fingers along it to his hand, where she laced their fingers together. "Hold on, Charles. Don't come before me."

He pumped inside her, and while she pretended to enjoy it, she let go of his hand and reached under the bed for the tie wrap. When he came, she'd loop it and tie him to the metal frame beside the mattress. He was in the perfect position now.

Just don't move that hand.

Harder, he rammed into her. She faked a scream, throwing her hair back and forth like a wild woman, clawing at his chest and tweaking his nipples. He exploded inside her, thrusting himself up with demonic urgency.

When he peaked, she leaned over and looped the tie wrap around his wrist. With a sigh of relief, she jerked it tight and bent over to toss his knife—still in his discarded boot—across the room.

Chapter 61

Murphy took a few minutes to come back to his senses. He lay slack beneath her, groaning and smiling. She pushed back to get off him, but in seconds he stiffened, and with his free hand he reached up and grabbed a hunk of her hair.

"Really?" he growled. "You tied me to your bed?" His eyes snapped open, and fury spilled from them. "No fucking way."

She yanked back, felt her hair practically rip from her head, then reached an elbow around and jabbed it into his neck. "Let me go, you big, ugly pervert."

She pulled back while he choked and reeled from the blow, but before she could escape, he grabbed her wrist and twisted. "You're not going anywhere. Woman."

He lay naked beneath her, now flaccid and exposed. Twisting in his grip again, she jumped up and with as much force as she could muster, aimed her knees at his crotch.

"Pretty big target. I can hardly miss it," she hissed. "Too bad you aren't man enough for what God gave you."

He let go of her wrist and reached to cover his manhood, groaning with his eyes closed. "You bitch!" he stammered. "You crippled me."

Free, she rolled off him, running to his stash of tie wraps on the other side of the room. She hurried back, and wrapped it around one ankle, jerking it tight. "You're not going anywhere, Charlie."

He wailed, still coddling himself and moaning, turning sideways. He tried to pull into a ball, but could only move the untethered leg. "I hate you!" he screamed. "You're just like her."

She backed away again, picked up his pants, and searched for the keys. "Like who? Your precious Momma?"

He screamed more obscenities, his metallic voice sending a shiver down her spine. "Don't talk about my mother. Nobody talks about her but me."

And then, he started to cry.

She stopped, stared, and flopped onto one of the chairs. "Really?" She sighed, starting to unbutton the hated uniform. She couldn't wait to get out of it. "I'm the one who should be crying, you bastard. I had to touch you. I had you inside me. I don't know how many showers it'll take to wash your stink off me."

She stared at him, trying to ignore the urge to do more harm to him.

She wanted him dead for what he did to Portia.

Dead.

She eyed the knife, leaned down to pick it up.

Could I? Could I end it right now? Stab him and leave him here where no one would find him for weeks? Maybe months?

With a fortitude borne of the knowledge that Anderson would never look at her the same way if she gave into these urges, she stopped herself.

No.

I've beaten the drugs.

I've beaten this bastard.

I can't give in to murder.

She shook herself, pushing away the tempting thoughts.

I just want to go home.

She got up, found her pajamas and damp underwear, put them on, and turned to him one more time. "I'll be back with the police. And if you have any other women stashed around here, we'll find them. And something tells me they'll sing like canaries at your trial." Looking at him over her shoulder, she winked. "I know I will."

Chapter 62

Grace walked through cement corridors for several minutes before she found an exit. In her bare feet and pajamas, she emerged into bright moonlight.

How the hell am I going to get home? Or even get to a phone?

She hadn't seen an office or phone on the way out, but wondered if she could possibly locate that room where Murphy had found the coffee maker. If people were using it, there had to be a phone hook up.

She missed her iPhone. It probably still sat in her purse in her bedroom at home. Battery dead. Wondering what happened to its talkative owner.

What about Murphy's car? She had the keys in her pocket, they jingled as she walked.

What color was it?

She had no idea. Just that it had a front and back seat, and a loud radio.

That's helpful, Grace.

She chuckled in spite of herself. He'd probably hidden it, she figured. Maybe over in the woods? She scanned the tree line that bordered acres of woods surrounding the facility. It was dark, so it really was useless to try to find something in those deep, dark woods now, anyway.

And where was the main road? She had no idea which direction to walk in.

Was that shining silver reflection through the trees the surface of Devil's Lake? Tempted for a moment to run toward the water and wash all things Murphy from her, she envisioned stripping and jumping into the cool lake water, stroking far out

255

into the middle of the lake, and just floating on her back with the moon shining on her face.

She stopped and sat on the stoop by the door where she had just emerged. Sat and thought. Sat and felt like crying.

A few tears trickled down her cheeks. She roughly wiped them away.

My God. I really did it.

If Portia's theories were right, Grace could've ended up as one of Murphy's castoffs. She might've been killed and buried out in those dark woods. She'd never have seen Anderson again. Or her parents and Portia. She would have just been a ghost, wandering the fields and barns of Bittersweet Hollow.

She wondered about her mother, and prayed that going back to the clinic would stop the cancer again.

How much is one person supposed to take, anyway? Beating the whole drug thing was hard enough. Trying to maintain a chaste lifestyle was another challenge, especially since she craved men so much and seemed to have a really hard time controlling it. Watching her mother wither away from cancer, month after month...Then getting kidnapped by a robotic-voiced moron.

What was that all about?

Something told her she was not going to crave other men so much now. Not after this whole charade.

She'd always been a good actress. That's how she met Anderson, when she starred in the lead role of her college production of "Grease." She'd made a fantastic Sandy, even if she did say so herself. And she'd fallen for Anderson, who'd apparently had it bad for her since the first day of auditions. Sure, he was fifteen years older than she was. But crap, who cared these days? If you found someone who loved you...what did it matter?

Anderson.

Would he understand? Would he think of her as tainted now?

No.

No, he had taken her back time after time when she'd cheated on him, when she'd fallen off the wagon. No. He'd take her back and love her, just like always.

I need to be much nicer to him. He's a gem.

Something moved in the woods to her right. A flashlight played along the path.

She froze.

Who would be out at this time of night?

Oh, God. Did Murphy have a partner?

⮞⭗⬿

Portia gripped Boone's arm, staying close to his side. He played the light along the narrow path in the woods.

"I told you to stay in the car, Portia." He stopped and chided her, knowing it was hopeless. "It could get dangerous."

"Jeez, Boone. I'm not your dog." She frowned and spit the words. "I'm armed." She brandished her father's rifle. "I know how to use this. My dad made sure of it when I was fourteen."

He flicked back a lock of his shaggy blond hair. "You haven't shot it in years."

"So? It's like riding a bike. It'll come back to me."

Anderson chuckled behind them, followed closely by Ned.

"Tell me this was a smart idea," Portia said. "We're doing the right thing, aren't we?"

Boone nodded and pushed toward the clearing where the gray buildings of the abandoned munitions plant sprawled for acres in front of them. "I'll tell you it was a good idea when we find her. She could be in any—or none—of those buildings."

Anderson took the lead. "We'd probably better split up. Do you all have a good signal?"

Ned held his up. "I've got two bars."

Portia and Boone did the same, nodding. "Good to go," Boone said.

Anderson lowered his voice as they approached the edge of the compound. "Let's check in every half hour. Boone, you call me. Ned and I will search together; we're taking the southern half of the plant. Portia, stick with Boone. Got it?"

The foursome had decided to investigate on their own after waiting for the police to act on the tip that had come in about some old drunk who said he saw Murphy driving a car in Baraboo with a girl slumped in the front seat. They'd acted skeptical about his report, even though Sheriff Dunne told them they'd already checked out the cabin by Devil's Lake and had found nothing new there. It was when Boone found evidence online that Murphy had worked at the old munitions plant over a decade ago that they decided to check it out.

They'd been on the road for twelve hours, and tired, cranky, and gritty-eyed, they'd all agreed not to wait until morning light.

They split into two teams. Anderson and Ned disappeared into the moonlit night, and Boone led the way toward the first building.

Chapter 63

Grace shrank back into the shadows beneath the overhang. Slowly, quietly, she shuffled to the corner and hid from the light in the woods.

She wanted to run and scream, wave her arms, and shout, "Here I am!" But she held it in, clamped her lips tight together.

What if the person in the woods with the flashlight was another nut job like Murphy? What if it was his brother?

Worse yet, what if it was his *mother*? What if she *took part* in his sick games?

She shuddered. She'd always thought of his mother as dead.

She hoped she was right.

With a deep, steadying breath, she peeked around the corner.

The light was coming closer, bouncing along the ground as if its owner was jogging toward the building. She pulled back a few more feet into the darkness and held her breath.

❧◦❧

Portia bent low and ran behind Boone, trying to keep a low profile. Soon she felt out of breath, and wondered if she could keep up the pace. Boone was in much better shape than she was, there was no question about that.

They approached a darkened building, but at the very end of the long building, she noticed a dim light spilling onto the gravel below a window.

She stopped him and pointed. "Over there."

"Come on," he said.

A shrill cry stopped Portia's heart beating in her chest. She froze, turned toward the noise, and was quickly enveloped by a shrieking tangle of arms and legs. Someone kissed her cheeks over and over again.

"Portia! Portia. Oh my God. It's you!" Grace danced in place, then jumped on Boone, both legs around his waist. "Boone! You guys actually found me!"

When Portia finally realized what was happening, she screamed Grace's name and hugged her and Boone in a three-person embrace.

Grace jumped down, wrapped her arms around Portia, and hugged and twirled with her for a full minute. "Oh my God. You're here!"

"Yes, we are, Baby Cakes." Portia laughed, relief flooding her so strongly that her legs almost buckled.

Boone was on the phone to Anderson, practically shouting the news. "We've got her."

In five minutes, the sound of scuffling boots grew louder, and finally, Anderson appeared in the light of his own flashlight. He stopped. Stared. And opened his arms for Grace, who threw herself on him with such passionate kisses that Portia almost had to turn away blushing.

"Baby, baby, baby," Grace muttered. "Oh God. You wouldn't believe what I had to do to get away from him."

When they finally stopped chattering over each other, the foursome stopped. Ned was the one who brought them back to reality.

"So," he said. "Where's Murphy? Did you have to kill him, Grace?"

"No," she said, looking pensive. She raised her eyes to each of them in turn. "But I was sorely tempted."

Boone gestured toward the light. "Is he down there?"

"Uh huh. Come on." Grace looped her arm through Anderson's and her eyes hardened. "I'll take you to the son of a bitch."

Chapter 64

Ned held his phone up in one hand. "Hold on a second. Shouldn't we call the cops first? Let 'em know we found Grace?"

Boone shook his head. "Let's wait, make sure we've really got Murphy, too."

Grace giggled, sounding almost hysterical. "Oh. We've got him. Unless he can chew through a plastic tie-wrap on his wrist and ankle, he's ours."

Portia's fists tightened at her sides and she leaned down to pick up the rifle she'd dropped. "I'd like a go at him." As soon as she said it, she wondered how those words could come from her own lips. But the pent up anger, the long-suffering pain, had been building up inside her for a long time. "Just five minutes. That's all I want."

Grace tossed her an empathetic smile. "I don't blame you. Come on." She took her sister's arm and led her into the darkened building, through the cavernous production lines and narrow green painted corridors. When they reached the locked door, Grace pulled the keys out of her pajama pockets. "Okay. Here we go."

The door squeaked open and Portia was hit with a sense of trepidation. She froze.

What if Murphy got loose? What if he was waiting for them, behind the door? With a knife? A gun?

Murphy's in there. So close. So stinking close.

She stepped inside after Grace and the men entered the room. Fear replaced her insane desire for revenge. She trembled all over.

Grace stood with hands on her hips, watching Murphy, who, indeed, was still tethered to the bed at the side of the room. Naked, he lay there for all to see, his face screwed into a furious mask with one hand trying unsuccessfully to cover his manhood.

"There's your man. Right where I left him," Grace said. "He's just kind of hanging out." Another too-bright laugh came from her lips and she covered her mouth with one hand, as if trying to control it. One raw sob erupted from her and she sucked in a deep breath, covering her eyes.

Portia moved closer and took her sister's hand. "You're safe now."

Grace leaned into her, sagging against her shoulder. "Thanks."

Boone edged forward carefully. "Let me double check his restraints." He leaned down, poked at Murphy's wrist and ankle with the tip of his rifle.

In a crazed burst of movement, Murphy lunged for the gun with his free hand. Shrieking with his metallic voice like a futuristic banshee, he reached it, struggled with Boone, and almost won control of the rifle. Boone streaked back, swung the gun around, and slammed the stock against Murphy's head.

Murphy lay still, eyes closed, body at rest.

Ned moved closer. "Is he dead?"

"God. I hope so." Portia let go of Grace and crept closer. "Check his pulse. But be careful." Bile rose in her throat and her fists clenched at her side.

She wanted to run. Run far away. Away from this monster.

Boone leaned forward and touched his fingers to the man's wrist, keeping his rifle an arm's length away. "Nope. He's alive."

Grace regained her composure and came closer, leaning down to look at him with fierce anger stamping her face. "*Bastard.* I'd like to get some answers before the cops take him away." She shook his shoulder. "Charlie! Wake up."

Anderson raised an eyebrow. "Charlie?"

Grace backed up and canted one hip, her saucy attitude firmly back in place. "He hates it when you call him that. Only his precious mommy was allowed to call him Charlie. He wanted me to call him Charles."

Slowly, Portia's anxiety settled, to be replaced by lava like anger. Her lip curled. "Really? Charles?"

Grace nodded. "Yup. If you wanna make him mad...call him Charlie."

"I can't look at that any more." Portia grabbed a blanket and threw it over his nakedness. "Hey. Charlie." She nudged his hip with her boot. "You awake?"

He didn't move.

"Too bad," she said, shaking with nerves. "I'd like to force him to tell us about the other girls. I know there were probably dozens. And I wonder if there are any more held in this place." She gestured to the abandoned buildings around her.

Boone put an arm around Portia's shoulder. She didn't flinch. She even leaned into him a little bit.

"Come on, Portia. Let the cops do the questioning. They're the experts."

She relaxed against him, leaning her head on his shoulder. "I guess you're right."

Anderson framed Grace's face in his hands and searched her eyes. "Do you need a doctor, honey?"

Grace placed both palms against his chest and rose up on her toes to kiss him. "No, baby. I'm okay, now that you're here."

Anderson's expression softened. "Well, then. Let's get you out of here."

Ned held up a hand. He'd been on the phone for several minutes already. "We can't leave until the police come." He turned back to his cell phone, head nodding furiously as he relayed the location and situation to Sheriff Dunne back in Vermont.

Chapter 65

"Come on. I need some fresh air." Boone led the way outside, where he sank heavily onto the edge of the cement steps, glancing over to the horizon. "Dawn's coming."

Portia sat beside him. She felt no fear, no nervousness. Her insides had churned when she'd seen Murphy again. She thought she was going to throw up. But then, when she realized he really was secured tightly to the bed, it had all fizzled out of her and she'd felt the fear drain away.

It's over.

She watched the cotton candy pink line grow thicker on the horizon behind the trees, dancing off the sparkling surface of Devil's Lake. She felt calm, calmer than ever before.

"Boone?"

He turned toward her. "Yeah?"

"Thank you." She took his hand in hers. "For finding my sister."

A smile slid onto his lips. "No problem."

He answered as if he'd just bought her a coffee, or handed her an apple. As if it were no big deal.

She loved that.

"I hear the police sirens," she said. "They're coming."

"Yep." He stretched his legs out. "We'll probably be here all morning."

"Probably." She turned toward him. "But after it's over, I have a request."

He cocked an eyebrow in her direction. "What's that, Peaches?"

She looked toward the lake, glistening in the distance. "I want to go for a swim before we head home." She paused, then continued in a rushed whisper. "I need to purge him from my system. I think I could do that by swimming for the last time in Devil's Lake, when I'm not running from someone, not swimming for my life. You know what I mean?" She took his hand in hers. "I want to float and relax. Swim without fear. Enjoy the feel of the cool water on my skin."

"Makes sense. And it sounds good." He eyed their clothing. "But we're not exactly dressed for swimming, are we?"

She shrugged. "I don't care. I need to feel clean again." She hitched a sob. "Can you understand that?"

Lights flashed in the distance, and the sound of the sirens grew louder.

Grace, who had been standing with Anderson and Ned behind them, plopped down beside her. "I totally get that. I want to swim, too."

The sisters embraced, cried on each other for a few minutes, and then sighed, linking arms and gazing toward the water through the trees.

"When I saw him again," Portia began, "it all came flooding back. I thought I'd crumple into a ball and die." She leaned over to kiss her sister's cheek. "But then I saw how brave you were. How you beat him in two days, Grace. Two days! Compared to my two years...I felt so proud of you. I drew on that pride and it gave me strength."

Grace swiped at her tears. "I kept thinking of you. How he'd hurt you. It made me so goddamned mad."

Anderson crouched behind Grace and rubbed her shoulders. "How *did* you do it, baby? In two days?"

Grace smiled at him over her shoulder. "I'll tell you some day, sweetie. But let me say all those acting lessons you gave me came in pretty handy."

Anderson nodded. "I should have known." He leaned over and kissed the top of her head. "You're our hero, Gracie. You're amazing."

She pulled him down beside her as the cop cars screeched into the yard. "I kept thinking of you. How much I loved you."

Portia and Boone exchanged smiles, then rose to greet the officers who ran toward them with weapons drawn.

Chapter 66

Grace and Portia stood at the shore of Devil's Lake, hand in hand, wearing gym shorts and tees Portia had thrown into her bag when she hastily packed to drive west in search of Grace. They didn't have towels, but she'd grabbed a big blanket from Boone's Jeep and it lay ready for them to share when they finished swimming. The men stayed back at the munitions plant, having offered to help the local police search the buildings for more kidnapped girls.

"I'm so glad this is over," Grace said, wading with Portia into the water.

"He won't be able to hurt any more girls, that's for sure." Portia shivered. "Oh! It's cold."

"We'll get used to it, Sweet Pea."

Portia turned to her with a trembling smile. "I love it when you call me that." She squeezed her sister's hand. "Grace? Will we ever forget Murphy?"

Grace squeezed her hand. "No. But we *will* get over it. We'll move forward."

"I don't know. I keep seeing his face in my nightmares. I wake up screaming to him standing over me."

Grace turned to her sister, locking eyes with her. "I want you to focus on replacing that image with the one you just saw. Murphy lying tied up. Helpless. Vulnerable. Naked to the world."

Portia nodded as they walked deeper into the lake. "Okay. I'll try. Or maybe I'll picture him in jail."

Grace let go of her hand. "Even better." She dove beneath the surface and came up a few yards away. "Come on. It feels great."

267

Portia followed her example, and when she felt the water streaming around her face and body, her entire being sighed with relief. She popped up beside Grace. "Wonderful."

Grace grinned. "Let's swim out a ways. You ready?"

Portia smiled back. "Ready."

They stroked side by side until their arms grew tired, then rolled onto their backs and floated. Mourning doves cooed from the shore, and birds flitted and chirped nearby. The sound of crickets came from the reeds in a nearby cove. Lulled by the feeling of security and peace, they linked fingers and drifted without saying a word.

Finally, Grace pulled up and tread water. "Portia? How's Mom? I've been worried sick about her."

Portia stayed on her back, gazing up into the blue sky above. "No worries. Dr. Kareem got her back on the IV drugs and she's starting to come back to where she was when she first was released. The doc said he can arrange a visiting nurse to come every other day to set up the IV, since the pills didn't work as well."

"Can we see her?"

"She'll be home in a few days, hon. We'll be together again. All of us."

Grace floated up onto her back again. After a few minutes, she said, "You like him, don't you."

"What?"

"Him. Boone. You like him."

"I—"

"Come on," Grace said. "I know you. I see the way you look at him."

Portia's cheeks felt warm. She had been avoiding thoughts about Boone for a while. Avoiding how she felt when she was around him. Her sense of irrational fear had pretty much disappeared. The anxiety had lessened. And now, when he touched her, or leaned a shoulder to hers, or turned to her with those gorgeous deep gray eyes, her heart thumped wildly and her knees went weak.

"I guess I do."

"What?"

"Like him. Kinda."

"Kind of?" Grace squealed a laugh and splashed Portia with a cupped palm. "Kind of?"

Portia giggled.

Grace grinned at the clouds above. "I see a cloud that looks like Boone's face. And I know you want to smother it in kisses." She paused for effect. "Don't you?"

Portia let the last of her anxiety go...up, up, away it floated, to the clouds above. She pictured it dissipating like vapors on the wind, gone for good. Never to torture her again. She began to sidestroke back to the shore. "Okay. I'll admit it. Maybe... maybe I'd like to kiss him."

Grace caught up with her. "Good. Because he's been in love with you since you were kids."

Portia snorted a laugh. "No way."

"Way."

"Seriously? Why didn't I ever..."

"Because you were blind, my dear sister. Blind and...um...stupid."

"Stupid?"

Grace chuckled and started to swim on her back. "Okay. Not exactly stupid, maybe dense."

"Oh, that's a lot better," Portia said, but she couldn't stop the smile that spread on her lips. "I'm just dense."

"It's just the truth, Sweet Pea."

It was Portia's turn to splash her sister. She drove an open hand across the water's surface, sending a shower over Grace's face.

Sputtering, Grace rolled over and stood in the now shallow water. "Really? You wanna go with me? Huh?" With a laugh, she jumped on Portia's shoulders and dunked her.

Portia emerged laughing, and collared her sister around the neck, giggling uncontrollably. "You're incorrigible, Grace."

"Incorrigible?" Grace snorted. "Oh, give me a break. You learned that word in *The Sound of Music*. The little boy. What was his name? Kurt?"

"Right. 'I'm Kurt. I'm eleven. I'm incorrigible.'"

"He was a boy."

"I know. But you're still incorrigible."

They reached the shore and wrapped up in the blanket, sitting side by side on a log.

Portia snuggled close to her sister. "I love you, Baby Cakes."

Grace leaned her head on her sister's shoulder. "Right back atcha."

They sat for a long time, until their hair was drier and their bodies were warm. With a satisfied sigh, they stood as one and walked back to the compound.

Chapter 67

Dirk helped Daisy out of the truck, amazed at how much stronger she'd grown in the past week. The intravenous experimental cancer meds had really turned her around, and for the first time in months, he felt a sense of relaxation, almost of...peace.

It was a foreign sensation. Peace. No worries. No wondering where his daughters were.

From Grace's druggie days, to Portia's abduction, to Daisy's cancer, he'd been in a constant state of anxiety that he fought to control and not show. After all, he was of strong Vermont stock. Farm men like him didn't cry. Didn't show their fear.

Except in private, when all the lights were out, when everyone was asleep.

When Portia had called him last night to say Grace had been abducted, but that they already found her and caught Murphy, he'd almost lost it.

They'd kept the news from him. His baby girl had been taken by that brutish monster, and he hadn't even known.

At first he'd raised his voice at her, told her she shouldn't try to protect him from life.

Then, when she'd explained that she didn't want him to fall apart with too much on his shoulders, he'd understood. What could he have done, anyway? Except worry some more. He wouldn't have left Daisy's side.

So, he apologized for his outburst, thanked Portia for loving him, and told her he'd see her as soon as he could arrange a flight home.

Now, both girls tumbled down the steps and ran toward them, throwing their arms around Daisy first and then him.

Boomer and Cupcake followed in their wake, and in seconds, Boone, Ned, and Anderson appeared on the porch steps, waving and watching. Mirage whinnied from his pasture, turning in tight circles and shaking his head as if he didn't want to be left out of the festivities.

"Mom! Dad!" Grace embraced and kissed her mom, then jumped into her father's arms, hugging him as if she'd never let go.

Portia kissed her mother's cheeks repeatedly, then put an arm around her waist, flashing a big grin at her father. "Mom. You look amazing. How'd you get better so fast?"

"Hi, darlings. It's so good to be home again." Daisy smiled at both daughters and waved to the men on the porch. "Dr. Kareem fixed me up good, girls. Now we know how to keep the 'good' going."

Dirk hadn't told her about the second abduction, and he'd cautioned everyone about that on the phone earlier. Daisy needed all her strength to get well.

He would tell her. In time.

After the kissing and hugging finally died down, they climbed the porch steps, shook hands and exchanged bear hugs with the men, and headed inside.

The aroma of roast chicken wafted up to him. What else was it? Rosemary?

Who the hell had learned how to cook since he'd been gone?

Portia grabbed potholders and opened the oven, and the aroma intensified to the point that Dirk's stomach growled.

"You hungry, Dad?" she laughed, glancing at his belly.

"Starving. Did you make this?"

She blushed. "I did. I hope it's edible."

He hugged her and whispered in her ear. "I'm sure it's gonna be great, sweetie. And can I tell you something?"

She nodded. "Sure."

"You look amazing. Completely different. You look...happy."

She leaned down to poke the chicken. "I am, Dad. I'm feeling like my old self again. Finally."

ॐ

Over dinner, the conversation eventually drifted to Murphy.

Ned, who'd been invited to the feast by Portia, scooped a second helping of mashed potatoes and plopped them on his plate. "Did you guys see the news this morning?"

Anderson wiped his mouth with a napkin and frowned. "Yeah. Unbelievable, huh?"

Daisy looked around the table. "What? What did I miss? Another school shooting? Oh, Lord, I hope not."

Dirk put a hand on hers. "Nothing like that, dear. It's just they caught that creep, Murphy, and they'd been discovering things about him." He sent a warning glance to Grace, who'd opened her mouth to speak.

Grace nodded in silent understanding. They'd talked about not mentioning her kidnapping until Daisy had been home for at least a few days. "There were others," she said. "Besides Portia, I mean."

Dirk grimaced. "I heard they're still uncovering the bodies. Around the munitions camp."

Boone forked another bite of chicken. "They're using dogs."

Portia nodded. "But they did find that one girl alive."

Grace rolled her eyes. "*Barely* alive. Poor thing."

Ned took another bite of potatoes and swallowed. "Where was she again?"

"Tied inside one of the old production facilities at the compound," Anderson said. "She was only sixteen."

273

Portia felt the old fear bubbling up inside her, but she pushed it down forcibly. *I am strong. I am whole.* "Her parents must be so happy to have her home again."

Dirk took a sip of water. "Damn. I know how that feels."

Ned pushed back his chair. "They're uncovering some pretty sick stuff about his childhood, too. His mother was bonkers. Rumor was she..." he looked at Daisy, then continued. "Um...she had inappropriate relations with her son. When the social workers found out, they took his mother away. She escaped from the home, came back to the house where her son lived with an uncle. The next day, they found her dead in the basement. They questioned Murphy about it. He was only thirteen, but they always wondered if he'd been responsible for the 'accident' when she fell down the cellar stairs."

Portia raised an eyebrow. "Really? I didn't hear that part. Was the mother by any chance a nurse?"

Ned answered again. "She sure as hell was. Go figure, huh?" He covered a belch with one hand. "Excuse me. Anyway, she worked at a nursing home before she got fired and ended up on welfare. The father left before Murphy was born."

Daisy laid her fork down and placed a napkin over her plate. "Well, it's sad to think of a child being abused like that. But that doesn't excuse his behavior. He's still responsible for his actions. He murdered people, for goodness sakes."

"Right you are." Grace stood and started to collect the dirty dishes. "At least it's over. We can rest easy again."

Anderson looked at his watch. "I've got an online class to teach, guys."

Portia glanced his way. "How much longer can you two stay with us?"

Grace answered for them. "I want to stay for the rest of the summer. We'll go back home after Labor Day." She smiled at Portia. "Long as that's okay with everybody?"

Portia got up to help her clear. "You bet it's okay. More than okay. Now, who wants coffee?"

Chapter 68

After dinner, Boone helped Portia with the dishes. He watched her with slanted glances, his heart heavy.

It's over. I'm going home.

No more seeing Portia every day.

No more watching her heal and learn to smile again.

No more bringing her cups of coffee or caring for her beloved horses.

It's really over.

It went without saying that he was glad she was safe now, that there was no need to protect her anymore. But still…

She reached up to put a serving platter away, straining to make the top shelf, but she couldn't quite reach.

"Here, let me help you." Boone took the dish from her and easily slid it beneath the fancy dishes stored up high. His shoulder brushed hers and he felt fire run through him, just like it did any time she was near. "There you go."

His shoulders slumped and he stood staring out the window to the fields beyond.

"What's wrong?" she asked.

"Nothing," he said, busying himself arranging the towel over the oven handle. "It's just I guess I ought to pack up my stuff. Ned's already gone home. I should get back to help with the chores. I've left my dad to handle all the work for long enough."

Portia froze for a minute, but didn't speak. "Of course. If you think that's best."

He glanced at her, but she was looking down. Did she feel it, too? Or was it just him?

"I wondered…" he began.

She raised her eyes to his. "About what?"

"Um. I was thinking maybe we could take a ride together? Now that everything's calmed down, and we don't need to worry every second. Just for old times sake. Before I get pulled back into my family farm."

Almost before he finished his sentence she flashed a smile. "Yes. I'd love that."

"Really?" His heart started to gallop in his chest. "You would?"

She glanced down at her shorts. "Let me change into jeans. Be down in a sec."

"Okay." He tried to stop the grin that spread over his face, but it was impossible. "I'll go get the horses ready. You want to ride Mirage?"

"Of course." She hopped up the stairs two at a time.

He watched until she disappeared, then turned and headed out to the barn.

༺∘༻

Portia led the way on Mirage, winding up the wooded hill that gradually twisted and rose to the top of the mountain. Her stallion pranced and shied for the first fifteen minutes, then finally settled down and focused on the climb. Boone followed on a big chestnut gelding. Rusty was surefooted and dependable. He clopped slowly behind Mirage, his head two feet behind the stallion's tail.

Halfway up the hill, Portia turned Mirage off the trail and started up a truck path that ended at a stone cliff. She stopped her horse a safe distance from the edge and tethered him to a bush. Boone followed her example.

She glanced down at an aquamarine pool glistening below, and her heart nearly froze. There it was. No Bottom Pond. The bottomless hole that spiraled into the earth. She stood staring into the bright reflection of late afternoon sun on the water.

"That's where they dumped the pickup," she said, her voice low.

"I know." Boone laced his fingers through hers and gently squeezed.

She glanced sideways at him; glad he'd taken her hand. It comforted her, made her feel safe. In the past, only her father could make her feel that way. But of course, this was different.

"That's how it all started. Me, racing home in that old beat up truck with my little mutt beside me."

"Seems like so long ago that I saw you coming up the driveway in a big cloud of dust," he said.

She snorted a laugh. "Yeah. And when you found me inside, you didn't even know who I was."

"Go figure. You shocked the hell outta me."

She leaned into him. "So much has changed."

"You've changed." He slid an arm around her shoulders and pulled her to him.

She relaxed into him. He smelled so good, of pine shavings and...what was it? Cinnamon?

Portia raised her eyes to his. "I have. I'm better now."

"Better than ever. You're relaxed, accomplished, and beautiful. The way you handled yourself this past week...it blew me away."

She cocked an eyebrow. "I love being called accomplished. But beautiful?" she said. "Really?"

"Yes. Incredibly beautiful, inside and out. And Portia, I can't stop thinking about you." He let it all out in a torrent of words. "I...I don't like being apart from you, Portia. I'm not...whole when I'm alone." He locked eyes with her. "I want to be with you. Always."

Portia took a deep breath. "It's time we talked about it, then."

"Okay."

She saw a shadow cross his face. She'd made him worry, but she'd fix that.

She looked across The Hollow, below. "I wanted to thank you for being so patient with me when I came home. I was such a wreck. So scared. And you were amazing."

"But?"

Pressing closer to his chest, she slipped her arms around his waist. "But nothing."

"Oh, thank God." He tilted her chin up and leaned down to place his lips on hers. Gently, he kissed her. When he pulled back, he looked relieved. "I thought you were going to say we could be good friends."

She melted into his arms, her heart racing against his ribs. "Boone," she said, lifting her lips for another kiss. "I'd love to be friends with you. And more."

He pulled back a few inches, surprised. "You never said anything. All these years. I've been desperately in love with you since you were sixteen. But I thought..."

"I know. I wasn't ready back then." She combed her fingers through his hair. "But now...I am. I'm ready."

Boone moaned. "Oh, God, Portia." He pulled her tighter, kissing her deeper. When they stopped to breathe, he whispered hoarse words in her ear. "I've wanted you for so long."

Heat raced through her, making her knees wobble. She slipped her arms around his neck. "Thank you for waiting," she whispered.

He shrugged. "It was the thing to do, Peaches. You were so fragile. So afraid."

"I know." Her eyes misted over. "And I might have moments. You know. In the future."

"No worries. I'll be here for you."

"Really?"

"Really. It doesn't bother me. I know why it's happening, and I'm proud of you. What you went through would have broken most women."

She frowned. "I know. It broke me for a while."

He kissed her again. "You not only survived, but you escaped that madman. You're a strong woman. And I'm honored to know you."

She fluttered little kisses over his face, kissing his nose, cheeks, and finally, his lips. "Thank you."

He slid an arm beneath her knees and lifted her with one swift motion. "No thanks necessary. But I have one favor to ask."

She thrilled to the feeling of him holding her. "And what's that?"

Turning, he faced the valley, motioning with his head toward their farms that looked like toys in the greenery below. "I love this land. And I want to spend the rest of my life working the farms, with you by my side."

She waited. Was he going to propose? Or ask her to live with him?

She felt him take a deep breath and let it out. "Portia. I don't have any fancy ring or speech made up. But this is something I've wanted to ask you for a long time."

"Yes?" Her heart beat faster.

"I'd like you to marry me. When you're ready."

Joy surged through her. She raised one hand to his fuzzy cheek, feeling the bristles of several days of stubble beneath her fingers. Smiling up at him, she kissed him softly.

"Well?" He laid his forehead against hers. "Was that an answer?"

She kissed him again. "It was."

He almost seemed surprised. "You'll marry me?"

"I will," she said. "I'll gladly marry you."

"Well, then," he said, carrying her toward a grassy spot. He gently laid her down, settling beside her. "We've got plans to make."

She snuggled closer to him, inhaling his musky male scent. "We do indeed." As if it were the most natural thing in the world, she laid her head against him and sighed with contentment, tracing patterns on his chest. "I don't want to move from this spot."

"Please don't," he said. "I might embarrass myself."

She chuckled, knowing exactly what he meant. "Okay, big guy. But I'm afraid you'll have to wait for the wedding night."

"You're killing me," he said. "But I'll try." A huge smile slid onto his lips. "So, wanna get married tomorrow?"

With a grin, she swatted him and pushed up to gaze into his clear eyes. "You're terrible, Boone."

"Is that a yes?"

"No, it's not. But soon. We'll set the date, and we'll be man and wife before you know it."

"Mmm," he said. "I like the sound of that. You and me, together forever." He lifted her lips to his and kissed her deeply.

"Together forever," she said. And she kissed him back.

- The End -

Acknowledgments

Huge thanks to Sonya Bateman, my long time critique partner, for her constant and unwavering support. I've learned more about writing from Sonya than from anyone else over the past decade. Generous and always open to frank discussion, she's been a port in the storm for me on many occasions. She also writes one heck of a synopsis. (Thanks again for this one, Sonya!) Please check out my favorite book of hers, *Broken Angel*, as well as her urban thrillers at: http://housephoenix.wordpress.com

To Joan Hall Hovey, award-winning author of some of the best romantic suspense novels out there today, including _The Deepest Dark_, her newest blockbuster. I have always loved Joan's work and consider her the ideal novelist. But be warned – if you start reading one of her books, you won't put it down! Thank you, Joan, for believing in my work.

To Robin P. Waldrop, who inspired me (okay, she nudged really hard) to try my hand at a new venture and who encouraged me along the way by offering insightful critiques and catching my dumb errors. See her very popular YA paranormal romance books at:

http://robinpwaldrop.com

Heartfelt appreciation to Sonia R. Martinez for her good-natured assistance and insightful edits. Sonia is my favorite food writer, who hails from Hawaii and never fails to bring a smile to my face. See her articles and photos at: http://www.soniatasteshawaii.com

Gabriela Scholter, you read this manuscript in less than one day and came back with a dozen excellent catches. I so appreciate your support and feedback, and thank you for your amazing speed and quality in your beta reading. Your ten years of teaching English as a second language abroad has made you an amazing proofreader. You've helped me remember a lot of my own eighth grade English, and I'm in your debt. Say hello to Stuttgart for me!

Joan H Young, we have just discovered each other's mysteries this year, and I must say I love your work. Thank you for taking a critical look at my manuscript even though you are as always swamped with multiple projects and many hikes across the great northeast woods! You really have an amazing knack for finding typos and mistakes, thank you for spending so much time on this. Joan's cozy mysteries can be discovered here: http://www.booksleavingfootprints.com.

Joan Miller, I truly appreciate all the hard work you put into finding my errors and inconsistencies. I wouldn't feel right unless you read through my manuscript multiple times before publishing, and I will always picture you and Gretchen's cat Jessie reading at night outside by the chiminea. From the bottom of my heart – thank you!

Linda Bonney Olin, if I didn't know better, I'd think you were a professional writing coach. Your sharp eyes and hard work with my manuscript have made it flow better. God has given you a wonderful gift, and I'm glad you honor him by writing those amazing hymns and more. Thanks for your deep reads and suggestions for improvement. Please visit her website here to learn about her creations: http://LindaBonneyOlin.com

Thank you, <u>Kellie Dennis</u>, of *Book Cover by Design* (www.bookcoverbydesign.co.uk), for your help with the cover art. I love the images you chose and stand in awe of your expertise. Way to go!

Maria Benzoni Lombardo lives on the same gorgeous ridge over the Genesee Valley that we do, and we have been friends for years. She is reading and reviewing my audio books, and recently offered to try her hand at beta reading. I'm very glad she did. Maria, thanks for finding the errors I made, especially the year that I skipped in the rough draft. I so appreciate your catches and value your input.

Deepest appreciation to Dina Von Lowenkraft, who writes Young Adult Fiction across the pond in Belgium, and whose new Twilight Times Book <u>*Dragon Fire*</u> was just released with a splash in the literary world. Dina, you are the ultimate finder of paradoxes. You have a brain like a steel trap and I appreciate your honest appraisal of the first part of this book before the rewrite. Kudos!

Jenny Woodall, who writes under the pen name of Victoria Howard, has become a wonderful author friend from "across the pond" in the UK. After we got past our UK/USA variances in writing styles, we have helped each other with stories, genre classification, and more. Jenny, I appreciated your insight into Portia's psychological state in the original first chapters of this book. Thank you for taking the time and for making the effort. Jenny's best-selling romantic suspense books can be found here: <u>http://www.victoriahoward.co.uk/</u>

Mary Alice Grimes, we have only recently "met" over the past few years, but I'm glad we did. I thank you for your painstaking attention to detail and presentation of opportunities to improve the work. My books are always better after you've had a chance to go through them, and I will be thankful to you for that forever.

Karen Vaughn, you have been reading through my Gus LeGarde series and other books so fast I can hardly keep up with your wonderful reviews! Thanks for reading through this book, too, to find errors. I'm glad you liked Grace in that last scene where she really gave it to Murphy. ;o) Check out Karen's books at: http://www.amazon.com/Karen-Vaughan/e/B004PRN7ZO

Sharon Pribble, thank you for offering to read this manuscript and for looking for my errors! Grateful for the time you took, and I wish you the very best.

About the Author

Aaron Paul Lazar writes to soothe his soul. A multi award-winning author of three addictive mystery series, writing guides, and more, Aaron enjoys the Genesee Valley countryside in upstate New York, where his characters embrace life, play with their dogs and grandkids, grow sumptuous gardens, and chase bad guys. Visit his website at:

http://www.lazarbooks.com

and watch for his upcoming releases, UNDER THE ICE and DEVIL'S CREEK.

You may contact him at:

aaron.lazar@yahoo.com or author@lazarbooks.com.

Books by multi-award winning author Aaron Lazar:

LEGARDE MYSTERIES
DOUBLE FORTÉ (print, eBook, audio book)
UPSTAGED (print, eBook, audio book)
TREMOLO: CRY OF THE LOON (print, eBook, audio book)
MAZURKA (print, eBook, audio book)
FIRESONG (print, eBook, audio book)
TREMOLO: CRY OF THE LOON (print, eBook, audio book)
DON'T LET THE WIND CATCH YOU (print, eBook, audio book)
THE LIAR'S GALLERY (print, eBook, audio book)
UNDER THE ICE (coming 2014)
LADY BLUES (2014) (print, eBook, and audio book)
THE LEGARDE MYSTERIES OMNIBUS (eBook)
MOORE MYSTERIES
HEALEY'S CAVE (print, eBook, audio book)
TERROR COMES KNOCKING (print, eBook, audio book)
FOR KEEPS (print, eBook, audio book)
TALL PINES MYSTERIES
FOR THE BIRDS (print, eBook, audio book)
ESSENTIALLY YOURS (print, eBook, audio book)
SANCTUARY (print, eBook, audio book)
BETRAYAL (print, eBook, audio book)
STANDALONES
THE SEACREST (print, eBook, audio book)
DEVIL'S LAKE (print, eBook, audio book)
WRITING ADVICE
WRITE LIKE THE WIND, volumes 1, 2, 3 (eBooks and audio books)

Aaron Lazar's Book Awards

The Seacrest

2014 Best Beach Book Festival WINNER, Romance category

2013 ForeWord Book Awards, Romance, FINALIST

Double Forté

2012 ForeWord BOTYA, Mystery, FINALIST

Tremolo: cry of the loon –

2013 Eric Hoffer Book Awards: Grand Prize Short List

2013 Eric Hoffer Book Awards: Honorable Mention, Eric Hoffer Legacy Fiction

2011 Global eBook Award Finalist in Historical Fiction Contemporary

2011 Preditors & Editors Readers Choice Award – 2nd place Mystery

2008 Yolanda Renée's Top Ten Books

2008 MYSHELF Top Ten Reads

For the Birds

2011 ForeWord Book Awards, FINALIST in Mystery

2012 Carolyn Howard-Johnson's Top 10 Reads

Essentially Yours

2013 EPIC Book Awards, FINALIST in Suspense

2013 Eric Hoffer Da Vinci Eye Award Finalist

Healey's Cave

2012 EPIC Book Awards WINNER Best Paranormal

2011 Eric Hoffer Book Award, WINNER Best Book in Commercial Fiction

2011 Finalist for Allbooks Review Editor's Choice

2011 Winner of Carolyn Howard Johnson's 9th Annual Noble (not Noble!) Prize for Literature

2011 Finalists for Global EBook Awards

Terror Comes Knocking

2013 Global Ebook Awards, Paranormal – Bronze

For Keeps

2013 Semi Finalist in Kindle Book Review Book Awards, Mystery Category

Websites

www.lazarbooks.com

www.murderby4.blogspot.com

www.aaronlazar.blogspot.com

www.aplazar.gather.com

http://aaronlazar.younglivingworld.com

www.pureoils.blogspot.com

Contact

You may contact the author via email, at aaron.lazar@yahoo.com.

Connect with Aaron Lazar

Facebook: https://www.facebook.com/aplazar2

Twitter:
https://twitter.com/aplazar

Goodreads:
http://www.goodreads.com/AaronPaulLazar

Amazon Author Page:
http://www.amazon.com/Aaron-Paul-Lazar/e/B001JOZR2M/ref=ntt_athr_dp_pel_1

LinkedIn:
http://www.linkedin.com/pub/aaron-lazar/4/b50/a2a/

Google+:
https://plus.google.com/106903480874581085678/posts

CPSIA information can be obtained
at www.ICGtesting.com
Printed in the USA
LVHW080953120722
723297LV00021B/241

9 781500 635039